Sarah M. Eden
BRITISH ISLES COLLECTION

A TIMELESS Romance ANTHOLOGY

Sarah M. Eden
BRITISH ISLES
COLLECTION
Six Historical Romance Novellas

Mirror Press

Copyright © 2015 by Mirror Press, LLC
Paperback edition
All rights reserved

No part of this book may be reproduced in any form whatsoever without prior written permission of the publisher, except in the case of brief passages embodied in critical reviews and articles. This is a work of fiction. The characters, names, incidents, places, and dialogue are products of the author's imagination and are not to be construed as real.

Interior Design by Rachael Anderson

Cover design by Mirror Press, LLC & Rachael Anderson
Cover image © Lee Avison / Trevillion Images

Published by Mirror Press, LLC
http://timelessromanceanthologies.blogspot.com

ISBN-10: 1941145639
ISBN-13: 978-1-941145-63-0

TABLE OF CONTENTS

A Friend Indeed   1

A Happy Beginning   61

The Road to Cavan Town   119
(Originally published in the Winter Collection)

A Christmas Promise   169
(Originally published in the Silver Bells Collection)

Dream of a Glorious Season   219
(Originally published in the All Regency Collection)

A Lesson in Love   279
(Originally published in the European Collection)

MORE TIMELESS ROMANCE ANTHOLOGIES

Winter Collection
Spring Vacation Collection
Summer Wedding Collection
Autumn Collection
European Collection
Love Letter Collection
Old West Collection
Summer in New York Collection
Silver Bells Collection
All Regency Collection
Annette Lyon Collection
Under the Mistletoe Collection
Mail Order Bride Collection
Road Trip Collection

A Friend Indeed

OTHER WORKS BY SARAH M. EDEN

Seeking Persephone
Courting Miss Lancaster
The Kiss of a Stranger
Friends and Foes
An Unlikely Match
Drops of Gold
Glimmer of Hope
As You Are
Longing for Home
Hope Springs
For Elise

One

Gloucestershire, England, September 1808

Poverty had prevented Caroline Downy from spending the Season in London. Her innate good sense had prevented her from crying about it. She was betrothed, after all, which bordered on the absolutely miraculous for a young lady without a dowry and nothing but her family's respectable standing to recommend her.

The match was an arranged one, which took all of the heart-pounding excitement out of the experience. A lady wished to be loved rather than settled for. She wasn't marrying a complete stranger, something for which she was unspeakably grateful. George Barrington and her brother Thomas had been the very best of friends since their days at Eton. George had spent most of his school holidays at Downy House, in fact. Caroline knew him and liked him very much. She simply didn't love him, and he didn't love her. Feeling true enthusiasm for such a loveless arrangement was difficult, to say the least.

"Is that what you intend to wear?" Mother eyed Caroline from across the sitting room. "You present a rather uninspiring picture, my dear."

The observation was not made in a spirit of criticism but of concern.

"I would love to don a new dress and slippers for the arrival of my intended, Mother, but I haven't had either in years. This is the best I was able to manage."

"Oh, Caroline." Mother sat next to her on the sofa and took her hands. "I loathe the necessity of this. A girl ought to be courted and treasured, not auctioned off."

"Was I actually auctioned off?" She sincerely hoped the arrangements had been undertaken in a less humiliating manner.

"Well, no, but this is hardly better. George is the very best sort of gentleman, but he wasn't of your choosing." Mother's eyes took on a far-off and weary expression. "I wanted so much more for you."

"And I expected so much worse." She squeezed her mother's hands. "Our financial situation has never been a secret. I have known for as long as I can remember that my chances of marrying were slim, and that, if I did somehow manage the thing, I would likely find myself attached to a cold and heartless man. George is a decided step above such a possibility."

Mother nodded, though her agreement was clearly hesitant. "We haven't seen him in more than a year. There is every possibility that he has undergone a fundamental change."

"Let us choose to be optimistic." As difficult as that choice sometimes was.

Over the course of her twenty years, she had resigned herself to never being truly loved by her future husband, had even convinced herself that she could find satisfaction in simply being treated with kindness and respect. But in the month since word had arrived that George Barrington was her intended, she'd struggled to feel content with what she'd always expected. Indifference from a stranger could be endured. Disinterest from a gentleman she counted as a dear friend would, she felt certain, weigh down her soul one indifferent glance, one dismissive gesture at a time, until the burden simply crushed her.

◦◦◦

"It's deucedly good of you to do this, George, but marrying a chap's sister to save his family from destitution is taking friendship a touch too far."

George reined in his mount. This misunderstanding needed to be cleared up before Thomas convinced Caroline that George was simply doing them all a favor. "For the last time, Tom, I didn't ask for your sister's hand as a favor to *you*."

Tom looked at him as though he were a loon. "But with the depth of your coffers, you could marry anyone you wished."

"And I *am* marrying exactly whom I wish." George speared him with a look. "So you can simply clear your brainbox of the absurd notion that my actions are the result of pity or charity or anything of that sort."

They both dismounted and handed their reins to waiting grooms before making their way up to the house. Some of George's happiest memories were connected with Downy House. For George's entire childhood, his own father worked on amassing his fortune, while George's mother had relentlessly pursued the elusive standing in Society she coveted. Only at Downy House had George not felt alone.

The early years of happy camaraderie with Tom and his brother, Edward, had paled in later years compared to Caroline's companionship. They'd not been in one another's company as often as he and the male members of her family had. Nevertheless, she, and she alone, was the reason he continued to return after his years at Oxford and despite having a country home of his own. She was the part of Downy House he'd missed most acutely over the past fourteen months.

"But why, Caro?" Tom had harped on this same topic for weeks, ever since he'd heard of the betrothal. "She's not what most would consider a beauty."

"The assessment of a brother," George replied. "Your sister happens to be a very lovely and fine-looking lady. More importantly, she is intelligent, possesses a witty sense of humor, is accomplished, an excellent conversationalist—"

"Enough." Tom held up his hands in surrender. "If you promise to quit making my bumbling baby sister sound like the Toast of the Town, I'll promise to stop quizzing you about your choice of fiancées."

"I will accept that offer, my friend."

They even shook on it. George's past had been far from picturesque, but his future looked brighter. Mr. Downy had accepted his offer. Edward, the oldest brother, had seemed enthusiastic at the prospect of the match. Tom didn't mean to make things awkward. And Caroline—his darling, beloved Caroline—had agreed to the match.

His future was bright, indeed.

Two

George and Tom were late. Mother again wore her all-too-familiar expression of pitying sadness. "I do wish we had arranged for you to have a new dress. George spends the Season in Town, and you must surely seem a dowd when compared with the well-to-do young ladies he interacts with there."

That was not a very comforting comparison. "Fortunately for me, George already knows our financial situation." Heat stained her cheek at just how aware he must have been of every aspect of their lives. "My thrice-mended sleeves and threadbare hem will come as no surprise."

"I suppose not." Mother fretted with the fringe of her shawl. "It is not as though he hasn't seen you in outmoded dresses and such all of your life."

Mother was not helping in the least. She made Caroline sound like the absolute worst marriage prospect imaginable.

"How did the arrangement come about?" Until now, Caroline hadn't yet had the courage to ask, not truly wanting to hear the answer. She felt, however, it would be best to know all she could before George arrived. "Did he ask Father, or did Father make the proposition to him?"

"I don't rightly know." Mother ran her fingers over the keys of the pianoforte as she passed. "The entire thing was arranged in London. At their club, I believe."

At their club? "Meaning, of course, they were likely drunk as wheelbarrows when the agreement was reached." Wasn't that terribly fitting?

"Do not use such an undignified expression, Caroline," Mother scolded.

"My apologies."

Before the silence grew overly long, Mother spoke again. "Between the two of us, I must say I am convinced that much of the reason for your fortuitous match lies in George's mother's ambitions."

Everyone knew of those. Mrs. Barrington's not-so-subtle eye was on more exalted rungs of the ladder of Society than she could ever hope to reach on her own.

"The Downys may not be wealthy," Mother added, "but we have a fair bit of cachet."

Although that was diminishing with each generation. Caroline's great-grandfather had been a duke. Caroline's father was the youngest son of the duke's youngest son, which made her one step removed from being an absolute nobody. Apparently, however, that one step meant something to the Barringtons.

Boisterous male voices sounded in the corridor. Though the family maintained an income sufficient enough for both a butler and a footman, the servants were never boisterous. The commotion, therefore, was likely the gentlemen arriving at last.

The last time she'd seen George Barrington, he was her friend. Now he was her betrothed. Caroline didn't care for the change one whit. She hadn't the slightest idea how she was expected to behave around him now.

"Caroline. You're woolgathering again." Mother's panicked whisper snapped her back to the present.

She watched the door, waiting for her future to step inside. She'd always liked George. Even when they were children, he had been good and kind. She sincerely hoped that had not changed.

The door opened, and the butler stepped inside. "Mr. Downy and Mr. Barrington, ma'am."

Mother rose and glided gracefully toward the door as Tom entered.

"My dear Thomas." Mother greeted him with an embrace.

Caroline's eyes remained glued to the doorway. She was happy to see her brother again, but he was not at all the most important arrival.

Oh, please let him not have fundamentally changed. If I must marry someone who doesn't love me, I need him to at least be kind.

George stepped inside. The absence of a year hadn't rendered more of an outward change in him than the difference between a twenty-one-year-old and a twenty-two-year-old. He boasted the same nearly black hair, brown eyes, and easy smile. He held himself confidently but without arrogance. He still pulled everyone's eye when he entered a room. That had been true of him for several years now, but never more apparent than just then.

Having known him as a child, Caroline couldn't quite clear her mind of the memory of him as a ten year-old boy, all knees and elbows, running about Downy House with more energy than grace. She had been all of eight years old and passing through a stage of clumsiness herself. He had, by his mere presence, eased much of her self-consciousness. If this boy, she'd reasoned, could be so gawky and yet be so universally doted on, then she need not worry about her lack of elegance.

He approached her with eyes narrowed in curiosity. "Dare I ask what has brought such an amused smile to your face?"

"I was remembering the first time you came to Downy House."

His smile pulled broad. "I was such a gawky boy, and I was absolutely gleeful at the prospect of spending Christmas with someone other than my governess. I am certain I made a nuisance of myself."

She had been well trained in the expected niceties of receiving a new arrival. "You were most welcome then, as you are now."

He offered the obligatory bow, which she returned with a curtsey.

"We are, indeed, very pleased to have you here with us again." Mother had abandoned her "dear boy" to offer her own curtsey and salutations. "How fares your mother?"

"She is well, thank you." George's manners had grown quite impeccable over the past year. "You appear to be in good health yourself."

"I am, thank you." Mother sat once more. With a quick widening of her eyes, she signaled for Caroline to do the same. The gentlemen could not, after all, be seated if the ladies were not. "Mr. Downy tells me your Shropshire estate is doing well."

Mr. Downy. Mother never referred to Father so properly when only the family was about. Until this visit, George had been considered near enough to family to be included in that exception.

"It is." George flipped the tails of his jacket upward as he sat in the spindle-back chair. "The tenants are prospering. The neighbors seem pleased to have someone in residence."

Mother nodded her approval. "An empty home can be a

burden when a neighborhood has been accustomed to a full selection of company."

"Indeed." George punctuated the response with a quick incline of his head.

Behaving so formally with a gentleman with whom she'd once spent rainy afternoons splashing in mud puddles was decidedly odd. She'd suspected interactions between them would be a bit awkward, especially at first, but this was worse than she'd anticipated.

She folded her hands primly on her lap, and in a voice of theatrical properness, addressed her brother. "Why, Thomas, is this not the mildest weather you ever remember experiencing in July?"

Tom could always be counted on to recognize a jest when she made one. "Indeed, sister dearest. I shudder to think what lies in store come winter. I may need to invest in new woolens."

Caroline dropped her mouth open in a look of shock and pressed her hand to her heart. "Why, Thomas. How scandalous of you to discuss such a thing."

"I offer my most humble apologies, sister dearest."

Mother's eyes darted from George to the others and back again several times. "Behave," she whispered harshly. "We have company."

Tom, bless him, laughed out loud. "It's only George, Mother."

"He is your sister's betrothed." Mother's eyes darted between them all. "If we misbehave so poorly, he is likely to change his mind, and then where will we be?"

"Very well. I will postpone the eulogy until after he's permanently shackled to her."

Tom's humor didn't often fall short of its intended mark, but it did in that moment. *Eulogy. Shackled to her.* If Tom was to be believed, her goal of simply being content in her match was doomed to failure. George, who had once been her friend, would come to resent her.

"How pleased we are that you are to be part of our family, George." Mother's attempt to salvage the conversation was not terribly graceful. "We knew Caroline would have to marry at some point, but I confess I assumed she would make a far less pleasant match, someone older and not terribly picky."

Being discussed as if she weren't present was always a wonderful experience.

"Then allow me to confess something as well," George said. "I am yet in shock at my tremendously good fortune. Your daughter might have married any number of gentlemen with far more to recommend them."

Mother sputtered a moment. She seemed to find that declaration nothing short of inexplicable. "Well, Mr. Farber was on her father's list of gentlemen he meant to speak with on this matter, and he is both wealthy and significant in the eyes of the *ton*."

"Don't forget his legendary love of brandy," Tom added with a laugh. "Besides, Mother, Farber is at least as old as Father. Surely Caro wasn't so desperate as all that."

Mother turned wide eyes to Tom. "Oh, but she was. Without a dowry, how else was she to secure an offer from someone better?"

Caroline stood, offering a benign smile. "I feel a bit of a headache coming on, so I mean to go lie down for a bit. Once the lot of you decide if I am to be declared fortunate or desperate, do send word with one of the maids, as I would very much like to hear the verdict."

She held her head high as she made her way toward the door. It was likely a more dramatic departure than she ought to have indulged in. But, heaven help her, the past month of knowing she'd been handed off to the highest bidder had proven a difficult reality to embrace. That weight only grew with George here speaking of her in the same dismissive way, as though she really was a commodity to be traded and evaluated. George, who had always treated her as a person worth knowing. Who had never seemed to devalue her because she was female. Even he seemed to have changed.

In light of all that, she'd earned a touch of drama.

Three

That had not gone well.

"Do you really wish to endure such a display for the rest of your life, George?" Tom's customary grin sat firmly in place. "Women are deucedly dramatic."

"That is not a word you ought to speak in your mother's hearing, Thomas," Mrs. Downy scolded. Her gaze darted from George to the now-empty doorway a few times before settling on him once more. "George, please do not hold this outburst against her. She has not quite been herself this past month, not since . . ." The sentence dangled unfinished, but George knew perfectly the words she'd left unspoken.

Not since she learned of our betrothal. He'd worried that the manner in which the match came about would give Caroline the wrong impression. But when Edward, the oldest of the Downy children, said that his father had come to London with the express purpose of finding someone willing to offer a bit of much-needed income to the family in exchange for Caroline's hand, George panicked.

His plan had always been to court her when she had her Season, to make his case in the traditional way, by convincing her of his love and devotion. But she never had a Season, and her family left her no opportunity to be wooed.

"Is she terribly unhappy about this?"

"Not at all," Mrs. Downy assured him. "She seemed perfectly resigned to it until today."

Perfectly resigned. That was nearly as bad. He hadn't expected her to be overflowing with excitement, but he'd hoped that knowing she was marrying someone whose company she enjoyed, and who was not several decades her senior, would have rendered the prospect a bit more appealing than "perfectly resigned" indicated.

And, it seemed, she wasn't even feeling *that* any longer. What a mess he had on his hands.

"Pardon me," he offered to the others before swiftly following Caroline's path. If he caught up with her before she reached her bedchamber, perhaps he'd have an opportunity to better ascertain the state of her feelings and do what he could to soothe them.

In a much appreciated bit of luck, he reached Caroline before she turned down the corridor to the family rooms.

"Caroline."

She stopped at the sound of her name and glanced over her shoulder at him. That particular posture had never failed to clutch at him in a way he couldn't explain. Something in the look, in the stance, seemed to warn him that she could leave him behind at any moment. He inevitably found himself both intrigued by the unspoken challenge of earning her affections and nearly frantic at the thought of losing her. For years he'd felt the pull of those competing emotions.

He reached her side in the very next moment. "I am sorry about your headache."

"It will pass with time and rest."

He'd developed a talent over the past few years of keeping his arms firmly at his side in the face of the almost overwhelming wish to reach out for her. "Is there anything I can do for you? I do not like the idea of you being unwell."

The tiniest of smiles flitted across her face. "You always were more felicitous than either Tom or Edward. But then, older brothers do have a tendency to be inexcusably inconsiderate of their sister's wellbeing."

"If I had been fortunate to have a sister, I would like to think I would not have been so blind."

Her smile grew by the smallest of degrees. "I do not doubt you would have been an excellent brother. You were always considerate of me during our childhoods."

Good heavens, did she think of him as a *brother*? A lady might learn to feel more than indifference for a match not of her choosing, but who could possibly find any excitement in the prospect of marrying her brother?

"At the risk of sounding rude, I would like to lie down." Caroline's patience was clearly being tried by the delay.

"Allow me to walk you to your door." He motioned for her to proceed him, which she did. "Has your maid been sent for? I would be happy to see that she is summoned."

"I will ring for her once I reach my room. I would rather lie down that much sooner than wait for her to arrive."

Was she more unwell than she'd admitted? "Ought I to send for the apothecary?"

"As I said, you are far more attentive than my brothers ever were. But no, I am not truly ill, simply worn thin. The past weeks have been quite trying."

A horrifying truth that was beginning to sink in. "Has this been so terrible for you?"

She tipped her chin upward in a show of firmness. "I have found I do not at all like being listed amongst my family's sellable assets."

Sellable assets? This grew worse and worse. "You have known me more than half of my life, Caroline. Do you truly believe that this, to me, is nothing more than a financial arrangement?"

"I am grateful that Father chose you. I truly am. I saw the list of gentlemen he intended to approach, and—" A sudden surge of emotion cut off her words. Caroline, who seldom grew overset, seemed unable to finish the thought.

She had seen the list? What had Mr. Downy been thinking to expose his daughter to the harsh reality of arranging a match? George allowed himself a momentary lapse in his iron-clad control and reached for her hand, holding it in what he hoped was a reassuring clasp.

But she quickly slipped her hand from his. "Despite my lack of social graces today, I promise I will do all I can to make certain you don't regret your"—she pulled in a shaky breath and stepped further away—"your purchase."

"Caro—"

But she had already rushed off, hurrying inside her bedchamber.

Her door closed with a sharp snap. She thought of him as a brother. A brother who had acquired her with the same level of tender emotion one calls upon when purchasing a horse or a bit of land. Far from pleased by their match, she was disheartened and resigned.

Mr. Downy had made the direness of her situation and the coldness of the arrangement apparent to her. How could she not assume he shared her father's view of things?

How much worse could the situation become? He hardly dared consider the possibilities.

What he needed was a plan.

 ~*~

George was elbow deep in ribbon when Tom wandered into his bedchamber.

"The birds aren't going to shoot themselves," Tom scolded. "I thought we came to the country for a bit of sport."

George didn't look up from the bow he was attempting to tie. "There are times, Tom, when I wonder if perhaps you have recently been dealt a blow to the head."

"What are you going on about this time?"

"Why would you think I came to your family home, where the lady to whom I have recently become affianced lives, in order to shoot birds?" George gave his friend a laughingly annoyed look. "This journey was always about Caroline."

Tom's eyes pulled wide even as his brows arched in surprise. "Boiled beans, man! You're not undertaking a courtship, are you?" He had always been something of a simpleton in matters not related to sport.

"I am not certain which aspect of 'betrothed' you haven't come to terms with." George set himself back to the task of adorning Caroline's present. "We're to be married, and I would much prefer that she be pleased with the prospect."

"Boiled—"

"If you say 'boiled beans' one more time, I'll boil *your* beans."

Tom chuckled. "What does that mean?"

"I have no idea." George examined his rather pathetic attempt at tying a bow. He could only hope Caroline would look past it.

"But the arrangements are already made." Tom sat on the chest at the foot of George's bed. "Seems to me that that ought to relieve a fellow from the necessity of making up sweet to a lady. A match of convenience ought to be . . . convenient."

"You needn't speak as though I've volunteered to spend an afternoon in close company with a rabid dog." George leaned back casually in his chair, grateful for a momentary reprieve from his heavy thoughts and worries.

Tom's nose scrunched as though he smelled something

particularly putrid. "You won't be making cow eyes at her, or anything equally disturbing?"

"What would you define as 'equally disturbing'?"

"As it turns out, this conversation." Tom fingered the discarded lengths of ribbon with a look of disdain. "Is gift-giving part of your courtship strategy?" Tom indicated the folded bit of fabric and its poorly tied bow on the end table.

"This is merely something I thought she would like." He pushed it a little away from him. The light blue shawl had seemed like the perfect engagement gift, but now he wished he'd chosen something a bit more impressive. Such a feeble offering was unlikely to increase her enthusiasm. "Do you think the gardener would let me pick some flowers?"

"I can't imagine why not."

That was good enough for him. "I'll see you at dinner," he said on his way out the door.

He knew that Caroline would assume his offering was out of expectation and obligation rather than out of the warmest, sincerest regards. He hoped she might sense at least some of the tenderness behind the gesture, that the offering would act as the first step in a successful plan to convince her of his regard. He no longer had the least confidence.

Four

Caroline tucked herself away near the empty fireplace in the library that evening, unable to force herself to join the family for dinner. Should anyone walk in, they would see nothing more worrisome than a calm and sensible young lady reading a book. They would never guess her heart and mind were in turmoil.

A quick knock echoed off the library door. Caroline dropped her gaze to the open book in her lap. "Come in," she said calmly.

"I commandeered your dinner tray."

Her gaze snapped upward at the realization that George, of all people, had stepped inside. Her tongue tied in knots, though whether by embarrassment or emotion or simple confusion, she couldn't rightly say. Gone were the days of feeling utterly at ease in his company.

George set the tray on the end table beside her chair.

"Thank you," she whispered, not looking directly at it or him. She settled her gaze on her book once more.

"Would you be terribly put out if I stayed for a moment or two?" he asked.

Yes. No. She wasn't at all certain what she wanted where he was concerned. But tossing him out on his ear seemed inexcusably immature. "Of course you may stay."

He wore the earnest expression she'd seen so many times: when she had been ill, when he'd helped search for her missing kitten, when he'd found her hiding in the orchard to avoid her brothers' teasing. He *did* care about her—she did not doubt that—simply not in the way a husband ought to care for his wife.

George sat gingerly on the far end of the sofa. He'd left the library door ajar, and they were affianced. Given the circumstances, few would have found anything amiss in his sitting directly beside her, but this long, awkward distance was more fitting. A chasm was growing between them, one they didn't seem likely to span.

"I understand your father and Edward are due to descend upon us from London tomorrow." It was as innocuous a comment as a mention of the weather or the general state of the countryside.

"Yes, I believe their business in Town is now complete."

Indeed, Father had found her a husband and, in so doing, had secured money enough to pay off the estate's debts and return home with hardly a care in the world.

"Have you ever wished to visit London?" George asked.

"It does not do to wish for things one can never have." That had been her reasoning for years.

"I spend a portion of every Season in Town," he said. "If you wish, you can as well, after we— once we are—"

He couldn't bring himself to even speak of their marriage in solid terms. How lowering.

"My family and my governesses were forever treating me as though I hadn't the intelligence for nuanced and layered conversations or the endurance for hearing uncomfortable news. But you, George. You never treated me that way. Until now."

He didn't speak, but neither did he look away.

"Is that what I have become to you? A lady with whom you cannot speak plainly, with whom you will never again be at ease?"

He slid across the sofa, directly beside her. "I am sorry to be making such a mull of this. But, my dear friend, things have changed between us, and I do not yet know what our new footing is."

So he was as lost as she was. That only served to cast more doubt on the success of this arrangement.

"Do you remember what you said when you were first told during my first visit that I would be spending the school holiday here?"

She shook her head, unable to recall her exact words in that moment.

"You said that you found it difficult enough sharing a house with *two* boys and could not possibly be expected to endure a third."

She likely had said that, as those had been her exact sentiments at the time. "I was only eight years old, you'll remember."

"And yet, in many ways not much has changed." He took her hand in his, a gesture of reassurance. "My first arrival here was an adjustment for you, for both of us. By the end of that holiday, we had made our peace with each other. We were even marginally fond of each other's company. By the end of my next visit, we were very nearly friends. As the years passed, we became precisely that—*dear* friends, in fact. Did we not?"

"We did." She heard the wistful note in her words. No doubt, he did as well. Did he mourn the impending loss of that decade of friendship as much as she did?

"We found our footing, Caroline, and I believe we can

again." He bent low enough to catch her diverted gaze. "Will you allow us to at least try?"

She raised her head to look at him more directly.

"Three weeks is all I ask," he said. "For three weeks, permit us the possibility of changing what has always been between us—not throwing it away, but building on it. See if in those three weeks you can find reason to believe we can make this a success."

"And if I cannot?"

"I could never be happy in this marriage if you were miserable. I will not force your hand, you have my solemn vow."

His words were so unexpected, she didn't at first know how to respond. "You would release me from our engagement?"

"I have only ever wanted your happiness."

She stood up, her thoughts colliding with one another at too fast a pace for sitting still. Her feet carried her to the fireplace, then the window, then past the sofa once more. "I am certain Father has already spent the money he received." Being perfectly honest with George seemed the best course of action.

"If you truly believe that money is more important to me than you are, then I have a greater task ahead of me than I realized."

He actually sounded disappointed in her. But how could she have believed otherwise? Her eventual marriage had always been about securing the family's future. Always.

"What is your decision?" he asked. "Am I to have three weeks?"

She stopped, facing him from her new position near the window. "Will you answer me one question first?"

"Of course."

Her courage nearly deserted her, but she rallied. "Do you truly want to marry me? I don't mean do you want to marry in the general sense, but do you want to marry *me*?"

He rose. Slowly, deliberately, and with measured step, he came toward her. No one would argue that he was still the gawky boy he'd once been. His movements had a masculine grace she could not ignore. He moved with purpose, with confidence, with a presence that filled any room he entered. And the way his gaze held hers without hesitation or uncertainty quickened her pulse with something bordering on nervousness but leaning in the direction of anticipation.

"Caroline Downy," he said once he'd reached her side. "I am not one to be forced into an arrangement not of my choosing—not by guilt or pity or intimidation. I asked for your hand because I very much wished to be granted *your* hand."

"But why?"

He closed his eyes and shook his head. "Three weeks, Caroline. Give me three weeks, and I sincerely hope that question will be one you no longer need answered."

The concern that had hovered in his expression when he'd first stepped inside the library had been replaced by sheer, unmistakable determination. He raised her hand to his lips and placed a kiss on her knuckles.

George had never done that before. Not once. She would have remembered the tingling sensation and the way her breaths came in sudden spurts. She would have remembered wishing he would brush those same lips along her cheek. If he had ever done that before, she would have remembered feeling this entirely confused.

He held her hand a moment longer. "I will see you tomorrow."

In the moment after George's departure, Caroline's eyes settled on the single white rose lying on the tray of food he'd brought for her. The staff would not have placed it there. Her family certainly would not have.

He must have thought of the rose—a white one, her favorite. The thoughtful gesture was reassuring. Perhaps he was correct in believing the awkwardness would ease with time and a little patient effort. He had asked her to grant him three weeks. She did not want to give up on her happiness—on *their* happiness. Three weeks seemed little enough to ask.

◦◦◦

Caroline added another white rose to her growing collection in a vase beside her bed. The chambermaid had brought one in that morning. Another had been waiting for her in the breakfast room. She'd found another just now tied with a ribbon to a small, folded bit of fabric left on the bench at the foot of her bed. Including the rose she'd received with her dinner tray the night before, George had given her five.

He'd not said the roses were from him, but she knew they were. The small tokens meant more than he likely knew. They served as reminders that he had a good heart, that she was fortunate to be marrying a man who was not unkind. He might not love her, but he was unlikely to mistreat her. More than that, he would treat her well. That was more than many women could say of their spouses.

She returned to the ribbon-tied fabric on the bench, running her fingers along the silky length of it. The deep shade of blue was exquisite, shimmering with the slightest hint of purple. Tucked behind the ribbon was a calling card. *Mr. George Barrington*, it declared.

She pulled it loose, unsure why he'd placed one of his cards inside. A quick perusal, however, revealed a note scrawled across the back.

> *My dear Caroline,*
> *I spied this in a shop in London, and its beauty immediately brought you to my mind. I hope you will enjoy it as much as I believe you will. I further hope the weather this afternoon will prove mild enough for you to undertake your customary walk in the gardens,*

as I know being denied that pleasure is particularly painful for you.
   ~Your George

"My George." He had never before referred to himself in that manner. Neither had he ever described her as beautiful.

She untied the ribbon and unfolded his offering. It was not, as she'd assumed, a length of fabric, but rather a shawl with intricate embroidery along the edges. She seldom saw anything so elegant, and she'd certainly never owned anything falling so firmly in that category. This was not the gift of a gentleman bought for a lady with whom he was merely a friend or an acquaintance.

"And he purchased it in London, long before our discussion last evening." So he must have been thinking of her in more personal terms already. But if she was not thought of as merely a friend, how was she thought of? There were so many degrees between "friend" and "true love." Where did she fit in his mind?

And where did he fit in hers?

She'd always prided herself on being focused and determined. How had she so quickly turned into this quivering mass of indecision? What was it about George's offer of marriage that had overset her in a way no one else's would have?

She wrapped the shawl around her shoulders as she sorted out her thoughts. If she could understand why she was struggling with her feelings so much, she might know how to best move forward. When Father left for London with his list of names, Caroline had simply reconciled herself to the inevitability. She formulated plans for making the best of her situation, for finding satisfaction in the usual, cold marriage of convenience. Discovering she'd been promised to a gentleman with whom she'd never had a cold or indifferent connection had upset those plans entirely.

With the other men on Father's list, she'd had nothing to lose. With George, she stood to forfeit a lifetime of affection.

She leaned her forehead against the window frame. She might have found some happiness in a loveless marriage to a man for whom she cared little, but that would never be enough with George. They would either be miserably aware that theirs was not a marriage of the heart, or they would love each other. There could be no middle ground.

She wanted him to love her, and she knew with sudden and terrifying clarity that anything less would be devastating.

She'd granted him three weeks to demonstrate that he was in favor of their marriage. But she needed to discover so much more; she needed to know if he could love her.

Five

George made a second circuit of the garden. Caroline never waited so long for her daily walk. He had joined her for this part of her day any number of times over the past five or six years, ever since he'd realized how fully she'd captured his heart. Those afternoons, along with a great many evenings spent playing cards and mornings spent in the library, discussing topics of interest, had rendered the state of his affections permanent.

He'd come to Gloucestershire fully expecting to be permitted those same indulgences. The night before, when her willingness to receive him had been cast into doubt, he thought his request for three weeks of leniency had secured his reception once more. It seemed he'd been mistaken.

"Is that you, George?"

He would have known Mr. Downy's booming voice anywhere. Indeed, his future father-in-law was striding up the garden walk toward him.

"I see you arrived here ahead of Edward and me."

"Tom and I reached Downy House yesterday." George offered the expected short bow.

Mr. Downy waved that off. "None of these formalities, boy. We're to be family." He chuckled. "Truth be told, I find it a little odd that we are not yet family. You've felt like one of us for so long."

"I do not know that I have thanked you and Mrs. Downy properly for having received me so warmly all these years." Indeed, they had been more of a family to him than his own ever had.

"Nonsense." Mr. Downy slapped him on the shoulder. "Having you as an honorary son was thank you enough. Though you'll not be honorary much longer."

At least Caroline's father was pleased at the prospect. "Another thing for which I need to thank you. I am certain what I had to offer paled in comparison to others you intended to approach."

Mr. Downy motioned for George to walk beside him. "I had held out some hope, George, that you meant to offer for her. Edward insisted you would."

"Edward? How did he know?"

Mr. Downy's sizable shoulders shook as his mouth turned upward. "Edward is not so thickheaded as his brother. He has sensed in you a growing fondness for our Caroline."

George hadn't realized that anyone had taken note of his growing devotion. "She is not at all happy about this, sir. I've had to enter into something of a devil's bargain, I am afraid."

Mr. Downy turned to George with drawn brows. "What is this bargain?"

They rounded the corner and passed the rose bower. George wondered if the flowers he'd sent to her had done anything to argue his case to Caroline. He'd heard nothing from her.

"While I had no guarantee that her feelings for me were

anything but that of a friend, I could not imagine her being satisfied with a marriage as uncaring and lifeless as she was likely to find with another gentleman. I am not saying she would have been mistreated; she simply wouldn't—" How could he put into words the fears he'd hardly dared voice even to himself? "I cannot be certain anyone else would have treated her with the kindness and thoughtfulness that she deserves."

"You wished to save her from that?"

George nodded firmly and decisively. "She deserves to be loved."

"Then what is this terrible bargain you have been forced into?"

"Coercing her to accept me would not secure her happiness. Indeed, I very much fear it would doom our marriage from the beginning." He inwardly cringed at the thought. "I asked for three weeks in which to prove that we could be happy together, that I did choose her for herself and not for reasons of social standing, or pity, or any of the many nonsensical notions she currently entertains."

"And should you fail in this lofty goal, what is the consequence?"

Again George swallowed the lump that never seemed to leave his throat. "I will release her from our engagement with no arguments, no bitterness, and no retracting of my financial pledge." He wanted to make certain Mr. Downy knew that the family would not suffer should George fail.

"Oh, good heavens, son." Mr. Downy released a long, drawn-out whistle. "You've set yourself to the task of fully wooing a woman in a mere three weeks? That is a devil's bargain if ever I've heard one."

"Especially considering she doesn't seem willing to let me try." He looked around the empty garden. "She's forgone her usual walk to avoid me."

"I know my girl, and I believe I know what she is struggling against." Mr. Downy tucked his fingers into the pocket of his waistcoat, his jacket pulling backward. "Caroline has a terrible fear of losing people. Ever since she was a child, whenever I depart for London she begs to know when I will return, pleading with me to be safe in my journey. When the boys began leaving for school, she cried and cried, insisting they would return having forgotten her and no longer allowing her to participate in their larks. She still grows teary when they depart. She fears being left behind."

George tried to reason out how that particular worry applied to his current predicament. "But I am offering precisely the opposite. I am asking—pleading—for her to make a future *with* me. She would not be left behind or forgotten."

"She would be if marriage means that you'd treat her differently from how you once did, that you resent her or dismiss her."

How could she possibly believe his adoration of her would change in any way other than grow? "I could never resent or dismiss her. I love her."

"Yes, but does she know that?"

"No, I do not believe she does."

Mr. Downy pointed a stubby finger at George's chest. "Then how can she think any differently? A wife chosen for any reason other than love can never feel fully valued in her marriage. That knowledge left me dreading my task this Season."

"Would you have chosen one of the others if I hadn't approached you?"

Mr. Downy took a deep, tense breath. "Only if I felt confident that they would have, at the very least, not mistreated her. I hope, George, that you do intend to be careful with your income and assets. It is a terrible thing for a father to see his daughter's future hang so precariously in the balance."

A wife chosen for any reason other than love . . .

"Ought I to tell Caroline of my feelings for her?" He hadn't done so out of fear of rejection, but he was already being turned away.

"I would advise against it at this point. She will likely suspect any declaration was an attempt to convince her not to break off your engagement."

"Surely she would not believe that I would lie to her."

They had nearly reached the garden gate. "I am only suggesting, son, that your actions will speak far louder than your words. Show her your feelings, and then the words you speak will have meaning."

"How can I show her if she never leaves her bedchamber?"

Mr. Downy grinned. "You are in luck. She is coming this way."

Indeed she was. And, though nothing in her posture spoke of true pleasure, she *was* wearing his shawl, which he chose to view as a good omen.

"Allow her to see the sincerity of your feelings, George. That will give her the confidence to move forward."

"I will do my best."

Only a moment later, she was beside them. "Welcome home, Father. We have missed you."

Caroline kissed her father's cheek. He patted her hand. "I have not yet greeted your mother. I will leave you with George. Be certain to set the dogs on him again if he misbehaves."

On the instant, color touched her face. "I was nine years old when I did that, Father."

"And," George quickly added, "I deserved it."

"You *were* teasing me rather mercilessly, and my kitten was unwilling to attack." Caroline, thank the heavens, sounded more like herself in that moment than she had in the past twenty-four hours. Perhaps all hope was not lost.

"Would it improve your opinion of my eleven-year-old

self if I told you that calling you Cry-o-line was Thomas's idea?"

He detected a smile beneath her continued discomfort. "I fully believe Tom was the instigator. But you fell in full step with his devious scheme, so you are just as much to blame."

George sighed dramatically. "He was a terrible influence."

"Perhaps that is why you spent more and more time with me as the years passed."

He nearly choked on the absurdity of that explanation. "That was not at all the reason."

Her continued light expression entirely dismissed the possibility that his reasons had been quite personal. She knew so little of his feelings.

He slipped his hand around hers, ready to pull away should she make the least objection. Much to his relief, she intertwined their fingers and, without the slightest protest, walked at his side as he undertook another circuit of the garden. At some point, Mr. Downy had slipped away, leaving them to the quiet solitude of trees and flowers and pebbled pathways.

"Thank you for this shawl," she said as they walked. "It is the most beautiful thing I have ever owned."

"I am pleased that you like it. You wear a great deal of blue, so I felt safe in assuming that it is a favorite color of yours."

She watched him with blatant curiosity. "I do favor blue, just as I prefer white roses. How is it you remember so many trivial things about me?"

"I would wager there is very little about our past time together that I do not recall. You have been, without question, the very best part of the last twelve years of my life."

Her smile blossomed once more. "You can hardly count the first years. We merely endured each other then."

Perhaps that had been true for her, but he had been top-over-tail in love with her even in those earliest times. "I have not spent any significant amount of time here this past year or more. Tell me, do you still ride in the mornings?"

"Most mornings, yes. Followed by a walk in the gardens after tea. Then after dinner, Mother insists on reading aloud to us all, sometimes for more than an hour at a time." Her tone and expression were equally rueful. "Do you not envy me my exciting existence? I have all of this whilst you have had to content yourself with the minuscule diversions of London."

"I will issue my promise once more. You have but to say the word, and I will take you to London myself, where you may enjoy those diversions to your heart's content." He felt he knew Caroline well enough to know she would never wish to spend her time in truly frivolous or scandalous behavior, but he suspected she would be thoroughly delighted with the theater and the opera, with balls and musicales. She would easily make friends amongst the other young matrons and would pass many cheerful afternoons making calls and receiving visitors.

"Where do you spend your time when the Season is over?" she asked. "Do you descend upon Bath or Brighton, or are those months passed in Shropshire?"

"Shropshire. I have at last managed to see the house refurbished and the estate fully prospering. I have time enough now to live as a gentleman of leisure, but have found myself most comfortable at home. I am afraid I am doomed to live a most dull existence."

She smiled at him. "I doubt your life will ever truly be dull. You have always possessed a knack for finding adventure wherever you may be. You are the one, after all, who found himself wedged into the tiny window opening at the back of the stables."

"Why is it that we are forever attacking each other with our childhood misdeeds?"

"Perhaps because there are so many of them." She nearly laughed; he could hear it in her tone. Oh how he hoped that meant she was feeling more at ease in his company. "And, more likely still, because we were always present for each other's disastrous failings."

"There have been good moments as well," George reminded her. "The time we convinced Cook to secretly give us tarts, and then we ran all the way here to the garden to eat them without anyone knowing."

She moved a bit closer to him, holding tighter to his hand. "You also danced with me at my first assembly. The first set, in fact."

"I remember. I had to punch Edward in the face to claim that privilege."

She stopped walking at once. "You did what?"

He laughed at the shock in her expression. "Did no one ever tell you about that row?"

"No."

"All of the male members of your family were terrified that you would have a less-than-enjoyable experience at your first assembly and had, therefore, concocted an elaborate scheme to ensure its success."

"And that scheme involved striking Edward?"

He slipped his hand from hers and set his arm across her back, guiding her around a puddle in their path. "I suggested that I ought to be permitted the first dance. Edward insisted on claiming it himself. In the end, I had little choice but to dim his lights a bit."

Once again she stopped walking to look up at him. "I am grateful you wished to help me, but coming to blows seems drastic."

"My and Edward's motivations were, I assure you, not at all the same."

She watched him, her gaze seeming to take in every inch of his face, as if searching for an answer in his expression.

With Mr. Downy's warning ringing in his ears about

not pressing his advantage too quickly, George kept to the least-revealing of his reasons. "I always did enjoy dancing with you. I haven't in quite some time, you know, and I would like to be able to again."

"A husband may dance with his wife anytime he wishes," she said.

"Anytime *she* wishes," he corrected. "A wife is not a slave, and a husband is not her master."

"How refreshing." She leaned her head against the side of his shoulder. "That is the best argument you have made for marriage thus far."

"Did you believe I would treat you poorly?" He most certainly hoped not.

"Of course not. I am simply pleased to know that I was right."

Progress, however small. "Do you still enjoy dancing?"

"I am so seldom permitted the opportunity that I hardly know."

He settled his arm more comfortably around her middle. "I have wanted to ask your mother if she would plan a ball, but in light of the undecided nature of our connection, I fear that would be presumptuous. One cannot, after all, throw a betrothal ball for a couple who may or may not remain betrothed."

"I suppose that would be uncomfortable." She sounded hesitant. "It is a shame, though. We haven't held a ball at Downy House since I was a little girl."

He had suspected she would enjoy a ball. "What if we did not declare it a betrothal ball? We could simply put it about that your family is celebrating being together again."

"It has been some time since all of us were here." She was at least a little in favor of the idea, then.

"We could plan it for three weeks from now." He knew he was pushing a little, but he had such little time that hesitancy was the enemy. "If you have decided to accept me and my hand, then we could officially announce our betrothal that night. If not, we need not say anything."

She pulled her shawl more closely around her shoulders. "And would I be required to dance the first set with Edward?"

"You will not be *required* to do anything."

She looked up at him and seemed genuinely pleased. "I look forward to the ball, George. And I hope that this time, you will not resort to fisticuffs with my brother."

"Let us both pray that does not prove necessary."

Six

"I fear I am beginning to regret our friendship, George." Tom spoke under his breath whilst his mother spoke at length of her plans for the upcoming ball.

"You and I have endured balls before," George reminded him.

"Not the planning of them. I have never heard anyone speak in such detail about fabric draping."

"Thomas, are you listening?" Mrs. Downy shot her son a look which sent both Tom and George immediately back to a proper posture and attentiveness.

"Yes, Mother. You were speaking of blue. A great deal of blue."

"Your sister likes blue," Mrs. Downy said. "Of course we will have blue at the ball."

"She also likes white roses," George pointed out. "We must make certain there are white roses."

Mrs. Downy looked to the housekeeper, who was dutifully writing down all the details of the upcoming event.

"Yes, ma'am. I've written it here: white roses."

"Excellent reminder, George." Mrs. Downy offered him a smile of genuine relief. She was far more concerned about the outcome of this ball than he would have guessed.

"You are encouraging her," Tom grumbled.

"I am attempting to be helpful. This ball means a great deal to her, and to Caroline."

Tom shook his head in apparent displeasure. "You talk of her as though she's the darling of Society. She's only Caroline."

"You, my friend, do not appreciate your sister as you ought."

"And I suppose you do."

He bit back a grin. "I do not, in fact, appreciate her as a sister."

"You two." Mrs. Downy's scolding tone hadn't decreased in the least. "Are you paying the least bit of attention?"

"Mother." Caroline spoke before either of them managed a response. "Why do we not allow the gentlemen to go about their day? I would far rather they save their best behavior for the ball itself than use it up now."

"You would not misbehave at the ball, would you?" Mrs. Downy eyed them all: her husband, both of her sons, George. "Not when it means so very much to us all?"

"I am certain they wouldn't," Caroline said. "But planning a ball is not really any of their areas of interest. Let us not torture them further."

Mrs. Downy shrugged a little and held her hands up. "I suppose—"

At that fleeting bit of hope, her male relations jumped to their feet, and with a few quickly offered words of farewell, practically flew from the room.

George remained behind. He had, after all, been the one

to propose the event. He could not abandon the ladies to the task of planning the ball. He approached the table where they sat.

"What can I do to help? Without Tom here to distract me, I may even prove myself an asset."

Mrs. Downy sighed. "Why is it that you are so much better behaved than those other three?"

"Perhaps I am simply a better person than they are."

She laughed, as he'd hoped she would. Even Caroline seemed amused. Her smiles had been too rare in the few days since he'd come from London. He wanted her to be light and happy, to be so pleased with the future spread before her that she, too, could laugh at absurdities and join in him in frivolity.

"I do thank you for your offer," Mrs. Downy said, "but I assure you we have this task very firmly in hand."

"You are certain?" he pressed.

"Quite."

"I had best go see how the gentlemen intend to spend their morning," he said, "and allow you ladies to return to your work. But, please, do send word if you think of anything I might do to assist you."

Mrs. Downy patted his hand. "Your mother must be so pleased with the gentleman you have become."

He forced a smile. "I sincerely hope she is." But he doubted it.

Mother's pleasure in any person was limited to their perceived importance. He, despite being well received amongst gentlemen and ladies alike within Society, could not claim a place of true social cachet, a failing which held great sway for her. Upon receiving word of his engagement, her congratulations were focused on the Downys' connections rather than on any hopes for his happiness.

He sketched a brief bow and made his escape. Why was it that thoughts of his mother's eternal disapproval always turned his mood sour? After twenty-two years of not meeting her expectations, he ought to have stopped allowing the realization to hurt.

He'd not gone far when he was stopped short by the sound of quick, slippered footfalls behind him. He turned about in time to see Caroline throw her arms around his middle. For a fraction of a moment, he stood paralyzed by shock. Then instinct took over. His arms settled naturally, easily, around her, returning her embrace with a sense of belonging he'd never felt with any other person.

"Your mother ought to be so very pleased with you." Her words shook with what sounded like a mixture of sadness and anger. "You are a good, kind, exemplary gentleman, and despite your evasive answer just now, I know that she does not see those things in you, or at least she does not allow those things to be enough to earn her approval." Her tender heart never ceased to touch his.

"Please do not allow my mother's coldness to upset you."

"How can I not? Every time she visits, she treats the lot of us as though we were nothing more than our ancestry. Far worse, she acts as though you are nothing at all because you haven't the social standing she wishes you did." Caroline still held tightly to him, her words muffled a bit by his jacket but spoken with such fervor that they could not possibly be misunderstood. "Your own mother, George, refuses to see the wonderful person you are. Of course that upsets me."

Was it any wonder he loved this woman so much? "Are you pleased, then, with the person I have become after such an inauspicious start? I was not so pleasant as a young boy, and I am well aware of it."

"You were always good," she said from within the folds of his arms. "Even when you teased me terribly, you were still kind."

"At the risk of sounding like the worst sort of son, I confess your good opinion means far more to me than any half-hearted approval my mother might be willing to bestow."

She leaned back enough to look up at him, though she made no effort to slip from his arms. "Why should my opinion matter so much?"

Though nerves sent his pulse into frighteningly rapid territory, George pressed on. This needed saying. "I am going to toss your father's well-meaning advice to the wind and tell you what I likely ought to have told you long ago."

He actually heard her swallow. Her coloring dropped off, and she took an absentminded step backward and out of his arms. He hadn't intended to alarm her but seemed to have done just that.

"My dear Caroline. I have loved you ever since I was old enough to understand what that meant. Your brothers are fine fellows, and your parents have been like parents to me, but it was you who pulled me here again and again. You, with your tender heart and quick mind, your beguiling conversation, your unparalleled company. I didn't blacken Edward's eyes simply because you are a fine dancer. I have loved you so long, I have lost track of the years."

She didn't speak, and didn't seem the least likely to. How he hoped Mr. Downy's words of warning did not turn prophetic.

He reached for Caroline's hand. Thank the heavens, he was not denied. "Did you never wonder why I have not come to visit these past fourteen months?"

"Tom and Edward are often gone. I assumed that without them here, you could not find a compelling enough reason to visit." Though she offered the explanation with a casual tone, the pain in her eyes could not be dismissed. She thought he hadn't cared enough to bother seeing her.

"I knew the time was fast approaching when your family would begin looking to arrange a match for you. I have been frantically addressing every aspect of my finances and estate and home, hoping that when the time came, I would have enough to offer that your family would accept my petition."

Was she hearing him? Accepting his explanation? Or, as her father had warned, did she fear he was merely telling her what he hoped she wanted to hear?

"Oh, no. No." She shook her head, stepping back. "I was afraid you would come to resent me because you didn't love me, but this—this is worse."

"Worse?"

She paced their small corner of the corridor. "You will be miserable. *We* will be miserable."

"Caroline?"

"You promised three weeks."

She kept a distance between them.

"I still have two and a half more. Please let me sort this out. Please give me the time and the space to do that."

She didn't answer, but rather turned and hurried away, something she'd done worryingly often of late.

He couldn't help a drop of his heart. Mr. Downy, it seemed, was right. Confessing his feelings had only made things worse.

Seven

"How was it I knew I would find you gazing forlornly out of a window?"

Despite Edward's tone of light censure, Caroline did not change her posture, nor her gaze. "I have had a great deal on my mind of late."

"A great deal more than necessary, if you ask me."

"I didn't," she pointed out.

He sat beside her on the window seat. "You have been playing least in sight this past week. Your absence has set Mother into hysterics, Father into hermitry in his library, and poor Tom has spent every waking hour consoling a nearly frantic George. That leaves only me to search you out and say what needs to be said."

She refused to meet his gaze. "Do not scold me, Edward. I am facing the entirety of my future. I have every right to be very careful about how I proceed."

"I never said otherwise. I only feel you ought to proceed with a perspective other than your own." Edward leaned back against the window, apparently settling in for a long and drawn-out discussion. "Do not give me that perturbed look so soon, Caroline. I am an older brother, and I mean to fill that role quite thoroughly just now."

She gave him the briefest of glances. "I suppose your thoughts couldn't hurt."

"Your confidence is overwhelming." He used the dry tone that never failed to bring a smile to her face. "Allow me to explain what I have observed over the years. You have always known that your marriage would be an arranged one, undertaken with the purpose of saving the family from financial ruin. Realizing this, you found it best to never allow yourself to fall even the tiniest bit in love with anyone. Losing your heart, even an inch of it, to any young gentleman would end only with heartache, so you wisely guarded yourself against that."

She nodded. She had been careful with her affections, for the exact reasons he'd stated. Courting heartbreak had never seemed a wise course.

"The mind and heart do not often discuss things as they ought. I realized a number of years ago that the walls you had painstakingly built around yourself had proven insufficient against the depth and sincerity of George's regard."

She pressed her cheek to the cool glass. "He told me he loves me."

"And he does. He has for at least five years now, quite possibly longer."

"Can you not see how terrible that makes everything? He will expect me to love him in return, and I have never thought of him that way. He is my friend, my kind companion. What if I am unable to love him the way he wishes? He will be miserable, and I will be miserable in return."

Edward tipped his head back, tossing his gaze at the ceiling. "You are being uncharacteristically thick about this."

Why was he scolding her?

"I remember your first assembly," he said, "and the absolute relief on your face when you were told that I would stand up with you for the first set. You were grateful to not be required to undertake that harrowing moment with a complete stranger." He looked at her once more. "But when you were told that George would be taking my place, it was not relief that I saw on your face, Caroline. Your very heart was in your eyes. I knew then that you loved him, but I didn't realize that *you* didn't know that you did."

She sat up straighter. "But I don't. He is my friend. He is only my friend." Why was it that the declaration brought a thickness to her throat and tears to her eyes?

"You have only ever allowed yourself to think of him in those terms due to your sense of self-preservation. But you are no longer saving yourself from hurt; you are causing it." He pulled her into a one-armed, brotherly embrace. "You have been told all of your life that loving someone was a risk you dare not take. Sweet, little Caroline, you must take that risk now. You have the opportunity to marry for love. Do you have any idea how rare that is?"

She leaned more heavily against him. "Surely you intend to marry for love."

"Though our estate is now solvent, I have no expectations of ever having a true income. Tom is in an even worse position. He and I both know we will likely never marry. We've known it as long as you have known the state of your future. We have nothing to offer a lady, nothing to truly recommend us. Please do not throw away your opportunity because you are afraid."

"I am not at all certain I am brave enough for this."

He squeezed her shoulders. "You needn't be afraid of George. He would move heaven and earth for you if he were able. Tell him of your worries and your fears, and he will hear you, and love you, and do all he can to walk this path with you. But you cannot begin that journey without a first step."

She took a deep, fortifying breath. "Is George terribly upset with me?"

"He is worried about you. Go put the poor man—and the rest of us along with him—out of our collective misery." He set her away from him, but held her gaze. "And be happy. Promise me you will be happy."

"Will *you* be?"

His usual smile returned. "When have you ever known me not to be?"

The bravado fell a bit flat, however. She'd heard real sadness in his voice as he'd admitted to his terribly slim chances of finding his own domestic happiness. She kissed his cheek as she'd done with him and father and Tom ever since she was a little girl.

"You are the very best of brothers." She prayed he could hear and see her sincerity.

"I know. Now go find poor George. He needs your reassurance far more than I do."

She took a moment to give her brother another hug. He shooed her off with a feigned show of annoyance.

Caroline searched the library, the gardens, the sitting room. She even peeked about the stables and orchard. She found no sign of George. Where could he have gone off to? Just when she'd convinced herself that he was off grouse shooting with Tom, she found her brother in the billiard room, alone.

"Have you seen George?" she asked.

Tom lined up a shot. "He left this morning for Shropshire to fetch his mother and bring her back for the ball."

"He's gone?" She had not anticipated that. "But, why did he not bid us farewell?"

"He did." Tom sent balls flying with a thrust of his cue. "But you were moping in your room, and he didn't wish to impose."

"I was not—" Actually, she had been moping a little.

And, it seemed, she had pushed him away in the process. "How long do you suspect him to be gone?"

Tom crossed to the far side of the billiard table. "Couldn't say." He tapped his cue against the table side, eyes narrowing in concentration. "He'll be back for the ball, I suspect."

"Did he seem terribly upset when he left?"

"I don't know." Tom never had been as helpful as Edward. "He's never in good spirits when faced with seeing his mother. She's a bit of a harridan, you know."

"I know." Everyone knew, in fact. "But he *is* returning for the ball, is he not?"

"I already answered that question." Tom didn't look up from his game. Indeed, he'd hardly acknowledged her throughout their conversation.

"Are you upset with me?"

"Everyone is upset with you, Caroline. You are making George miserable, and none of us likes it." He took another shot. As the balls rolled, he looked at her at last. "But George made us solemnly vow to be patient with you, or else he'd pummel the lot of us when he returned. We, being intelligent, believe him."

How like George. And how like her to have never seen more in his fiery defense of her than staid friendship.

"Odd that the first smile I've seen from you in ages comes upon hearing that your brothers' well-being has been threatened." Despite his protestation, Tom sounded amused.

"I was only thinking how often George has been my champion."

"The poor bloke loves you, for all the good it's doing him." Tom set his billiard cue in the rack on the wall. "You're torturing him, you know."

"That has recently been brought to my attention." She had meant to try harder to sort out her jumbled feelings. But she'd meant to do so with George there. He would have listened, and understood. He would have held her hand as she struggled.

Good, kind George. Lovely, wonderful George.

Her George.

Eight

"With a bit of effort, the Downys could make this approach far more impressive." Mother eyed the facade of Downy House as though it were a hovel surrounded by mud and muck. "One would never guess they were kin to a duke."

She treats the lot of us as though we were nothing more than our ancestry. Caroline had been quite astute in that observation. Mother reduced everyone to their respective bloodlines, for better or for worse. The irony, of course, was that her own ancestry did not stand up to scrutiny.

"I am certain the Downys have far more pressing matters to see to than the appearance of their home."

Mother waved that off. "First impressions are crucial, George. Remember that."

How could he help but remember something she never let him forget? "I do hope you will be civil to the Downys, Mother. They have received me warmly these many years and deserve warmth in return."

"I am always civil." Mother's declaration didn't entirely hit its mark, delivered as it was down the length of her haughtily upturned nose.

The carriage came to a stop at the front portico. The carriage door was opened. The Downys' footman handed Mother down. George waited a moment longer, needing to brace himself for the coming few days.

Mother would, no doubt, be nearly impossible.

The Downys would be in a frenzy of planning.

Caroline would be . . . He didn't know what to expect from her. She'd gone from hesitantly friendly to a hermit in the short time he'd been here. She'd cried more and talked less than she ever had before. It worried him. Deeply.

But he'd made an ironclad bargain with her, one he was honor-bound to see through to the very end, whatever that end might be. He squared his shoulders and stepped down from the carriage. Their trunks were already being unloaded. The stable hands were seeing to the horses. When he stepped into the entryway, the housekeeper was already being berated by Mother. All-in-all, a typical arrival at Downy House.

"George!"

His heart leapt to his throat at the sound of Caroline's voice calling his name with such excitement.

"You've come at last!" She ran down the stairs, enthusiasm emanating from every inch of her.

"Have you missed me?" he asked.

She answered by simply throwing her arms around him, much the way she had in the corridor the day her mother had enlisted them all to help plan the ball. Except this time, there was no pity or sadness in the embrace. She seemed overwhelmingly happy to see him.

Holding fast to her in return, he said, "This is the best welcome I have ever received."

"You were gone so long, George."

"Only a week." He rested his cheek on the top of her head.

"It was a very long week. Mother kept predicting you wouldn't return. Tom insisted you'd joined the navy to get away from me."

He rubbed his hand in large circles on her back. He breathed in her sweet, flowery scent. "I hope you didn't believe either of them."

"Edward told me not to."

He had always thought her oldest brother was smarter than the rest of them combined.

"I must say, for a young lady of such exalted standing, this is a rather unseemly display." Mother had been so quiet George had all but forgotten her.

Caroline rose to her own defense. "Your son left without bidding his fiancée a proper farewell. Is that not rather low-class as well?"

Mother offered a confused humph before gliding up the stairs, dignity rolling off her in waves.

"Mrs. Barrington?" Caroline called after her. "Would it be terribly unseemly of me to kiss your son here in the entryway?"

Mother picked up her pace.

"What has come over you, Caroline?" George wasn't complaining; he was simply confused.

"I've missed you."

He settled her in the crook of his arm, walking with her slowly toward the back terrace. "I have missed you as well, my dear."

"Without you here, I had no one to talk with. No one to walk with me in the gardens. No one to sit with in the library or laugh with about the oddities of life." She leaned her head on his shoulder as they walked. Though she had done that on occasion before, there was something different in it now. "There was no *you*, and I didn't like that at all."

Please let this be more than her pining for my friendship.

"I've had no one to hold my hand, or to put an arm around me when I was afraid."

He stopped up short. "You've been afraid? Of what?"

"You." She was so much more at ease with him than in the weeks before; even that answer didn't overly concern him. "I worried you were marrying me for the wrong reasons. And then I worried that I was marrying you for the wrong reasons. And I worried that all of those wrong reasons meant that our marriage was ill-fated, and then if our marriage fell apart, that I would lose you."

"Is that why you were so opposed to this match?" He turned to face her. "Because you thought it would . . . ruin our friendship?"

"I couldn't bear the thought of losing it—of losing you."

He slipped an arm around her waist. "And what do you think of the match now?"

"It will change things between us, but it doesn't have to be a bad change. You will still be a wonderful, lovely, integral part of my life."

George pressed a kiss to her forehead. "And you will always be the best part of mine."

"I want to try, George. I want to try thinking of you as something more than a friend." He could hear hints of nervousness in her voice. "I don't know if I can, but I would like to make the attempt."

He kept his arms around her. "You will allow me to take this next week before the ball and court you as I'd hoped to? Really, truly court you?"

"Yes, please."

At the earnestness of her response, he couldn't help a grin. He'd been given something more than a mere chance at winning her regard; he'd been granted eager permission to do so.

He didn't mean to waste the opportunity.

Some of Caroline's earliest memories were of reminding herself not to daydream about courtship and love. Now as a young woman, she'd spent so long convincing herself that she didn't care about such things that *un*convincing herself was proving something of a struggle.

George brought her flowers every morning at breakfast. He never failed to kiss her hand anytime they parted company. He smiled warmly at her from across the table every evening at dinner. He sat beside her each night whilst Mother read long, misery-inducing passages of poetry, and he never looked the least unhappy about it.

Each show of affection from him prompted in her an instinctual response of dismissal, a reaction learned out of self-preservation. With each loving gesture George made, Caroline forced herself to remember that she needn't hide behind armor any longer. Slowly, inch by inch, that armor was slipping away.

The night before the ball, George sat beside her, as usual, in the drawing room after dinner. He'd taken to sitting close, very close. So close, in fact, that the chill of approaching autumn in the air didn't reach her at all despite the lack of a fire.

Mrs. Barrington clearly didn't approve. As she had the last few nights, she eyed them with pursed lips and narrowed eyes.

"I suspect your mother thinks I'm a heathen," Caroline whispered.

"And a bad influence."

The introduction of a courtship between them hadn't diminished their ability to laugh together. She was infinitely grateful for that.

Mrs. Barrington turned to Mother. "Do you not intend to say anything to them? I, for one, find this display appalling. There is something unacceptably intimate about a couple sitting so very close, smiling so warmly, laughing so unabashedly."

"I, for one," Father answered, "find 'this display' unspeakably reassuring. They are happy, and that puts this father's heart at ease."

"Are you?" George whispered to her. "Happy, I mean."

"I am. That's not to say I'm not still a little nervous, a little uncertain. But I'm not afraid, and yes, I am quite happy."

George pressed a kiss to her forehead.

"George Edmund Barrington!" Mrs. Barrington's usually controlled tones turned ear-shatteringly shrill. "You take your lips off of that girl this instant. How unseemly you have become."

He looked anything but chastened. His hand took gentle hold of Caroline's, and he remained as close to her as ever. When her eyes met his, she saw such fond contentment. Her heart both settled into a place of warm relief and sped its beating.

Though she had no experience with love—she'd never been permitted the luxury—Caroline knew instinctively that these moments of quiet contentment mingled with eager anticipation were the result of finally allowing herself to feel that long-dreamed-of emotion.

Nine

Upon arriving in Gloucestershire with Mother one week earlier, George had fully prepared himself for heart-wrenching disappointment. But the past few days had left him at a loss for words . . . in the best way. Caroline sat beside him, held his hand, laughed with him. She looked at him with real affection. She was happy.

His head wasn't so firmly in the clouds that he thought Caroline had fallen in love with him in only a matter of days. But at last he had hope that someday she would.

He stood at the base of the stairs, watching as his beloved slowly descended, dressed for a ball at which they might very well be publicly announcing their betrothal. Even if she wasn't ready to take that step yet, he wasn't worried. He was being permitted the chance to court her. That was all he'd ever wanted: the opportunity to attempt to win her heart.

"You look very handsome this evening." She stood only two steps from the bottom, smiling at him. How easily he could grow accustomed to moments like these.

"And you, my beloved Caroline, are a vision." He offered her the bouquet of white roses the gardener had helped him assemble. "I know you can't hold them while you're dancing, but I wanted you to have them all the same. I know how much you love white roses."

She accepted the offering with such obvious enjoyment. She held the bouquet to her nose, closing her eyes as she savored the fragrance. "I will never see another white rose without thinking of you."

"Then I am glad I didn't give you a bouquet of stinkweed."

Caroline called over a passing maid. "Would you have these placed in a vase?" she asked. "And place the vase near the receiving line?"

The maid curtsied. "Yes, miss."

Caroline's hands were empty once more, the perfect opportunity to take her hand in his. "Are you excited about the ball?" he asked as they walked toward the entry, where her parents would be waiting for her.

"I am," she said. "Are you?"

"I once pummeled a good friend for the sole purpose of securing your hand for a single dance. Of course I am excited about this ball."

She threaded her arm through his. "You are assuming, then, that I will dance with you."

"I certainly hope so."

Her parents and brothers had already assembled in the receiving area, anticipating the arrival of their guests. George deposited her in their midst and offered them all the expected bow. "I will see you all in the ballroom."

"George?" Caroline stopped him with a hand on his arm. "Will you not join us in the line?"

His eyes darted to her parents before returning to her. "Doing so would negate the need for a betrothal announcement. It would be an announcement in and of itself." He watched her more closely, unsure if her request meant what he hoped it did. His pulse pounded high in his neck. "Have you decided to make this a true betrothal?"

He held his breath, and he firmly suspected her family did as well.

"I—" Her gaze fell on her brothers. George didn't think he had ever seen her blush so deeply. "This is—" The blush only deepened.

"Pardon us," George said to her family and, after taking quick hold of her hand once more, he hurried her in to the drawing room, where they could be alone. "Tell me what is worrying you, dearest."

"Nothing now," she said. "My brothers would tease me mercilessly if I said any of this in front of them."

"Any of what?"

"I love you, George Barrington."

Those five words froze him on the spot.

"Not in a life-changing way," she added. "Not yet. But thinking of you as anything other than my friend is a new undertaking for me. I understand these things take time."

"Are you saying that you believe you *could* love me in that way?"

She held fast to his hand. "I am saying that I believe I might already, I simply have no practice in recognizing it. I'm still sorting it all out."

Not a terribly difficult obstacle to overcome. "Then allow me to show you every day what it is to be loved and cherished and treasured. Allow me the opportunity to make that experience so clear that you need never doubt it again."

"I would like that very much."

Was she saying what he thought she was saying? He studied her face, her smiling, contented, happy face. "Does this mean your father will be announcing our betrothal this evening?"

"Only if you will grant me the first dance, and the last, and all of the dances in between."

He brushed a hand along her cheek. "As well as join

your family in the reception line? There will be a great many whispers by the time your father finally explains things."

Her smile grew tenfold. "How very unseemly of us."

George slid his arms around her waist. "So long as we are treading that path, I believe I shall kiss you. And I do not at all mean a staid, brotherly sort of kiss."

She set her hands on his shoulders. "I am ready to be thoroughly scandalized, George."

He leaned in, savoring the long-awaited moment and the promise it held. His lips brushed hers once, twice. Breathing proved a chore, as did hearing anything above the pounding of his own pulse. But the feel of her tucked up to him, in his arms at last, wiped away any doubt, any worry.

He kissed her just as he'd promised he would, right there in the drawing room. And long afterward, he simply held her, blessing fate and the heavens for bringing her into his life.

His darling, wonderful friend.

His sweet, loving Caroline.

A Happy Beginning

One

Stirlingshire, Scotland, 1850

Against all odds, Sophia Pemberton had fallen in love. With Scotland.

For six months she had resided on a large estate with Loch Lomond to the west and Ben Lomond to the east, and she already thought of the wild and untamed countryside as home. The estate was not hers. The land was not hers. Yet somehow she had come to think of the view as belonging to her.

The children she tended, however, were far more difficult to love.

"I will not be spoken to that way by a servant." Seven-year-old Ella Haddington sniffed at the stable hand holding her pony's lead. She, along with her brother, were undertaking their riding lessons.

"You were kickin' the pony, miss," the beleaguered

young stable hand explained. "She don't like when you do that."

"It does not matter what I was doing," Ella snapped. "You are not permitted to order me about." The girl sounded like her mother.

Sophia had learned early in her time as the Haddingtons' governess that correcting any of the family in their treatment of the servants only made the situation worse. Though the servants weren't overly fond of her, she didn't want to cause trouble for them. She'd learned to bite her tongue, no matter how much she wished to speak.

"I do not like this pony." Nine-year-old Joseph never liked any pony the stable master chose for him. "Give me another, Buchanan."

Dermot Buchanan, the Haddingtons' stable master, simply kept chewing on the length of straw between his teeth. "I'm fully certain the animal don't care for you either, laddie. He manages to endure it, though."

Sophia bit back a smile as she bounced almost one-year-old Jane on her knee. Dermot never allowed the Haddingtons to run roughshod over him. He never allowed *anyone* to run roughshod over him.

"Well, I don't like the pony." Joseph tipped his chin upward.

The stable master gave a firm nod and pulled the straw from his teeth. "Fair enough." He tossed the straw aside then stepped up to the boy and pony. He reached up and pulled Joseph from the saddle and set him on his feet.

"What are you doing?" Joseph demanded.

"You can walk," Dermot said. "A fella who doesn't appreciate his pony doesn't deserve to be carried about by the animal."

"I will tell my parents that you didn't allow me to finish my lessons."

"I've no doubt you will." Dermot jerked his head in the direction of the house. "Best get on with your tattling, boy."

Joseph huffed away from his pony in high dudgeon, slowly making his way toward her, his scowl reaching monumental levels. He would be impossible for the rest of the day, more so than usual. Still, Sophia couldn't begrudge Dermot his scolding. Joseph deserved the sharp words; he received them far too seldom.

The little tantrum didn't distract Dermot at all. He gave a quick, sharp whistle. The pony turned its head in his direction. He clicked his tongue and motioned for the animal to follow, and it did. They always did. The animals heeded him. His stable hands heeded him. Sophia had even seen Mr. Haddington subdued by nothing more than a sharp look of censure from the self-possessed master of his stables.

Dermot never said much to anyone but kept very much to himself. Still, everyone within a several mile radius knew and respected him. Sophia also kept very much to herself, but all she had to show for it was eating every meal by herself and having no one to talk to.

Joseph reached her and set his fists on his hips. "I am hungry."

"You may have milk and biscuits after your sister has finished her riding lesson." Sophia continued bouncing Jane, hoping to stave off the usual noonday fussing.

Joseph's fussing generally couldn't be staved off. "I won't wait for her."

"You have little choice."

His little mouth turned down in a monumental pout. "Why do you never do anything helpful?"

When she'd accepted the position as governess to three young children, Sophia had imagined that her days would be spent imparting wisdom to eager learners, going on morning walks and afternoon outings, singing, and laughing. Not one of those predictions had proven accurate. The children disliked her, and she worked hard not to return the sentiment.

"Dermot," the stable hand called out. "The lassie's kickin' her horse again."

A second stable hand emerged, taking up the reins of the pony that Joseph had been riding.

Dermot turned to face Ella and her mistreated mount. "Am I needing to set you on your feet as well, missie?"

Ella was a bit less blustery than her brother, but only a little. "The pony is too slow."

"That is because you are practicing riding at a walk today. Of the two of you, only that beast is managing the thing."

Oh, to have the ability to speak that way to a member of the Haddington family. Dermot Buchanan had an air of inarguable authority about him. She could not imagine Queen Victoria herself arguing with Dermot.

In the early weeks of her employment, Sophia had been rather intimidated by him. But she'd watched him, likely more often than was seemly, and had discovered something else about the stable master. He was stern, yes, but he was also kind. She'd never heard a sharp word spoken to his staff that was not both necessary and deserved. He had never mistreated the animals in his care, even those whose stubbornness must have been exceedingly frustrating. Though he told the children in no uncertain terms when their behavior was unacceptable, he never did so with anger or malice.

Dermot Buchanan was something unique and wonderful.

Ella had twitched her chin up to a haughty angle, an expression she had most certainly learned from her mother. "I do not want to ride at a walk any longer," she told Dermot.

"Very well."

Quick as anything, Dermot pulled Ella from her saddle and set her on the ground, just as he had Joseph.

Ella approached Sophia's chair with her lips pursed and her eyes narrowed. "I meant I wanted to ride fast."

"Mr. Buchanan will allow you to ride fast when he feels you are ready to do so." Sophia had spent much of her six months at Haddington House attempting to teach the children to be concerned with the welfare of others rather than only themselves. The effort hadn't yielded results, but she didn't know what else to try.

Jenny, a maid from the house, arrived at precisely that moment. She always came to fetch the children at the end of their lessons. She must have noticed that Joseph's ride had come to a premature end.

"Jenny is here," Sophia told the children. "You are to wash before your milk and biscuits, as always. Cook will not send up your tray until I tell her to, and I intend to check your hands when I reach the nursery. Is that understood?"

They grumbled, which was all they ever did when given instructions to do something they did not find enjoyable.

Sophia handed Jane to Jenny. "Thank you for fetching them."

"You're welcome, Miss Pemberton." She curtsied as she spoke and kept her eyes diverted.

Though Sophia no longer claimed a spot on the upper rungs of Society, the servants at Haddington House treated her as if she did. Even the upper servants, with whom she was on more equal footing, treated her like a stranger around whom they didn't quite know what to do or say. Of course, to the Haddington family, she was every bit as dismissible and lowly as a scullery maid or a knife boy.

She had been warned that such was the plight of a governess, to never belong in either world, but the reality of the situation had proven more difficult than she'd anticipated. She had never in all her life felt so utterly alone.

Usually Sophia spent the fifteen minutes after Jenny took the children up to the house leisurely making her way to the nursery. But this day, she'd come to the paddock with a plan, one she hoped she had courage enough to see through.

She approached the gate, watching as Dermot instructed his stable hands in their tasks. Her eye couldn't help but be drawn to him whenever he was near. He was handsome, yes, but the pull she felt was far more than the appeal of his dark hair and piercing brown eyes. His posture was one of a man confident in his abilities and sure of his place in the world. Everything about him told a person that his respect had to be earned and could be just as easily lost. Such an obvious and palpable degree of confidence was an unusual thing in a member of the servant class, who were taught to appear subservient even if it went against their natures.

What was it that made Dermot so different from others of his station? How was it he communicated so much when generally saying so little? And would he, as she suspected, and desperately hoped, prove to be the one person on the entire estate who might be willing to toss aside conventions and treat her like a real person?

A moment later, he spotted her at the gate and stepped over to her. The tiniest change in his expression asked the question he didn't speak out loud: What was it she wanted?

"May I ask a favor?"

Dermot nodded, a fresh piece of straw moving up and down between his lips. She didn't know why he did that, nor why it was so mesmerizing.

"I have Friday afternoons to myself," she said. "And, I—" Heavens, this seemed presumptuous now that she was actually asking. "When I was growing up, I used to ride a great deal. I would very much like to do so again."

"You would?" He didn't speak often, but she never tired of hearing his gravelly, Scots voice.

"I never learned how to saddle a horse, and I realize that means one of your stable hands would be inconvenienced. I am, however, able to brush a horse down after a ride. I don't mean to leave the estate, so I wouldn't need any help riding, or anyone to accompany me. I am simply hoping for a moment of . . ." She wasn't sure how to finish the sentence.

A HAPPY BEGINNING

She hoped for a moment of enjoyment? Of peace? Happiness?

"How long has it been since you rode?" he asked.

"My father sold the horses four years ago—all but his, that is, but I was never permitted to ride his gelding."

Dermot leaned against the gate frame. "Was the horse too powerful for you?"

She shook her head no. "I am an excellent horsewoman. My abilities were not in question; he was simply never very good at doing without."

The straw moved about as he watched her, silently. Had she asked too much? Presumed too much?

"So you've not ridden in years," he said. "You'd be wise to keep to quiet mounts early on, until you've accustomed yourself again."

Hope tickled at her heart. "Then you'll allow me to ride?"

"That favor's not mine to grant," he said. "The master and missus dictate such things."

"Oh." That was not good news.

She couldn't ask Mr. Haddington for permission; he had an unsettling way of looking at her. His presence was only bearable in locations where she knew every possible exit. With Mrs. Haddington's tendency to insult and demean, she was not a much better option. Still, Mrs. Haddington didn't feel threatening in the same way her husband did. She was unkind but not dangerous.

Sophia would simply have to choose the lesser of the two evils. "I will ask Mrs. Haddington."

"Truly?" His brows shot upward and his eyes pulled wide.

"It seems the only choice if I wish to ride again."

Dermot made a deep sound of contemplation. "If Mrs. Haddington says aye, I'll see to it you've a horse to ride come Friday afternoon. Kelpie would give you a fine ride. Mina would as well."

"Truly?"

He nodded.

"You won't change your mind? People are forever breaking their word to me."

Another communicative nod.

"And please assure whichever of the stable hands assigned to help me that I am far better behaved than any of the children."

He stepped back from the gate. "Aye. I'll do that."

"Thank you, Mr. Buchanan."

He offered no words of welcome or farewell. He simply nodded again.

She watched him walk back to the stable, her heart leaping about. She'd found the nerve to approach him, to speak with him on a personal matter. How long she had wanted to do that.

Her mind spun with possibilities. He would see how well she rode, how much she knew of and enjoyed horses. They would have something to talk about. Perhaps, sometime in the future, he would even ride with her. Perhaps she would be permitted to come by the stables to visit with him. In time they might come to be friends, perhaps more.

Perhaps.

Two

Sophia Pemberton was a surprise. Dermot had watched her these past six months as she'd struggled with the Haddington children. He had assumed she was no different than the handful of browbeaten, lifeless governesses who had preceded her. But she'd stepped forward two days earlier and asked a favor of him, one that benefitted no one but her—the others had seemed terrified to even acknowledge their own existence, let alone their right to some happiness—and she'd further declared her intention of taking the request to their dragon of an employer.

This governess had a bit of steel to her. A surprise, indeed.

Aiden, the most experienced and reliable of the stable staff, spoke as he cleaned out the hoof of Barnaby, Mr. Haddington's prized gelding. "'Tis Friday afternoon, Dermot, and we've seen neither hide nor hair of the governess. Do you wager Miss Proper'll make an appearance, then?"

"Aye."

"Then you think the Missus gave her permission?"

"No."

Aiden set Barnaby's foreleg down. "Then why d'you believe she'll come?"

"Civility."

The Scots tended to fight things out; the English preferred irritating their enemies into submission with ceaseless propriety. Miss Pemberton would come to the stable, not to ride a horse but to apologize for not coming to ride a horse, or something equally English.

"You ought to have put a bit of blunt on that wager, Dermot. You'd've won handsomely." Aiden motioned with his head toward the doors.

Miss Pemberton was but a few steps from the stable. She always wore dark, subdued colors. One would think she was forever on her way to a funeral.

She stepped inside, and her eyes immediately found him. He'd never seen her smile. For reasons he couldn't yet identify, that bothered him. She seemed like the sort who ought to smile.

"Mr. Buchanan." She stepped up to him, meeting his eye without hesitation. "I am sorry to have not come sooner. No doubt someone has gone to trouble on my behalf, but I have only just received Mrs. Haddington's answer regarding my ride this afternoon."

"And are you to ride?"

Though her shoulders remained squared and her demeanor calm and collected, unmistakable disappointment flickered through her dark, expressive eyes. "She feels my time would be better spent on less frivolous pursuits."

"Isn't Friday afternoon *your* time to spend as you choose?" he asked.

"It is, but the mares are *hers* to lend out as *she* chooses, and in this case, she chooses not to."

So Miss Pemberton was to be denied this simple pleasure. Even the stable hands were permitted to ride now and then in the name of exercising the mounts or cooling them when the family didn't care to take the time to do so.

How could the family treat her with less consideration than they did their lower servants? She was English, after all. And well born. Refined.

"Would you mind terribly, Mr. Buchanan, if I stayed a moment and simply looked?"

Looked? "You mean at the horses?"

"Yes, please. I do like horses." Her gaze slid to Barnaby and lingered a moment, admiration and eagerness touching the planes of her face. "I will be no bother; I'm particularly good at keeping out of the way."

What an odd sort of lady she was, putting forth her invisibility as an asset when her class generally found being unnoticed a disagreeable experience. That, he felt certain, was the reason the other governesses had worn their forced quietude with such discomfort. Miss Pemberton seemed determined to bear it with pride.

As a governess, she was more than merely a surprise; she was a niggling question, tickling the back of his mind. She was a mystery.

"I'll show you about m'self," he said.

She shook her head without hesitation. "I could not ask that of you."

"You didn't. I offered. If you'd asked, I'd likely have turned you down."

She accepted his reply with neither offense nor humor. On first acquaintance, one could be excused for thinking her rather emotionless. She hid her emotions well; that was all. He sensed that despite the thick aura of England about her, Miss Pemberton had a bit of fire smoldering beneath the surface.

He jerked his chin in the direction of the gelding. "This here's Barnaby."

"His markings put me in mind of Odin, the stallion at Tockwith Grange," she said.

She'd seen Viscount Cattal's famed stallion? And at Tockwith, it seemed. Perhaps she came from a more exalted family than he'd suspected. That might explain why she never seemed wholly intimidated by anyone. People were forever puzzling over his reasons for being so sure of himself. He'd wager his reasons and hers were one and the same: despite the current state of their employment, they'd both experienced moments when they were the most important people in the room.

He took her from one stall to the next, to whichever animal she indicated a wish to visit. He gave her the name of each animal and a few details. She asked insightful, intelligent questions and actually listened to his answers, something the Haddingtons and their occasional guests seldom did.

He stopped in front of the stall housing Miss Ella's pony. "I believe you recognize this tortured soul."

"I do, indeed. Poor creature must relish the days when Miss Ella does not have riding lessons."

Will, one of the younger stable hands, approached, but at the sight of Miss Pemberton, stopped abruptly. He hung back, eyes diverted like a lower servant approaching a member of the fine and fancy elite.

"Forgive me," he muttered. "I only meant to ask what you're wanting me to do now that I'm done with the tasks you gave me."

When was the last time anyone on his staff had waited for instructions? Dermot made a rule of keeping a close eye on what each hand was doing so he could assign another job before the first was finished. He'd ushered Miss Pemberton all around the stables when he had a load of other work to do. He couldn't remember the last time he'd been so fully distracted.

She must have sensed the direction of his thoughts. "It appears I have interfered with your work, Mr. Buchanan."

"That you have, lass." He had no one to blame but himself, yet he meant to do a fair bit of blaming.

Her brow pulled downward, and her wide mouth turned down in disappointment. "I asked too many questions, didn't I? My father forever told me not make a nuisance of myself by asking questions." She clasped her hands. "My apologies, Mr. Buchanan. And" —she turned to Will—"to you, as well. I will leave all of you to your work, as I ought to have done from the first." She gave a quick nod to them both. "Good afternoon."

Miss Pemberton left swiftly, not looking at anyone as she went.

I should get back to work. Dermot eyed the now-empty stable doorway. *There's loads to do.*

Yet his feet carried him from the stable, following the route Miss Pemberton had taken. She'd already reached the path leading back to the house. The lass moved swiftly.

'Twould be easy as anything to simply go back to the stable. Why, then, were his feet ignoring his mind entirely?

"Miss Pemberton." Apparently his voice was equally as disobedient.

She stopped and looked back. He reached her in the next moment.

"Did I forget something?" How could she look so serene while sounding so uncertain?

"No. You didn't forget anything."

Her eyes darted about a moment before settling on him once more. "Did I do something wrong?"

"You left upset."

"And that was . . . wrong?"

"Not wrong."

She turned her head a bit away, eyes narrowing. "I don't understand."

This was exactly why Dermot avoided conversations: too many ended in confusion. "You left upset. I didn't like it."

"I'm s—"

"I wasn't lookin' for an 'I'm sorry.'" Crivins, she apologized a lot. "I only need to know why you're unhappy." Though why he needed to know, even he couldn't say.

"Oh." She blinked a few times, as if his concern surprised her as much as it did him. "I disrupted your day and made a burden of myself."

"You weren't a burden." A disruption, perhaps. A confusion, yes. But not a burden.

"A bother, then. And for that I am sorry."

He heard himself answer with words he'd not intended to speak. "You're welcome to come visit the horses at any time."

"Thank you. I promise not to interrupt anyone's work to do so, especially yours."

More words slipped from his lips unbidden. "I'd hope you'd offer a 'good day' at the least."

The tiniest hint of pleasure entered her deep brown eyes. "I will."

She no longer appeared upset or embarrassed or whatever it was she'd been when leaving the stables. That was good enough to satisfy him. He gave a quick dip of his head in anticipation of returning to work.

"Mr. Buchanan?" She, apparently, wasn't finished.

He paused and silently gave her leave to continue.

"Would you—Might I—" Though she'd never seemed overly talkative, Miss Pemberton was not generally so tongue-tied. Just what favor did she mean to ask this time? "Would you mind if I came and talked with you now and then?" Her words rushed out, quick, almost flustered. "I would be careful of your time and obligations, and I promise not to pester you with questions."

Talk? With a high-born lady? "What on earth would we find to talk about?"

"Well . . ." She clasped her hands once more. "I have wished ever since my arrival to learn more of Scotland, and you have lived here all your life. We share an interest in horses. We work on the same estate. Those topics would likely suffice for a time."

That sounded painful. "I don't talk."

"But we have talked quite a bit today," she said.

He shook his head at such an argument in favor of more conversation. "Idle talk'd only keep me from m' work."

"I could help. I do know how to curry and brush a horse."

That was near about the most ridiculous thing he'd heard: a governess with white kid gloves and silk dresses and fine manners doing the work of a stable boy. "We've hands enough to see to those tasks."

"I wasn't petitioning for employment." Her clasped fingers fidgeted and tugged at one another. Though she didn't look away, she grew noticeably uncomfortable. "I was hoping to . . . make a friend."

A friend? Of him? And her an Englishwoman? She might have deemed him worthy of her notice and conversation, but he had spent enough time interacting with the English and, worse still, the upper classes, to know that such a thing was not a good idea. He'd rather not endure more of the condescension he'd received all his life.

"I'm not in need of friends, Miss Pemberton," he said.

Heat touched her face and her gaze dropped away. "A good afternoon to you, Mr. Buchanan."

Humility never seemed to sit lightly on the shoulders of those born to privilege. Miss Pemberton, however, wore it more like sackcloth than a sack of rocks, as if accepting the dismissal of others was unavoidable, as if she almost deserved punishment rather than this moment of discomfort, which would be shed as quickly as possible.

Dermot knew he'd done the right thing. A friendship between them was not a wise idea. He'd seen far more of the world than she likely had and knew more of the pitfalls of her suggestion.

Why, then, did the necessary rejection of her offer sit with such weight on his chest? Why did he feel like he'd made a mistake?

Three

I'm not in need of friends. The look in his eyes when he'd said that . . . Sophia's face burned at the memory. Until that moment she'd honestly believed that Dermot Buchanan thought of her as being on even footing with him. But a man did not respond to an offer of friendship from an equal with such easy dismissal.

She poked her fork at the venison on her plate. Jenny had the onerous task of putting the children to bed, nearly the only unpleasant task relating to their care that Sophia was not charged with. Sophia always set her tray aside and waited to eat until she was alone in her room. She'd thought early on in her time at Haddington House that she would take her meals below stairs with the housekeeper and Mrs. Haddington's lady's maid. But she hadn't been welcome there.

So her meals were spent alone. Very, very alone.

She pushed her tray a bit away and crossed to her

bedchamber window. If she knelt on the window seat and pressed the side of her face against the pane, she could just make out the edge of Loch Lomond. Her bedchamber did not boast the most breathtaking view the house had to offer, but she still loved it. The lake was difficult to see, but the rest of the prospect was lovely. Trees. Hills. In the mornings, a marvelous array of birds.

"I may not have any friends or anyone to talk to, but I am living in a beautiful place." She chose to find some comfort in that.

Turning her head in the other direction, she could see the paddock. It was from this vantage point she'd first come to know Dermot Buchanan. She'd watched him care for the horses with expertise and compassion. She'd seen for herself the authoritative, but respectful way he interacted with his stable hands. He was generally quiet, tending toward the solemn, but from her window, she'd witnessed rare moments when he'd laughed out loud, happiness lighting the features of his face.

If he had any idea she watched him when he worked, he'd have done far more than reject her friendship. He'd have sent for the squire and seen her tossed into jail. Loneliness had made her desperate. And pathetic.

Someone knocked at her bedchamber door.

"Come in," she said.

One of the chambermaids poked her head inside. "Beggin' your pardon. Mrs. Haddington wishes to see you in the library."

That did not bode well. Mrs. Haddington almost never sent for her and hadn't once done so to offer a compliment or pass along good news.

When Sophia stepped inside the library, both Mr. and Mrs. Haddington were there. She hadn't been expecting that. Avoiding *Mr.* Haddington had become a daily goal of hers.

"You sent for me?" Sophia addressed Mrs. Haddington quite specifically.

"I understand you caused a disruption at the stables this afternoon."

A disruption? "I only went to relay the message that you had not granted me the use of any of your mares and would not be riding."

Mrs. Haddington smoothed the fabric of her dress. "I might have granted you the privilege of riding if I had been at all hopeful that you would not be a disruption. Clearly, I was right to assume you would cause trouble."

"I didn't cause any trouble." She *had*, in all honesty, prevented a couple of men from completing their tasks in a timely manner, but she hadn't been truly disruptive.

"That is not the report I received." Mrs. Haddington's mouth pursed in disapproval.

Who had reported that she had caused difficulties? One of the stable hands? Or—or Dermot? She had accepted his rejection with grace and swiftness. And he had gone to the trouble of following her after her first departure to make certain she was not upset. Why, after showing her such kindness, would he feel to then denounce her to their employer? It was cruel.

"I believe it would be best for you to stay away from the stables," Mrs. Haddington said.

"But what of the children? Surely you do not mean for them to discontinue their riding lessons."

Mrs. Haddington raised her chin and looked down her nose at Sophia. "One of the other servants can sit on a chair doing absolutely nothing for an hour. *Any* of the other servants could accomplish that."

If the Haddingtons believed Sophia did so little, and performed her tasks so poorly, it was a wonder she still had a job. "I cause no disruption whatsoever during their lessons. As you said, I sit in a chair at a distance from the paddock. I do not even converse with the children during the lessons. There should be no problem with my—"

"Are you questioning my instructions?" A hardness had

entered Mrs. Haddington's expression. She was being more than overbearing in that moment; she was upset. Just what had she been told about Sophia's time at the stables?

Mr. Haddington jumped into the brief pause in conversation. "I am certain Miss Sophia will be well behaved at the stables."

He always called her Miss Sophia, with a disconcerting emphasis on her Christian name. Yet even when he used the formal version of her name, he made it sound unnervingly intimate.

Mrs. Haddington's eyes narrowed, her gaze not wavering from Sophia in the least. "I think it would be best if you kept mostly to the nursery, Miss Pemberton. There is little reason for you to be wandering the estate."

"I have never been prone to wandering," Sophia said.

"Then this should be an easy adjustment for you." Mrs. Haddington took up her sewing. "That is all. You may leave now."

But she didn't go immediately. "I am not entirely clear on my instructions."

"You do not know what the word 'leave' means?" Mrs. Haddington didn't look up from her sewing, but if her tone was any indication, her mouth twisted in a sneer.

"I do not know if you have ordered me confined to my bedchamber, or simply relieved me of my obligation to accompany the children to their riding lessons."

"All I have asked is that you stop making a nuisance of yourself." Mrs. Haddington snipped a thread. "And in case I wasn't clear, that includes leaving now without further argument."

Sophia didn't care to remain anyway. She gave a quick dip of her head and left. Footsteps followed her. She didn't look back, having her suspicions about who followed.

"Miss Sophia."

Her prediction was correct. Civility dictated that she pause and hear what her employer had to say—one of the reasons she did her best never to cross paths with him. "My sincerest apologies for my wife's dictatorial attitude, as well as her restrictions."

Sophia responded with a quick, simple, silent dip of her head. She took a step away, only to be stopped yet again by the unnerving sound of "Miss Sophia" on Mr. Haddington's lips.

"Now that you have every other afternoon to yourself while the children are at their lessons, you are welcome to avail yourself of my library. I am certain you can find something there of interest to you."

He stepped closer. Not so near that she clearly had grounds to object, but near enough to make her excessively uncomfortable.

"You do like to read, do you not?" He put her in mind of a cat offering cheese to a mouse.

"I am not a great reader, I am afraid." The lie was more than justified.

He came closer still. "You will never be one unless you put your mind to it, Miss Sophia."

Rude or not, she needed to make good her escape. "A good evening to you, Mr. Haddington."

She left as swiftly as she could without looking as though she was fleeing. Like a cat stalking a mouse, if he sensed she was even the slightest bit afraid of him, he would likely hunt her even more aggressively.

Only after dropping into her window seat once more did she realize the full extent of her predicament. If she kept to her bedchamber during the children's afternoons at the stables, Mr. Haddington would know precisely where to find her. There would be no avoiding him, no escape. Mrs. Haddington had warned her not to wander the estate. But was it wandering if she was actually hiding?

She felt the frustration of her situation more acutely than usual. She needed a means of supporting herself. Were she to quit, she would have no recommendation to help her find another position. But staying meant enduring Mr. and Mrs. Haddington and their varied means of making her miserable. What she wouldn't give for just one friend, one person she could confide in. But the only person she'd thought might be willing had turned down her offer without hesitation.

She was well and truly alone.

Miss Pemberton hadn't been present for the Haddington urchins' last three lessons. She was far too responsible to simply be shrugging off her duties, so Dermot was certain something had happened.

"Where's Miss Pemberton?" he asked Ella.

"She doesn't come with us anymore." Ella's smile was a bit too haughtily satisfied for Dermot's peace of mind.

"I'd figured that much on m' own. But *why* doesn't she come?"

Ella shrugged. "I don't concern myself with the servants."

Dermot would wager Mrs. Haddington was behind Miss Pemberton's glaring absences. The family was so convinced of their own superiority that they treated even others of their class as if they were the lowliest of petitioners.

"Where does she go instead?" he asked.

"I do not want to talk about Miss Pemberton. I do not care where—"

"You'd best decide to care, lass, or you'll spend the rest of your lesson sitting on the grass next to the maid."

The children had quickly learned that he was not one to make idle threats. "She goes to the garden or the orchard. Father offered her the use of his library, but she doesn't go there, likely because she is not bright enough to be a reader."

Dermot called over a stable hand. "Aiden, see to it Miss

A HAPPY BEGINNING

Haddington makes another circuit of the paddock at a walk. If she's well behaved, she may try a slow trot after that. Only if she's well behaved."

"If she's not?" Aiden asked.

Dermot gave Ella a pointed look as he answered Aiden's question. "Then her lesson'll be over."

Ella nodded her understanding. Dermot left similar instructions with Will, who was overseeing Joseph's lesson. His staff knew that if the Haddingtons voiced any objections, he'd take responsibility for the shortened lessons. The staff's trust allowed him to trust them in return, and today, it gave him the freedom to go do what needed doing.

Garden or orchard? The weather was unusually cool. The shade would likely make the orchard a far less-comfortable choice. He'd try the garden first.

And why am I hying after this lass in the first place? She'd managed to wriggle her way into his thoughts and concerns these past months. He'd watched her struggle with ill-mannered and headstrong charges with determination and patience. He'd heard whispers of the monumental scolds Mrs. Haddington had subjected her to, though he'd never heard Miss Pemberton speak ill of her employer. The quiet governess had a quiet strength that, despite his feelings for her fellow countrymen, had earned her more than a small measure of Dermot's respect.

Upon arriving in the garden, Dermot spotted her quickly. Her dark-blue dress contrasting against the light-green shrubbery gave her away. She sat on a bench near the star-shaped fountain, reading a book.

"Miss Ella doesn't think you read."

Miss Pemberton didn't look up. "Let us hope her father believes the same thing."

Mr. Haddington must have at least suspected she liked to read, else he'd not have offered her the use of his library. Of course, that likely meant enduring his company as well, and Dermot could easily understand the displeasure of that prospect.

"Are the children's lessons finished early?" Miss Pemberton asked.

He shook his head.

She set her book on her lap. "Are they causing you difficulties?"

He shook his head again. The Haddington children were little terrors, but he knew how to handle them.

"Then what brings you here whilst they are at the paddock?" she asked.

"You."

Her eyes pulled wide. "Me?"

"You've not been present for the last few lessons. You didn't come Friday to visit the horses." He'd fully expected her to.

"I find your surprise . . . surprising. I thought you would have been pleased."

Now that was near about the oddest thing she could have said. "Why would I have been pleased?"

"Because your report was taken seriously."

He dropped onto the bench beside her. "You're not making a bit of sense, woman."

"Mr. and Mrs. Haddington were told that I disrupted the work at the stables during my brief visit last week. Thus, I have been banned from returning, even for the children's lessons."

She took up her book once more. He slipped it quickly from her hands, which brought her gaze to him.

"You think I told 'em you were making trouble?"

"I cannot imagine our employers holding court with a lowly stable hand, and outside of your staff and I, you were the only other person at the stables that day." She shrugged as if it were a natural conclusion, one that ought not surprise anyone.

He, however, was far from satisfied with that

explanation. "If I've a rat amongst my staff, I'll sniff him out and give him a piece of my mind." The very idea that one of his workers might be slippin' up to the house behind his back to make trouble for Miss Pemberton was insupportable.

"It wasn't you, then?" The possibility had clearly never occurred to her.

"You weren't any trouble that afternoon. You never are, I'd wager. And I'd certainly prefer having you accompany the children. They're better behaved when you're there."

She looked away, shaking her head. "I doubt that."

"They are. You don't allow them to browbeat you, so they're less horrible when you're about."

She still looked doubtful. Dermot slid closer to her, leaning forward a bit in an attempt to catch her eye.

"I saw them with all of their previous governesses, so I know how awful they *can* be. You've made a difference, Miss Pemberton. You've helped."

"At least someone has benefited by my being here," she said quietly.

Her posture slipped, something he didn't think he'd ever seen. She held herself so properly all the time. While he often scoffed at the English for their adherence to etiquette at all costs, he found he didn't care for the sight of her abandoning the armor of civility. It felt too much like defeat.

"You don't think anyone else is happy to have you here?"

She shrugged a shoulder as she stood. "The other servants more or less ignore my existence. Mrs. Haddington seems determined to punish me for imagined misdeeds." She ran her fingers along the leaves of a bush as she walked past. "Your staff, it seems, find me a nuisance. I'm rather convinced you do as well. And Mr. Haddington—his feelings on the matter are best left unexplored."

She'd taken a great deal too many tangents there to explore them all. He chose the one he felt most qualified to answer. "What makes you think I find you a nuisance?"

"What else am I to think? You hardly ever speak to me—this conversation is by far the most words I have ever heard you utter—and you were very, very clear in your desire that we not consider ourselves to be on friendly terms."

"When have you ever known a man and a woman from such differing backgrounds to be friends?" Surely she understood the difficulty.

"I suspect we are really not so different, Dermot Buchanan."

That was more true than she knew, more true than anyone knew. Had she discovered aspects of his history he'd kept hidden? He didn't think so, yet she seemed so certain that they were on relatively equal footing. Had he given himself away without realizing?

"Why is it you want to be my friend?"

Though her mouth didn't turn upward, something in her eyes hinted at a smile. "You are kind and considerate and thoughtful. We share a few interests. Your conversation is intelligent and interesting. And, though I don't know you well, I'd be willing to wager that you are a good man. To me, that makes you a very good choice for a friend."

"Even though I'm only a lowly stable master?"

She shook her head. "I am only a governess."

The difference in their positions—his claiming nothing more exalted than being a lower servant and her hailing from the upper classes—truly didn't bother her. With only one exception, he'd never before met an English person who felt that way.

"A friendship between us might be difficult," he warned. "You, after all, are not permitted to come to the stables."

A palpable relief settled on her. Relief, of all things. She truly wanted to be his friend. She, an Englishwoman of the upper class, wished to associate with him, a man inarguably beneath her. How very . . . refreshing. "I am permitted to come to the garden, though. Perhaps if you have an evening to yourself, you might come here. We could walk the paths for a time and talk. The garden is public enough to not cause any scandal."

He stood and joined her at the fountain. "I'm free most evenings other than Sunday. Perhaps you might make your way here to the fountain tomorrow after supper."

She smiled at him, and at the sight, something decidedly odd happened: his heart, an organ he'd managed to ignore for a great many years, lurched. Warmth trickled over him even as a smile of his own threatened to break free. His breath caught in his lungs, and anticipation tiptoed over every inch of him.

He'd spent evenings in the company of friends before, but had never once looked forward to the experience with such eagerness. Miss Pemberton had asked for his friendship, but Dermot suspected he had already begun to feel a bit more than that for her.

Four

"I grew up about an hour from here, closer to Ben Lomond." Dermot hadn't spoken much about himself over the week they'd spent walking through the garden in the evenings. Sophia was pleased he was finally doing so. "Aiden, who's my right hand in the stables, and I have known each other since we were children."

"Did he follow you here, or did you follow him?"

"I came first." Dermot plucked a flower from an obliging bush and gave it to her.

Sophia did her utmost to hide the surge of excitement the off-hand gesture created. The more she knew him, the more she liked him. Though she wished for more than merely his friendship, she was not willing to lose that by revealing the depth of her feelings for him.

"Did you always want to be a stable master?" she asked, carefully holding the delicate flower.

"No. My mother had hoped for greater things, though I think she's learned to be proud of how I'm living my life."

"How could she not be?" Sophia couldn't imagine any mother not being inordinately proud of a son who was good and kind and hardworking.

"You'll puff me up if you're not careful with your compliments."

He set his hand on her back to guide her around a puddle in their path. Moments such as these, his mannerisms resembled those of a gentleman more than a servant. He was a wonderfully intriguing contradiction.

"I've learned much of you this past week," he said. "What do I not know yet?"

She pulled her shawl over her shoulder once more. "You are good at asking questions. I can't imagine anything about me you haven't discovered yet."

His dark-eyed gaze narrowed on her. "There is one topic you have neatly avoided every time we've inched near it."

A lump formed in her throat. "What topic is that?"

He stopped and turned to face her. His expression wasn't frustrated or commanding. He was, without a doubt, concerned. "Why are you afraid of Mr. Haddington?"

"I never—I didn't say I was afraid of him."

Dermot took her hand in his, still watching her closely. "You didn't have to say it, Sophia. His name surfaces now and then, and every time, you grow as rigid as a tree and as pale as a snowy owl. How is it he scares you so much? Has he done something he ought not to have?"

She shook her head no. "He makes me uncomfortable, yes. But he hasn't done anything in particular. Not really. He simply –" How could she explain her reaction to Mr. Haddington when she hadn't solid reasons for it? "Something in his eyes worries me."

"Promise me this, my friend," he said, squeezing her fingers. "Do not ever hesitate to come to me if that 'something in his eyes' ever proves to be too much for you, if it ever becomes something more."

She nodded.

"I need to hear you say it. I need to know that you know you can come to me if you're ever worried or afraid."

"I will. I promise."

His smile sent shivers from her head to her feet. "Now, you'd best hurry along. I've seen a face looking down from the window a time or two. I'd wager you're needed somewhere."

It was far more likely someone was looking down in disapproval. She was forever earning someone's disdain. "Will you come back to the garden tomorrow?" she asked.

He shook his head. "Tomorrow's Sunday. I'll be away all day."

"Monday, then?"

"I'd not miss it for the world."

Her breath caught a moment. "Do you mean that?"

"You'll find, Sophia Pemberton, that I do not say anything I don't mean."

⚘

"You are not paying attention." Ella's shrill voice cut into Sophia's distraction. "Mother will not like that you are woolgathering during our lessons."

"Imagine how she would feel if she were to discover that *you* have woolgathered so much that you are still unable to locate Prussia on the map of Europe," Sophia replied.

Ella's nostrils flared. "That is your fault. You are supposed to be teaching me geography."

Sophia refused to be cowed by the petulant child. "Joseph has managed to learn his maps. Clearly this is not a matter of *my* neglecting lessons." If she had for one moment believed Ella's lack of knowledge was the result of anything other than the girl's own laziness, Sophia would not have pressed the issue. But Ella, despite being bright, refused to apply herself to learning anything.

"Yes, well—" Ella sputtered a moment, clearly struggling to find a way to make this Sophia's fault. "I do not wish to learn geography today. I want to study French."

Ella had a natural aptitude for French. If only the girl would put in a bit of effort, she could become remarkably proficient. Effort, it seemed, was entirely out of the question when the subject matter was the countries of the world.

"We will study French tomorrow," Sophia said. "Return to your maps."

No sooner had Ella bent over her paper than a voice broke the silence, a voice that set Sophia's skin crawling. "Miss Sophia. A moment of your time."

She turned toward the nursery doorway. She dipped her head to indicate she was listening.

Mr. Haddington's smile of amusement was anything but pleasant. "In private," he clarified.

Sophia had no intention of ever being fully "in private" with Mr. Haddington. She followed him out as far as the corridor, then stopped. "What was it you needed?"

"We can speak in the library."

She shook her head. "I won't be away from the children any longer than necessary. We are in the midst of geography lessons."

"Geography can wait." Mr. Haddington moved swiftly toward her, forcing her to step backward. A wall impeded her escape. "Why is it you never come to the library during the children's riding lessons?"

Because I know you did not offer the invitation out of concern for my literacy. She couldn't say that, however. She knew too well the precariousness of her situation. "Their lessons were nearly the only time I was out of doors. I mean to continue spending it that way."

One of his eyebrows arched, and the side of his mouth

turned upward. "You needed only tell me that, Miss Sophia. I didn't know where you were."

That had been the point, really.

Mr. Haddington set his hand on the wall near her face. He leaned in close. "But now I know where to find you."

She tried to move the other direction. He set his other hand on the other side of her, stopping her.

His gaze slid over her in an unnervingly possessive manner. "Playing coy has its appeal, but I've grown weary of this game. Do not pretend to be innocent in the ways of the world. I have seen you making up sweet to Buchanan. You are no delicate flower, and he is not the only one looking for nectar."

He stepped closer, all but pressing her against the wall.

"I would ask you to keep a proper distance, sir."

"I am master of this house." He touched her face with the tips of his fingers. She flinched. "Any distance I choose is 'proper.'"

She ducked away, trying to slip around the side of him. "I must return to my duties."

He took firm hold of her wrist. "We *are* speaking of your duties, Sophia."

Her lungs and heart froze, petrified. Mr. Haddington expected this of her. Demanded it.

"I came here to be a governess. Nothing else." She attempted to pull free, but his grip tightened.

"I can make life exceedingly difficult for you."

She yanked her arm once more, but his grip was firm. "Release me, sir."

His other arm slipped around her waist. This was escalating quickly. She had to get away. Far away. She couldn't break his grip with her own strength; she needed another way to force him to loosen it. Sophia could think of only one way.

She slammed her boot onto the top of his foot. The

surprise sent him backward a step. Sophia jerked her knee upward with all the strength she had.

He doubled over, moaning in pain. But he'd released her wrist. Sophia waited not even a moment. She ran, not slowing her pace all the way down the stairs and to the back corridor. She pushed open the doors to the terrace and ran the length of the topiary path. Her lungs burned with the effort. The weight of her full skirts pulled heavy on her.

Where am I to go? She had no money, no possessions, no family to turn to. But she had a friend, one who had only two days earlier made her promise to turn to him in precisely this scenario.

The paddock was as busy as ever. The staff were putting a few of the horses through their paces. Sophia didn't see Dermot. He was likely inside.

She hurried around the side of the paddock, continually glancing back to make certain Mr. Haddington hadn't come after her. A stable hand led a horse out, momentarily blocking the stable doorway. Sophia tried to glance around, hoping to catch sight of Dermot.

She slipped inside, behind the exiting horse and into the warm, damp air of the stable. The smell of horses and hay washed over her. Dermot kept his stable mucked and cleaned, so the other less-pleasant smells weren't nearly as strong as they might have been. Stable hands filled every imaginable space. Horses nickered and moved about their stalls. Where was Dermot? The business of a working stable didn't usually bother her, but in that moment, she felt trapped.

She stopped halfway to the back of the row of stalls, then turned around to see if she'd missed him. Again and again she spun, hoping for a glimpse. Into her thoughts, unbidden, came Mr. Haddington, his humiliating and infuriating expectations, his clawing closeness, his painful, possessive touch. Her wrist still throbbed.

She needed to get away from Haddington House. The

view no longer held any pleasure. The land she'd fallen in love with had betrayed her.

She took a shaky, thick breath. The threat of emotion squeezed every drop of air from her lungs.

"Miss?" Aiden stepped into her blurry line of sight. "Are you unwell, miss?"

She didn't know how to answer. "Where is Dermot?" The question broke as she spoke it.

His expression changed from curious to concerned. "This way, miss."

She followed him back outside and around the side of the long, stone building. "I'm sorry to pull you away from your work."

Aiden shook his head. "Dermot'd have m' neck if I'd left you there looking about, ready to cry."

They came around the back side of the stable to a small, enclosed paddock. Dermot was inside with a young filly, leading it around and talking softly. Some of Sophia's panic eased simply at the sight of him. She felt less alone.

When Aiden called his name, Dermot turned. His gaze moved quickly to her. She felt her chin quiver, so she firmed her resolve to remain strong and collected. He led the young horse to the paddock gate.

"Aiden, walk the filly about for a few minutes more."

He and Aiden switched places, Dermot's gaze not leaving Sophia for more than a moment. "What's happened?"

"Mr. Haddington—" She managed nothing more than that. Fear, humiliation, exhaustion, all conspired against her. The weight was nearly crushing.

Dermot set his hand on her back and led her to the far side of the small paddock, out of view of the house and stables. Sophia focused on walking and breathing, and not thinking about all that had just happened and, worse still, might have happened if she hadn't escaped.

They stopped behind the stables, and Dermot turned to

face her fully once more. "Now tell me what's happened. Did he hurt you?"

"My wrist."

He took careful hold of her hand and inched back the cuff of her sleeve. "He's left marks." Dermot looked up at her once more.

"He held it so tight. I couldn't break free. He—" She pushed out a tight breath, attempting to fully calm herself. "He said that you weren't the only one who ought to be permitted a taste of my 'nectar.'"

Dermot's expression hardened. "He said that to you?"

"I knew what he wanted, and that he'd insist upon it. I kicked him and struck him with my knee." The enormity of what she'd done slowly washed over her. "He may very well be coming for me or sending the squire to drag me back. No one would ever believe I was defending myself, not if he says otherwise."

"*I* believe you," Dermot said.

She'd known he would. "I don't—I don't know what to do. I have nowhere to go."

"Well, then, it's a fortunate thing for you that I know most everyone for miles around."

He would help. Relief inched over her. "I likely shouldn't allow you to be bothered with this."

He held her hand between his two large ones. "How many times do I have to tell you, woman? I'm not one to be made to do something I'd rather not."

"And you'd rather help me?"

He nodded firmly. "I'd very much rather."

Sophia did not know why, but his eager assistance undid what little control she'd gained over her emotions. A tear dropped from the corner of her eye more quickly than she could wipe it away.

"Don't cry, Sophia. You're not alone in this. We'll find a place for you to lay your head."

She swiped at a second tear, hoping it would be the last.

"I would happily live in a cave so long as I need not return to that house."

"You need never go back there again. And further, you need not live in a cave."

"A hole in the ground, then?" The attempt at humor might not have been expertly managed, but making the effort lifted her spirits a little.

"Or a mud bank," he answered. "Whichever is handier."

She took her first steady breath in thirty minutes.

"We've a fair distance to travel," Dermot said. "We'd best get started."

He kept her hand in his as he walked, urging her along with him toward the front of the stables once more.

"Am I permitted to know where we're going?"

He nodded. "I'm taking you to stay with someone."

"Someone you know?"

Another nod.

They stepped into the stable. Dermot pulled one of the stable hands aside. "Hitch my horse up to the cart. When Aiden returns with the new filly, tell him I've put him in charge for the remainder of the day."

The stable hand gave a quick, deferential bow. "Are you going somewhere?"

"I'm takin' Miss Pemberton to meet the queen."

"You are acquainted with Queen Victoria?" Sophia asked, not believing it for a moment.

The stable hand answered before Dermot did. "Not *that* queen."

"Do we have another?"

Dermot pulled a knapsack from a hook near the back. "Mary, Queen of Scots. Heard of that one?"

Sophia had come to adore Dermot's sense of humor the past week or more. "I hadn't realized Queen Mary was still wandering about. She must be quite ancient by now."

He tossed her a smile over his shoulder. "Don't let my mother hear you say that."

A HAPPY BEGINNING

"You refer to your mother as Queen Mary?"

"You'll meet her soon enough. Then you'll understand."

Five

'Twas a very good thing for Mr. Haddington that Dermot was occupied with driving Sophia to his mother's house, elsewise he'd likely have tracked the man down and beaten him to a bloodied mess. He'd long suspected Haddington was a blackguard of the worst sort, but hearing the proof of it from Sophia's lips and seeing the fear in her eyes had ended all doubts.

Though Sophia had worked hard to hide it, she cried off and on during their drive. The tears had only fully stopped when she had fallen asleep.

Haddington had made her cry. That, Dermot could not forgive.

She sat tucked up beside him, her head resting on his shoulder. It was a position of such utter trust. A number of women had thrown themselves at him. Those who knew him as the stable master generally saw little beyond a handsome face and strong build. Those acquainted with his life away from the stables were far more intrigued by his holdings and connections. None of them ever bothered to see the man he was.

But this woman, this high-born lady with her impeccable manners and precise civility, had seen *him*. More than that, she liked the *him* she had seen. What would she think when she realized how much of his life he'd kept secret from her?

The wind picked up, as it often did in the Highlands. Dermot pulled her closer, hoping to lend her a bit of warmth. She fidgeted a bit before her eyes fluttered open. Whether it was the chill or his movement that woke her, he didn't know.

"We've a fair spell left to drive yet," he said. "You can go back to sleep."

She didn't lift her head from his shoulder. "I fear I am not a very enjoyable traveling companion."

"I wouldn't say that."

She pulled the wool blanket more firmly around her shoulders. "You prefer your companions asleep?"

"Quiet, anyway." He smiled down at her.

She took a deep breath and settled more snugly against him. "Will your mother be upset to have us descend upon her without warning?"

"She enjoys visitors."

"Even visitors who are English?"

The thought of his mother, of all people, being put out over Sophia's Englishness pulled a laugh from him.

"Why should that amuse you so much?"

He shook his head. "You'll simply have to meet her."

"Why do you call her Mary, Queen of Scots?"

"Again, you'll have to meet her."

She sat up straight but turned a bit to face him more directly. "You are making me more worried, not less."

He slipped the reins into one hand, then took hold of her hand with his free one. "My mother is a goodhearted lady who not only lives alone and longs for visitors, but who rather dotes upon her only son and will be smotheringly affectionate toward anyone he chooses to bring to see her, especially if he happens to be fond of that visitor."

"You're fond of me?"

Of all he'd said, *that* was what she'd latched on to? "Of course I am. Do you think I'd spend six evenings out of seven wandering a garden chatting with you if I wasn't?"

"Or driving me to meet the queen."

"Indeed."

She wove her fingers through his. He liked that. "Are you pleased, then, that I begged you to be my friend?"

"I'd not say you begged, but I am pleased."

"Are you truly?" She slid closer to him. He could feel the weight of her gaze. "Please don't say that if you aren't in earnest. So many people lie to me about things." It was not the first time she'd said that.

"'People'? Would that be your family, then?"

She turned forward once more. "I don't believe my father ever said a truthful thing to me in all my life. My aunt promised to take me in after my father lost our home, but she changed her mind. A friend of my grandmother's offered me a position as a lady's companion, but then told her butler to refuse me entrance to the house. Mr. Haddington hired me for what he said was the role of governess, but he lied about why I was brought to Haddington House. People are forever lying to me."

He raised their entwined hands to his lips. "I'm sorry people've hurt you, Sophia. But I swear to you that I'm not one of them. When I say I'm pleased to be your friend, I mean that I'm very much pleased to be your friend."

"Do you kiss all of your friends' hands?"

Nothing slipped passed this woman. "M' first time." And, he hoped, not his last.

He guided the horse up a pebbled path and under the columned portico of a house he knew well indeed. "Let us hope the housekeeper has a fire built in the sitting room."

Sophia's eyes darted from him to the house again and again. "*This* is your home?"

"It is."

Johnny, who looked over the animals and stables, stepped up to the cart. Dermot tossed him the reins then hopped down.

"But—" Sophia looked all around, her expression only growing more confused. "But this isn't a cave."

Heavens, he enjoyed her sense of humor. "The cave is in back."

He came around the cart and reached up for her. Without hesitation, she set her hands on his shoulders and allowed him to lift her to the ground. He kept his hands at her waist even after she'd firmly regained her footing; he enjoyed both her confusion over his home and her nearness.

"You are employed by another man when you own your own house and land?" She looked up at him. "I don't understand."

"We've stumbled upon a new idea up here in Scotland. We call it work, and we consider it a mark of a worthwhile person."

"Is there not work enough to do here? In my experience, most estates require a great deal of effort to run."

"It's not the same."

She watched him closely, clearly pondering his answer. Few people had truly listened to him the way she always did. He'd found himself anticipating their walks in the garden hours beforehand, knowing he had both a listening ear and an enjoyable conversation to look forward to. "You took the job to prove yourself, I'd wager," she said. "To convince someone—I have my theories about whom that someone is—that you were more than the fortunate son of a land owner."

She'd pieced that together quickly.

"And what do you think of my efforts? Have I been wasting my time on a pointless pursuit?"

"That depends on whether you convinced your harshest critic."

He tucked a stray hair behind her ear. "And who is my harshest critic?"

"I think" —she stretched up on her toes—"that would be you, Dermot." She pressed a quick kiss to his cheek, sending warmth straight to his very heart.

The front door flew open and Mrs. Green, the housekeeper, rushed out, arms waving, eyes wide with excitement. "Master Dermot! We were not expecting you." Her eager gaze fell on Sophia, whose hands yet rested on his chest, whilst his hands were still at her waist. "What is this? A sweetheart? Did you marry and not tell anyone?"

He laughed out loud at the immediate look of panic on Sophia's face. "No, Mrs. Green. I'm not married. This is my dear friend, Sophia, who has come to meet your mistress."

Mrs. Green clasped her hands over her heart. "Mrs. Buchanan hasn't had a visitor in weeks and weeks."

"Not even her son?" Sophia asked.

Dermot slipped his hand around her back, guiding her toward the house. "I'm here every Sunday without fail."

"This is where you go. I wondered about that."

They stepped into the sitting room where Mother always spent her evenings. This evening was no exception. She rose from her usual chair, her blue silk dress flowing in elegant waves as she stood.

Dermot slipped away from Sophia's side and crossed to his mother, placing a kiss on her cheek. "I've brought you a visitor, Mother." He indicated Sophia. "She has until recently been employed as the governess at Haddington House."

"How very unfortunate for the young lady. Employment at Haddington House, no matter the roll, is an occupation I would not wish upon anyone." Mother glided across the room, her hand outstretched in invitation, her words and tone as refined as ever. "You are most welcome to Greenborough. I trust your journey was a pleasant one."

A HAPPY BEGINNING

Sophia's startled gaze sought and found him. "You didn't tell me that your mother is English."

Mother looked as shocked as Sophia did. "Dermot, you've brought me an Englishwoman."

"More than that, Mother. She is my friend. And I hope that she'll become yours as well."

⁂

"Now, son, no more of your stories. Tell me what is truly happening here." Mother sat in her favored armchair, eying him with the very knowing look of wisdom that had always brought a gleam to Father's eyes.

Mrs. Green had led Sophia up to a guest room under strict instructions from Mother to provide her with a few gowns to try on, since Sophia didn't have any of her own. Now Dermot was alone with his mother and, as was her tendency, she'd not waited more than a moment to ask questions.

Dermot had learned from his late father that delaying an answer was pointless. Though it was the Scots who had the reputation for stubbornness, his very English mother had long ago taught him that they weren't the only ones with backbone.

"Mr. Haddington threatened her," he said. "'Twas no longer safe for her to stay."

Mother's mouth turned up in a subtle smile. "You sound even more Scottish than usual today, Dermot. Miss Pemberton appears to have affected you more than you will admit."

"How could an Englishwoman's influence make me sound more *Scottish*?"

She reached over and patted his hand. "Even as a little boy, whenever you were excited or worried or overwrought, whatever influence I had on your diction disappeared. You have sounded like Johnny ever since your arrival. Miss Pemberton's presence here must be indicative of something more than the moral depravity of Mr. Haddington."

"She is my friend."

His usually regal mother actually rolled her eyes. "Aiden MacAllister is your *friend*. When was the last time you sat with his hand in yours for a full quarter hour as you did with Miss Pemberton this evening?"

"I am fond of her, but she was born to a family of privilege and refinement."

Mother pushed out a heavy breath. "Now you truly do sound like your father. He made the exact same objection early in our acquaintance. Tell me, did I ever believe myself above him, too refined for a Scotsman?"

Dermot shook his head and leaned back against the sofa. "But you, dear Mother, are the universal exception to most every rule."

"Would it help if I told you that whilst I watched Miss Pemberton this evening, I saw a fondness in her eyes every time she looked at you that went beyond mere friendship?" She smoothed the front of her skirts.

"You've been trying to find me a wife for years and years, Mother. Knowing your growing desperation, I'll not allow you to be the judge of any woman's fondness for me."

"Then allow me to be the judge of my son's idiocy."

He chuckled. Mother never was one to mince words.

"With her, you smile and you laugh, something you haven't done often since your father died. And though my difficult relations convinced you long ago that the English hold unflattering views of Scotland and her people, please do not allow that to convince you to paint all the English with the same hateful brush."

He let his shoulders sag. "She said something like that to me not long ago. I don't care for the idea of the both of you being right about that part of me."

A HAPPY BEGINNING

Mother tucked a stray hair back behind her ear once more. "I, for one, am impressed that she possesses enough fortitude to tell you when you're being mule-headed. You are rather intimidating, you realize."

"So I've been told." 'Twas one of the reasons the Haddingtons allowed him full run of the stables with few questions asked, and one of the reasons they didn't dig too deeply to discover his origins. He needn't tell anyone he owned a small but fine estate of his own; his demeanor alone convinced people to heed what he said. He far preferred being respected for his work and self-possession than for the value of his land and his mother's family's connections.

"Does Miss Pemberton find you intimidating?" Mother asked.

"She seemed to at first, but not any longer."

Mother nodded. "I like her."

He had hoped she would. "Do you like her enough to allow her to stay while she finds her footing again?"

Mother clasped her hands on her lap, her bearing as royal as if she'd actually been a queen. "She may stay as long as she wishes, under one condition."

He narrowed his gaze on her. "What's the condition?"

"You must come visit her, and do so more often than once a week."

He opened his mouth to object, to explain all of the many reasons why that was unreasonable. But she held up her hand and cut him off.

"It is only an hour's drive. And, Dermot William Buchanan, a woman who liked and valued you before knowing of your relative wealth and assets, who saw past the fearsome demeanor and quiet grumpiness you exude, is well worth the effort."

Six

"I first met Dermot's father at a ball in London, if you can believe that." Mrs. Buchanan always lit up when speaking of her late husband.

In the fortnight Sophia had spent living with the dear woman, she'd grown exceptionally fond of her. The regal bearing that had earned the older lady the teasing title of "Mary, Queen of Scots" had grown thin over those two weeks, revealing a tenderhearted and caring woman. It seemed that Dermot had inherited from his mother the tendency to wear a protective mask. Sophia had learned to see beyond both.

"You have told me many times that Dermot is much like his father," Sophia said as they turned a corner of the garden path. "And I cannot for the life of me imagine Dermot at a Society ball."

"Fingal had been there on forfeiture of a wager," Mrs. Buchanan explained. "And I was introduced to him by a young lady who, as it turned out, rather disliked me and thought that obligating me to dance with an unsophisticated Scotsman would be a humiliating experience."

Sophia could easily picture the situation, having known a great many ill-mannered young ladies. "Clearly, she made a significant miscalculation."

"Clearly." Mrs. Buchanan stopped to take in the fragrance of bright-yellow rose. "His Scottish manner of speaking was nearly as pronounced as Dermot's has become, and he was as rough and unrefined as the land he called home. While I was, at first, merely curious, I quickly became enthralled, and, quite unexpectedly found myself deeply in love with him."

"What did your family have to say?" If Sophia's family had been in any position to object to the direction her heart was leading her, they would have done so loudly and incessantly.

"They were properly horrified." Mrs. Buchanan's mischievous smile filled in the gaps: Her family objected, but she hadn't cared one whit.

"Did you ever regret marrying your rugged Scotsman?"

"Not for the briefest of moments." Mrs. Buchanan's slow, fond gaze slid over the garden, the house, the distant land. "I fell further in love with him every day of our lives. His home became my home, his people my people. Those first few years, I traveled to my family's estate, hoping to maintain that connection, but they were horrid to my husband and son. That, I am afraid, is where Dermot gained his distrust of the English. It is the only thing I regret about my life here: not putting an end to those visits before my relations soured him so fully."

"How could you have known?"

Mrs. Buchanan nodded slowly. "Mistakes are always easier to see when looking backward."

Sophia picked a small, pink flower from an obliging bush, spinning the bloom between her fingers. "Do you suppose Dermot will ever fully let go of his distaste for the English?"

"As a whole, likely not." Mrs. Buchanan slipped her arm through Sophia's and leaned in a bit closer as they walked on. "But on an individual basis, I know of one instance in which he already has."

She forced down a smile, not wanting to appear too eager, or desperate. "The first time I asked him to be my friend, he turned me down on the instant. He seemed almost horrified at the idea."

"He has made the journey here nearly every night these past two weeks," Mrs. Buchanan said. "A man does not go to such effort for a lady whose company horrifies him."

"He has told me several times that he is fond of me."

Mrs. Buchanan laughed out loud. "I promise you, he is far more than merely *fond* of you; he's simply unwilling to admit it, stubborn man."

"Why does he continue working at Haddington House? He certainly doesn't need the income; he has told me himself that this estate is profitable. I know he doesn't stay out of loyalty to his employers."

Mrs. Buchanan indicated a nearby stone bench. Once the two of them were comfortably settled, she answered Sophia's question. "That is also the fault of my relations, I am afraid. They spoke at length of the lazy Scots, which convinced my little boy that he had to prove himself a hard worker to dispel that impression. And to compound matters, he became keenly aware of how very English it was to live off one's inheritance without making contributions to the outside world."

"Above all else, he did not wish to be seen as English." Sophia was coming to understand him better all the time. The more she knew, the more miraculous it felt that he'd ever agreed to interact with her, an Englishwoman from the gentry. She must have seemed to him the embodiment of all he disliked.

"You have been good for him, you know," Mrs. Buchanan said. "He is happier than I ever remember him being. He smiles, and he laughs, and he speaks of this as home again, as a place where he means to live and not simply visit."

"I am happier with him as well." Sophia found her hostess to be an easy person to talk with. The past fortnight had been delightful. The only way she could imagine improving her situation would be to have Dermot home.

"It seems, Sophia, that you are about to be very happy." Mrs. Buchanan motioned up the garden path.

There he was. The man who had laid claim to her heart, not through grand gestures or flowery speeches, but through weeks and months of constancy and goodness. She never tired of his company and never grew less eager to see him again.

"I hope you will not think me rude if I eagerly and unrepentantly abandon you," she said to Mrs. Buchanan.

"On the contrary. I will find you utterly ridiculous if you do not."

Sophia needed no more encouragement. She leapt from the bench and rushed toward Dermot. His eyes danced when he saw her, and his smile formed on the instant. He held his hand out to her as she approached and she slipped hers into it. That had become their greeting whenever he returned. She spent her days looking forward to that moment.

"We were not expecting you until later tonight," she said.

"I can leave and return in an hour or two if you would prefer."

She shook her head at his teasing. "Your mother has been saying flattering things about you. You had best be well behaved, or I will be inclined not to believe any of it."

"Will you trust that I am a wonderful person if I tell you that I have good news?" They walked along the garden path, their interwoven hands swinging between them.

"What is your news?"

"I will be late tomorrow," he said.

She stopped and looked up at him. "That is not good news at all."

His grin could not have contained another ounce of mischievousness. "You do not yet know the reason why I will be late."

"It would need to be an exceptionally good one for me to feel at all happy about it."

He raised her hand to his lips and pressed a kiss to her fingers. "Tomorrow I am resigning as stable master at Haddington House."

Her first response was relief on his behalf, then excitement that he would be free of the misery of that place. But just as quickly, she realized another unsettling possibility. "Where will you work? Will you be farther away? Will you still come back and see m—see us?"

He brushed his fingers along her cheek. "I'm not leaving you, Sophia. After tomorrow, I'm coming home."

◈◈◈

Dermot didn't pause long enough to hand his outercoat to Mrs. Green as he made his way to the sitting room the next night. His last day as stable master at Haddington House had been as chaotic as he'd expected it to be.

If not for his concern for the stable hands, he'd have left the Haddington family high and dry the moment he'd learned of Mr. Haddington's treatment of Sophia. Instead, he'd spent the two weeks since planning a thorough mutiny.

"Why, Dermot. This is a surprise." Mother rose from her armchair. "We were not expecting you until tomorrow at the earliest."

"Where is Sophia?" He'd hoped she would be here when he arrived, knowing as she did that he was returning to stay.

Mother laughed. "I would be offended if I weren't happy to know that you've missed our dear houseguest."

"*Missed* her? That feels like a terribly inadequate word." The room was empty other than him and his mother. "Where is she?"

She hugged him fiercely. "She is a lovely and good and kind young lady."

"I know all that, Mother. What I don't know is where she is." Had his mother taken leave of her senses?

She patted his cheek. "I'm only happy that you are happy. Sophia is in the back garden, waxing silently poetic over the view of Ben Lomond."

That sounded like his Sophia. He'd seen her love for this land in her eyes long before they'd first spoken. "I'll be back shortly."

She simply smiled. "Take your time, son."

Sophia was, indeed, precisely where Mother had said he'd find her. And her gaze was, as predicted, fondly focused on the mountain Dermot had spent his childhood memorizing.

"'Tis a lovely sight, is it not?"

Her head jerked in his direction. Immediately, a smile curved her lips. "Dermot, you're here at last. How did your day go?"

Dermot dropped onto the bench beside her. "Haddington House is in turmoil." He wasn't hiding his glee at their former employers' distress. "There has been a coup."

Her mouth dropped open a moment. "Good heavens."

He could hardly sit still, he was so excited to tell her all that had happened. "Knowing Mr. Haddington for the snake he is, I couldn't imagine that you were the first or only member of the staff he had imposed upon. A few subtle, vague questions in the right ears revealed the horrid enormity of his conduct."

Her sudden pallor concerned him.

He took her hands. "I did not ever mention you, nor your situation. I swear to you."

But she shook her head. "That was not my concern. I hate the idea that he has caused other people pain."

"Mrs. Haddington has been rather horrible as well. It seems you are not the only one who has been forbidden from moving freely or attending certain activities. And the entire family are terrible to the animals, as well."

Sophia's mouth and brows turned down. Life inside the house was likely even more miserable than it had been in the stables.

"I have spent the last two weeks finding new positions for my stable staff," Dermot said. "The housekeeper and butler heard whispers and began searches of their own, finding new positions for the household staff."

"Did they?" Amazement lit her expression. "What did the family say as this all came about?"

"They didn't have the opportunity to say much. Only I remained behind long enough for comment."

A triumphant smile tugged at Sophia's mouth. "What did *you* say?"

"A great many things I can't repeat in a lady's company. Suffice it to say, Haddington now knows that if he mistreats his staff, should he manage to hire any and I hear about it, he'll find himself in dire straits—more dire than a mere loss of staff." It had been an extremely satisfying exchange, actually.

Sophia stretched and placed a kiss on his cheek. "You are a good man, Dermot Buchanan."

"Yes, I am." He settled his arm around her and pulled her next to him. She laid her head against him, her gaze forward once more. "My mother tells me you've been enjoying my mountain."

"Ben Lomond is yours, is it?" The song-like quality her voice took on when she was amused had quickly become one of his favorite sounds.

"Not the entire mountain, just this view of it," he said. "But I might be willing to share."

"Which is a good thing, because you will be here often now." She shifted in his arms, looking up at him. "Won't you?"

"Every day, love."

She leaned into him once more, settling there as naturally as anything. There was really only one thing for a man to do when a woman held him that way. He wrapped his arms around her as well. Heavens, she felt good in his embrace.

"We have missed you so much," she said.

"We?" he pressed.

"Nothing is the same without you here. I hadn't realized it until I came to Greenborough, but your presence at Haddington House was what made life there bearable. Seeing you, if only from my bedchamber window, was a gift and a joy. I have missed that, and I have missed you."

Hearing things like that from the woman who'd stolen away his heart did a man's pride a world of good. "Spied on me from your window, did you?"

"Unrepentantly."

He slid ever closer to her. "And if I promise to spend time beneath your bedchamber window here, will you spy on me some more?"

"Spend time *with me*, Dermot, and I'll have no need to spy."

That was an offer he would gladly accept. "But what'll we find to do?"

"I imagine we can think of something," she answered, her voice quiet and low.

He slipped his hand around the back of her neck, pulling her to him. "I'm thinking of something already, love."

She sighed, her breath tickling his lips. "I love when you call me 'love.'"

He brushed his mouth over hers, kissing her slowly. She slipped her arms around his neck once more. He settled his arms around her waist. The late evening sun shone warm on them as he held her and kissed her and thanked the heavens for bringing her to Scotland.

"I have something for you," he said.

"You do?"

He held her hand in his and led her out of the garden. "I explained to Squire Reynolds that you were owed back wages—that Haddington wouldn't pay what you are owed."

"I was afraid he would refuse."

They turned the corner of the house and took the path leading to the stables. "Squire Reynolds is a good man. He insisted that Haddington either send with me the money he owed you, or that he pay you in kind."

"I'm to be paid?" She'd grown so accustomed to being mistreated that a good outcome fully surprised her.

Dermot slipped his arm around her waist and tugged her up next to him. "Haddington owed me wages as well, so we worked out an agreement."

He led her into the stables, past Will and Johnny, past Aiden, and to a small, windowed stall at the back of the building. "I accepted this as payment of his debt."

"The filly?" She looked up at him, eyes wide.

"She is yours, my dear. Yours to raise and train and make your own."

"Where will—*she* live?"

There was far more in that question than the stabling of a horse. "She will live here, my dearest, sweetest Sophia. She will live here with us."

A sudden redness rimmed Sophia's eyes. "Us?"

He pressed a kiss to her forehead. "Will you stay with me, love? Will you stay?"

She took a shaky breath. "Us?"

"We've a tradition in the Buchanan family, one only recently adopted. A cantankerous, stubborn Scotsman finds himself desperately in love with a warm, caring, beautiful Englishwoman, whom he somehow convinces to marry him."

Her heart leapt to her throat.

"I'd like to continue the tradition, my dear," he said. "Would you consider it?"

"Marrying you?"

He brushed his thumb along her jaw. "I'd be the happiest man in all the world if you would."

Joy bubbled through her, filling the aching voids left by a lifetime of heartache. "And I'd be the happiest woman."

He kissed her fully, truly, then pulled her into his arms. "I love you, my darling."

She nestled more snuggly into his embrace. "Ours is to be a happy ending, it seems."

"A happy *beginning*, love. A tremendously happy beginning."

The Road to Cavan Town

One

County Cavan, Ireland, 1864

The roads leading to Cavan Town boasted a fine collection of young bachelors hying themselves to that gem in the midst of the lake county. They made the journey, not to conduct business, not to shop at market, not to worship. The men came to pay court to the belle of the county, each hoping to have a single word, a single glance from the object of their universal affection. Unfortunately for Alice Wheatley, she was not that belle.

Alice hadn't a particular taste for the attentions of hordes of men at one time. Her heart belonged to but one man, a certain Isaac Dancy, whom she'd met on the road to Cavan. He walked the dozen miles around the lakes from his home near Killeshandra every weekend to join the throng of besotted men. Alice walked nearly as many miles herself, returning home to Cavan from her weekday job as a maid-of-all work for a farm family of very comfortable means.

They'd struck up a conversation and a friendship quicker than a change of weather in autumn. He'd shown himself intelligent and thoughtful and kind. They laughed together and smiled together, yet their conversations were known to take serious turns as well. She knew his worries, and he knew hers. She felt closer to him than any other person on earth.

Yet he was making the weekly walk into Cavan to court another woman. Even knowing the reasons for his weekly journeys, Alice had fallen quite deeply in love with him. If her parents had given her a middle name, it likely would have been "Terribly Unlucky."

Still, as she followed the turn in the road that she walked each weekend and approached the spot where Isaac waited for her every Saturday morning, she didn't regret her lack of luck. He stood there as usual. Her heart smiled to see him. Unlucky she might have been, but she had his company twice each week and felt grateful for that.

"Good day to ya, Isaac Dancy."

"And to you." He rose from the rock he'd been sitting on.

Alice sometimes wondered if she'd ever grow accustomed to the sight of him. His hair could not have been a darker shade of black. Deep brown were his eyes, and full of intelligence and a love of living. And a life of working the land had left him broad of shoulder. What woman could help admiring the very sight of him?

"Have ya noted our fine view this morning?" he asked. "The last bits of autumn color are on the leaves."

She had noticed it. A fine prospect the lakes offered all the year 'round. Snow hung on bare branches in the winter. Buds of green brightened the landscape in spring. Foliage was lush and plentiful during the summer. She'd developed a fondness for the road in the two years she'd walked it. But the past four months, walking with Isaac, she'd hardly noticed the beauty around her.

"How went yer week, Isaac?"

Thus began their usual stroll. He spoke of having finished his harvest and preparing his home and land and animals for the coming winter. She spoke of her own work and the growing coldness at night, how her tiny closet of a room at the farmhouse hardly kept any of the night air out. He suggested she might want to begin bringing blankets with her as the seasons changed. She wondered aloud if the market would yet have apples or if the picking season had entirely ended.

'Twas always that way between them. Conversation came easily. They could speak on anything or nothing and thoroughly enjoy themselves.

In time, she told herself, he would recognize that for the wonderful thing it was. In time, he would give up his courtship of Miss Sophia Kilchrest and move on to higher pastures, as it were.

Sure, he'd been lured, like so many others, by Miss Kilchrest's lovely face and fine figure. He'd been pulled in by her flawless manners and twinkling eyes. He'd even found a bit of motivation in the dowry she'd bring with her, though, to his credit, he'd not mentioned that but once, and even then, as an off-hand observation. And, Alice had noted, having set his mind on the pursuit of such a highly prized treasure, Isaac had taken on a certain single-mindedness where Miss Kilchrest was concerned. Alice doubted he gave his pursuit much thought of late. He simply continued because it was a goal he'd worked on so long.

"Do ya plan to keep making this walk after the snows come?" Alice asked, praying and hoping and feeling generally quite desperate that he would.

"I don't plan to give over the progress I've made with Miss Kilchrest, if that's what ya mean."

'Twas not in the smallest bit what she meant. But life had taught her that men could be terribly thickheaded, and a woman had no real choice but to be patient with them.

"Are ya making progress, then?"

Isaac nodded. "She spoke to me quite particularly the last few weekends, though the other men vying for her attention were ready to rip me apart over it."

"And men enjoy that, do they, the look of violent loathing in the eyes of another man?"

Isaac grinned. "Indeed."

I will never understand men. Was it the loathing and the sense of victory Isaac liked, or was it the attentions from Miss Kilchrest? Surely he was intelligent enough not to court a woman simply out of pride. "And what did ya talk about during this jealousy-inducing conversation with Miss Kilchrest?"

He buttoned his coat against the growing wind as they continued down the road. "She spoke of her friends and fashion and the weather."

"Fascinating." Alice only just kept her tone less dry than she felt the comment deserved.

He laughed a little. "She and I aren't the friends that you and I are. We've not endless topics to discuss yet."

So stop trying to converse with her and start spending more time with me. She'd convince him one day; she swore she would. He'd realize Sophia Kilchrest was not for him. More important still, he'd realize she absolutely was.

"Can I let ya in on a secret?" he asked.

Alice couldn't help a smile. He'd shared "secrets" with her before. Sometimes 'twas nothing more than a teasing story, though on a few occasions, he'd told her of plans he had for his home and land. He told her personal things, important things, things she felt certain he hadn't told Miss Kilchrest.

He'd piece it together. He'd realize in time she was his match and not the Belle of Cavan.

"What's this secret?" she asked.

"This weekend in Cavan," he said, earnest excitement in his voice, "I mean to ask Miss Kilchrest if she'll consider me her exclusive suitor. I mean to see to it we're on the firm path toward making her my bride."

With that declaration, Alice Wheatley's world ended.

Two

Isaac would never, as long as he lived, understand the female mind. He'd told Alice of his plans to move quite seriously forward with Miss Kilchrest. Rather than offer immediate congratulations or encouragement, she'd looked shocked. *Shocked.*

How could she have been even a little surprised? They'd spoken of his pursuit of Miss Kilchrest nearly every weekend since he'd first crossed Alice's path some four months earlier. She knew as much about his plans and thoughts as anyone on earth, *more* even. And yet she clearly hadn't expected his declaration.

Women will never make the least sense.

They reached Market Square, where the weekly crowd of men gathered to jostle for position alongside Miss Kilchrest as she wandered about the vendors' tables. Over the months Isaac had been at the task of courting her, he'd planned out his efforts quite meticulously. Those plans seldom needed review or second thoughts.

Alice, on the other hand, was near constantly throwing his understanding of her entirely out the window.

"Have we made good time?" Alice asked that question every Saturday as they came in to Cavan Town. She needed a timepiece of her own, she did.

He checked his pocket watch. "'Tis only just noon. Ye've time to reach yer grandparent's house for luncheon."

Her nod was one of relief.

"Have they taken a turn for the worse?" She'd spoken often of her grandparents and their failing health. They were the reason she returned to Cavan every weekend—to take over from a cousin the task of caring for them.

"No more than expected. They're growing old fast, is all." She gave him a sad smile, but with more than a hint of her usual optimism. He didn't like how it dulled her usually sparkling brown eyes. "I'd best not keep ya from yer efforts. There's a market full of men needing tripping up and pushing aside."

There was the laughing encouragement he was used to receiving from his friend. Perhaps she'd only been distracted earlier by worries over her family. That would certainly account for her unenthusiastic response to his news. 'Twas a logical explanation, something Isaac far preferred to confusion.

"Is there anything I can do to help with yer grandparents?"

"Bless ya, no. There's no immediate crisis, only the hardship of waiting and watching them fade."

He could appreciate that. "Ya know where to find me if ya need anything."

"Yes, I simply follow the crowd," she said dryly, with a bit of a twinkle back in her eyes.

"Indeed. And ye'll find me at the very front of it." He set his eyes in that direction, in fact. 'Twas time and past to get on with the weekend's goals. "Wish me luck."

She hesitated the briefest of moments. "I'll wish the best for ya."

There was some difference between that and what he'd asked for, though he couldn't put his finger on just what that difference was.

"Until tomorrow, then. Farnham Street after church."

She smiled. "I'll be there."

He watched her a moment as she made her way down Market Street, away from the square. She didn't attract the attention Miss Kilchrest did, but she was a fine-looking woman. Her light brown hair didn't capture a man's gaze the way a head of fiery locks did. But she didn't fade into the scenery. He'd wondered many times while walking at her side just why it was that no man had snatched her up yet.

His weekly walk to Cavan had improved drastically with the addition of her company and friendship. Even as the weather had turned colder, he'd not minded waiting at the point in the road where she always joined him. Her company was well worth the discomfort. She would certainly be the first person he told when someday Miss Kilchrest accepted his proposal. Likely only his mother would be happier for him, though she didn't live close enough for telling in person.

But he would have nothing to tell either of them if he didn't focus on his goal. The list of things to accomplish was clear and precise in his mind. He'd purchase a few foodstuffs to eat over the weekend whilst making his way to the coveted position at Miss Kilchrest's side. Once he had accomplished that, he would speak with her about furthering their connection. After her acceptance, he could see to some business he needed to undertake. While courting Miss Kilchrest was reason enough to come to Cavan, he found that justifying the time away from his farm was easier when he added business with pleasure.

'Twould be his most productive trip into Cavan yet.

He purchased a bit of bread and cheese from stalls along

the market road. A few of the men he saw every weekend trailing Miss Kilchrest noticed him there. Their faces fell a bit upon seeing him arrive, a sure sign his progress with Miss Kilchrest had not gone unnoticed. She was a fine catch, to be sure. Her dowry was something any man would wish for, but her kind heart and gentle spirit even more so. That those arguments in her favor were combined with a strikingly pretty face and a fine figure had secured her more suitors than she likely knew what to do with.

She'd not have to worry over that long, though.

His sack upon his back and his eye on the thickest part of the bachelor crowd, Isaac set his mind to the task at hand. Some assertive weaving in and around tables and vendors and spectators set him within a few feet of his goal and well within sight of the lovely Miss Kilchrest as she walked at her leisure among the stalls. She did seem to take a great deal of delight in shopping and glancing coyly at the men who trailed her.

He'd thought it a very good sign during his twelve-mile walk from home that the last remaining autumn leaves were a shade of red that quite perfectly matched the color of Miss Kilchrest's hair. The glimpses of sky he'd spied between the ever-growing clouds reminded him of the brilliant blue of her eyes. A very good sign, indeed.

Today would be his day. Of course, first he'd have to actually come close enough to her to speak the words.

The past months had taught him to be more forward than he was by nature. Standing about waiting for Miss Kilchrest to notice him hadn't worked very well.

He stepped in front of one of the other men, moved around a few others. Miss Kilchrest was fully in his sight and lovely as ever she'd been. What man could help but notice her, especially when she wore a bright smile as she did in that moment?

The rising wind rustled the few curls she'd let hang loose about her face. She was sweet to everyone, charming them and easing even the most nervous of her suitors. The women, too, seemed happy to see her when she crossed their paths. At vendor stalls, she stopped to enquire after their goods and compliment their offerings, though she rarely made a purchase. Her friendly nature would make a good addition to his neighborhood.

He caught her eye in the next moment. She smiled welcomingly. 'Twas all the encouragement he needed.

Isaac slipped up to her side near a vendor's table with a small spread of braided watch fobs.

"A good afternoon to ya, Miss Kilchrest."

She laid a light hand on his arm. "How are you, Isaac?" She'd taken to using his first name, though he'd not felt comfortable calling her "Sophia." Perhaps after she accepted his coming request he would.

"It seems we are in for a bit of weather," he said.

She nodded, glancing briefly up at the sky. Her gaze returned quickly to the men standing about. Some held hats in their hands. Others stood with airs of confidence. Isaac had made a study of which men she gave second and third looks to. Those who arrived ragged or dirty she seemed less than impressed with. She preferred a smile to a somber expression.

The men who met those expectations were the ones to receive an invitation to call at the Kilchrest home. Isaac had seen at least a dozen men receive that coveted invitation. His turn was coming; he knew it was. After all, if she agreed to consider him her primary beau, his presence in her home would be a natural thing.

Miss Kilchrest, he had quickly learned, preferred to make the conversation than follow it. Isaac usually obliged her in that, but if he were to pose his question, he'd have to take control of their short time together.

"I wondered if I might have a word—"

One of Miss Kilchrest's particular friends arrived in that

exact moment. Isaac stood back, waiting, while the women exchanged embraces and quick-paced words.

He looked over those men who hadn't yet given up for the day. O'Leary from Drumora, who'd received ample attention from Miss Kilchrest. Kelly from Pullamore Far. Others he'd not met in person but recognized from their many weekends jostling one another about. Malone and Sheridan, both Cavan men, who Isaac knew were his greatest rivals. They alone had been granted as much of her time as he. Others had, early on in Isaac's courtship, but they'd fled the field, apparently having been deemed not quite what Miss Kilchrest wished for.

Her friend moved along with one last wave goodbye.

Isaac began again. "Miss Kilchrest, I wished—"

"Buy a flower for the fine lass, will ya?" a little flower girl, likely no older than ten, implored with a bit of forward cheekiness, but wearing the dimpled smile of an angel.

He could hardly resist such a request, especially seeing the acceptance of the offering already hovering on Miss Kilchrest's face. Whether the flower girl had anticipated it or not, she'd made a clever suggestion. Given the sheer number of men still trailing after Miss Kilchrest, all the little girl's flowers were purchased and offered in a moment's time.

"Oh, I do love flowers," Miss Kilchrest said, her arms laden with blooms, likely the last they'd see in a while. The chill of late autumn hung heavy in the air.

A light sprinkling of rain began as it so often did. Usually, Isaac didn't even note it. But the timing today might actually prove helpful.

"There's an overhang just this direction," he said, motioning toward a nearby building. "If ye'll just step that way, ye'll be out of the rain."

"How thoughtful." She shifted the flowers into one arm. She offered a wiggly-fingered wave to the other men then slipped her arm through his.

Isaac took a deep breath as they walked swiftly away.

His moment had come. Months of working to gain her notice were about to pay off. Soon she'd send the other men packing, and he could move on to the next part of his plan.

Safely under the overhang, he charged ahead. "Miss Kilchrest, I feel we've come to know one another these past months."

"Indeed." She smelled her flowers, obviously at ease with him. A good sign.

"I think ye've come to feel something of a preference for my company."

She touched his arm briefly. "Of course, Isaac. Who could possibly not enjoy your company?"

With that extra encouragement, he cut directly to the heart of the matter. "I wish to ask you, then, if ye'd be so good as to consider me yer beau, rather exclusively."

She did not appear nearly as shocked as Alice had, though perhaps a bit surprised. Her smile, however, remained serene. "You sweet man," she said. "I didn't realize you were so fond of me."

"Who could possibly not be fond of you?" He echoed her words of a moment earlier, thinking she might laugh at the sally.

Miss Kilchrest shrugged a single shoulder, returning her attention to her collection of flowers.

"I don't wish to press ya, but is there an answer to my question?"

A flattering bit of color touched her cheeks. "Of course there'll be an answer, I'm only uncertain what answer to give."

"Might I suggest 'yes'?"

She swatted at his arm. "You sweet man. 'Tis not a matter of yes or no."

"It isn't?" Isaac didn't think there was a third option.

"This is only unexpected, is all."

Unexpected? What did she think he'd intended with his four months of pursuit, if not an eventual proposal? The sensible assumption was that he meant just this, to further their connection.

She gave him such a heart-tuggingly uncertain look. "Can my answer be 'perhaps'?"

Perhaps. A third option, after all. "'Perhaps,' but not 'no'?" he clarified.

Miss Kilchrest looked quite pleased with that. "Yes, exactly."

Not no. He could accept that. For the time being.

And, he thought with some burgeoning hope, Alice would help him think of ways to win Miss Kilchrest over for good. Alice would help, and he'd have Miss Kilchrest's hand for sure and certain.

Three

Alice generally looked forward to her Sunday afternoon walk toward Killeshandra. For those few hours, she had sole claim on Isaac Dancy's time and attention. For that brief time each week, she could imagine he fancied her, that he thought her more than merely a friend. Walking the road as they wound about the lakes felt like coming home.

But, standing with her childhood friend, Billy Kettle, waiting for Isaac to arrive, Alice couldn't summon enough enthusiasm to even smile. Her favorite time in the entire week, and she was dreading it.

"Why do ya have to go, Alice? Can't ya stay here? We could have fun." Billy asked the same question and made the same arguments every week. He generally did so in the first moments after she left her grandparents' home and long before she left the street where both their families lived. He'd been more overset than usual that day and had followed her all the way to Farnham Street. "No one else will feed the ducks with me."

She patted his hand. When they were both little, she would pat his shoulder, but he'd grown far too tall. "The ducks have all flown away now. They'll not be back until spring."

"*Ducks* go away. *You* go away." His forehead creased deeply as he pouted. Though he had the look and build of a grown man, little else about him had changed over the years. "I don't like all the going away."

He kicked a pebble with the toe of his boot, his hands shoved into his trouser pockets. Poor lad. 'Twas the same difficulty, the same sadness every week. The only thing that changed was how easily he could be reassured.

She looked up into his handsome face and almost painfully innocent eyes. "I'll be back on Saturday as usual. We'll have grand fun then, we will."

"How far away is Saturday?"

"But six days. Not even a whole week. And yer da says he's found a bit of work for ya to do." She smiled encouragingly. "Ye'll be quite busy, and I'll be back before ya even have time to miss me."

His mouth twisted about, brow still furrowed. "I can miss ya fast."

He'd always been so sweetly loving, like a dear younger brother.

Billy's worried pout transformed instantly to a laughing grin. "Here comes yer beau."

He'd teased her about Isaac from the very first time Billy saw her arrive in Cavan with him. Billy gave her a quick hug, laughing like a child who'd heard a particularly entertaining tale. She couldn't help smiling at his antics. He rushed away, throwing grins back at her as he did.

She yet had a smile on her face when Isaac arrived at her side. Thank the heavens for Billy. She'd not have been able to greet Isaac with anything resembling cheerfulness without him.

"Who was that?" Isaac motioned with a small twitch of his head in the direction Billy had gone.

Had he never met Billy? Alice couldn't remember introducing the two. "He's Billy, m' dear friend."

"Yer *dear* friend, is he?" Isaac's mouth pulled down, his eyes narrowed, still not looking at her.

Feminine instinct can be a wonderful thing. Useful, at the very least. The man, Alice realized on the instant, was a touch jealous. And if he could be jealous of her friendship with another man, he couldn't be quite as determined to court Sophia Kilchrest as he professed to be. Part of him, at least, must have some feelings for *her*.

Alice clasped her hands behind her back and walked slowly down the road, not looking back, but certain he would follow. "Aye, my dear, dear friend. He welcomes me to Cavan Town each Saturday and sees me off every Sunday."

Isaac caught up to her. "Why is it I've never seen him?" He looked back over his shoulder several times.

She shrugged. "Ye've been a bit distracted, ya must admit. Fighting off hordes of fellow knights in shining armor takes all the concentration a man can muster."

"But ye've never even mentioned him."

Aye, jealous he was, and no doubting it. "I'm certain I have."

She kept up her somewhat brisk pace, quickly leaving behind the outskirts of Cavan. That Isaac kept up with her without protest seemed a good sign.

Alice picked up a topic other than Billy. 'Twould do Isaac a world of good to let things spin about in his mind a while. "You were to have a monumental weekend, if memory serves. How did things go with Miss Kilchrest?"

She'd dreaded the conversation for two days but now found herself equal to it. Perhaps she hadn't lost her opportunity after all.

He buttoned his coat higher as they walked further from town, the chill of approaching winter stronger even than it had been the day before. "I had a chance to speak with her during that bit of rain we got yesterday."

Alice's heart stumbled a bit in her chest. She did her utmost to keep her expression and her tone light and unconcerned. "A proposal in the rain? 'Tis hard to set a more romantic scene than that. Perhaps if ye'd arranged for a dusting of snow."

Isaac yet watched her with creased brow. "Yer *dear* friend, he is?"

A smile tipped one side of her mouth. The situation wasn't entirely hopeless. "Never ya mind about Billy. Tell me how Miss Kilchrest answered yer question. Has yer courtship become etched in stone?"

Please say no. Please say no.

"Well . . ." He didn't seem to know just how to answer. "I asked if she'd consider me her one and only suitor and . . ." Again his face twisted in thought. "She didn't say 'no.'"

"Did she 'yes,' then?"

Isaac shook his head.

"Not yes, but not no." Alice took some comfort in that. "And ya mean to ask again, do ya?" But how soon? How insistent did he mean to be?

"I mean to go back and try my hand again." He gave her a quick but earnest look.

"Even if she makes that effort difficult?"

"The difficult things are often the most worthwhile." He nodded just off the path in the direction of the lake. "Like this here." He stepped off the path and bent over, plucking a bright yellow flower from the ground. "Blooming so late in the season is hardly an easy thing, and yet this daisy here has managed it."

"'Tis a sowthistle." She smiled through the light correction.

The look he gave her was utterly amused. "Daisy.

Sowthistle. *Colaimbín*. Ya can't expect a man to know the difference."

"Perhaps that is yer problem with Miss Kilchrest. Perhaps she's a flower expert and is disheartened by yer ignorance."

Isaac eyed her hair a moment. Her hair? What was the man about? He pulled a few low leaves off the stem of the sowthistle he'd picked and tucked the flower into her bun. Alice ordered her cheeks not to heat, but they only paid her the tiniest heed.

A tender gesture it was. A man couldn't be entirely indifferent to a woman and have such a thought even cross his mind.

Isaac didn't linger over the moment as Alice would have loved him to do. He simply nodded and continued on down the road.

"Ye'll help me, won't ya?" he asked.

Alice shook off her scrambled thoughts. "Help ya with what?" She lightly fingered the flower in her hair. She'd never look on a sowthistle the same way again.

"Help me work out just what will turn Miss Kilchrest's head? I'm all at sea in this."

He wasn't the only one. How could the man act so fond of her in one moment—acting jealous of another man, picking wildflowers for her—and determined to claim Sophia Kilchrest's hand in the very next instance? It seemed men were thicker in the head than she realized.

"Ya wish me to help ya win her over?" Her heart dropped at the thought.

He nodded enthusiastically. "What better person to help me than you? Ye're a woman."

"Noticed that, did ya?" she muttered.

"So what do ya suggest?"

Thickheaded, foolish man!

She picked up her pace, tension pushing her ahead. "I've

no advice for ya, Isaac. Ye'll have to sort this one out on yer own."

"No advice at all?" He spoke from a bit behind her, no longer keeping pace. "Because ya can't think of anything? Or because ya don't want to help me?"

Not want to help him? He made her sound selfish, petty. Could he not even guess at her reasons? She was jealous and heartbroken. But she was also worried. She didn't know Sophia Kilchrest personally, but there was something about her she didn't like. But she *did* like Isaac, more than seemed advisable, in fact.

She slowed her steps enough for him to reach her side again. "Can ya tell me what it is about Miss Kilchrest that has captured ya?"

Something like relief entered his expression. He thought her question a sign she meant to help rather than a moment of self-inflicted pain. To know why she'd been passed over wouldn't necessarily help ease her regrets. She only hoped knowing the whys would lead to some degree of acceptance.

"Well," Isaac said, his tone filled with pondering, "she's beautiful."

There was no arguing that. Alice knew she was no beauty, though she'd not thought herself wholly plain.

"And she is genteel and sophisticated."

All things Alice knew she was not, and yet that ought to have been an argument in her favor. "What in heaven's name is a genteel and sophisticated woman going to do living on a farm?"

He shook his head firmly, eyes turned directly ahead. "Ya make me sound as though I live in a tiny crofter's cottage on a half-acre of barren soil."

"I said nothing of the sort." She'd learned over the four months she'd known Isaac Dancy that he could be a bit touchy about his land. "I know ya have some of the best land in all of County Cavan. And I further know ya've built a fine home for yerself. But in the mind of a woman like Sophia

Kilchrest, who has lived all her life in a town the size of Cavan in a fancy house with all the comforts she must have there, the life of a farmer's wife will be entirely foreign to her."

Isaac didn't appear to even ponder her very logical argument. "She has a kind heart and giving spirit. Such a woman wouldn't turn her nose up at the life I have to offer her. I've told her enough of my home and life. If she hated the idea, she'd not have continued acknowledging me week to week. And she certainly would have answered my question yesterday with a no."

Alice wondered if Miss Kilchrest was simply stringing Isaac along. She couldn't prove it, nor make any argument that would likely convince him. Neither could she force herself to help the man who'd captured her heart win over another woman.

He'd long since set his mind to courting Miss Kilchrest. Though his determination and dependability were among the reasons Alice liked him so very much, his stubbornness could, at times, be so very frustrating.

"I wish ya luck of it, Isaac. I've a feeling Miss Kilchrest will not be easy to win over."

He shoved his hands once more into the pockets of his coat. "Then how do I go about it? I gave her flowers yesterday, but so did everyone else. My offering didn't seem to stand out to her."

Sophia Kilchrest is a fool. Alice once again brushed her fingertips along the petals of the flower Isaac had only just given her.

The road made its lumbering turn around the lake, a wind blowing off the water that made her shiver. She'd need to start wearing her heavier coat as the season turned. Winters were not generally bitter in Ireland, but they were decidedly cold and, more often than not, wet.

"Do women have a favorite flower?" Isaac asked. "Perhaps if I chose better, she'd appreciate it more."

Isaac is a fool too, it seems. "Giving a woman flowers isn't about *the flowers*. A woman who really loves a man will love any flower he gives her, not because of the flower, but because of him. She'd not even need offerings. Simply being with him would be enough." Isaac had picked flowers for her now and then during their walks to and from Cavan, but she hadn't *needed* such things. He treated her kindly. He shared his thoughts and his worries. They'd found an ease with each other and, she thought, a closeness unique to the two of them. "If a woman really loved a man, she'd light up simply because he was nearby and think of him when they're apart. She'd be just as happy talking with him as she would be spending an afternoon in silence. 'Twouldn't matter in the least, so long as they were together."

She'd all-but bared her soul, nearly confessed what she never intended to. But did Isaac realize as much?

If his distant expression were any indication, he'd not made the connection. "I'm competing with half the men in County Cavan. I have to think of some way to stand out."

Alice shook her head, both out of frustration and sadness. How could he not see what was so obvious? "If she loves ya enough to marry ya, Isaac, then none of those other men would matter in the least."

He picked up a pebble off the road and skipped it over the rippling water. "Ya don't understand."

"What don't I understand? I'm a woman, like ya said."

He pulled his hat down more snugly on his head. "A woman, aye, but not one who has men clamoring after her."

The man might just as well have slapped her for all the sharp, immediate pain of that observation. No, she hadn't hordes of men desperate to enjoy the pleasure of her company. She hadn't even one.

"Billy likes me, so I suppose that's something." She knew if Isaac pressed her about Billy, she wouldn't be able to lie to him, but admitting the only man who thought her special actually thought of her the way a child did a playmate would only humiliate her that much more. She rushed her words, not wanting to give him a chance to ask questions. "I'm meaning to stop here a bit, spend some time at the lake before winter comes."

When she stopped, so did Isaac. Thoughts flitted across his face. His mouth moved without sound. She set her gaze out over the water, grey with the clouds hovering above. She'd rather look at the scene in front of her than see rejection in the face of the man beside her.

"You can go on ahead." As soon as the words left her mouth, she knew that "going on ahead" was what she desperately needed him to do. Being with him while his heart was elsewhere, listening to him sing another woman's praises, was more than her battered heart could bear.

"I can't leave ya all by yerself."

Ya already have. "I know my way, I assure ya."

"But—"

"Ya have animals to see to. We've spoken of them all, I'll remind ya." Indeed, she knew the name of his horse, both his cows. She knew exactly how many chickens he had, how many pigs. She knew just what was planted in every acre of his farm, despite never having actually been there. Sophia Kilchrest likely didn't know any of those things. Alice would wager Sophia didn't care, either.

"Ye're certain ye'll be fine here alone?"

Alice nodded. She needed to be alone. *Needed* it.

Isaac hesitated. "But ye'd have to walk the rest of the way by yerself."

She managed to smile at him, though her heart wasn't in it. "I'll be fine."

"Then, I'll see ya on Saturday, I guess."

Alice knew in that moment she couldn't endure another walk like she'd just had. Listening to him speak at length about his plans with Miss Kilchrest, hearing him tick off a list of how ideal she was, would be torture. Even making her walk in to Cavan alone would be better.

"Actually, I need to make the walk early this next weekend. But I know ya can't leave sooner than ya always do, what with yer chores and all. So ye'd best just make the walk and not wait about for me."

"But we always walk together."

That he would miss her, at least a little, was only small comfort. Her company was not dear enough to him to push Miss Kilchrest from his mind and plans. 'Twas best to make a clean cut.

"If ye're hopes for Miss Kilchrest come to be, ye'll not need to make that walk at all." She tried to look encouraging.

He asked a few more times if she was absolutely certain she wished him to leave her there. He finally seemed to accept her insistence and continued down the road alone.

In the silence he left behind, Alice sighed. She ought to have realized at some point in the last four months that Isaac was determined to continue with his courtship of Miss Kilchrest, and that no amount of wishing and caring on her part would turn his thoughts to courting her instead.

Alice pulled the sowthistle from her hair, spinning it about between her fingers. He'd given his intended flowers, but the woman hadn't cared. This tiny wildflower to Alice was a treasure. But it was also something of an arrow to the heart. He'd given it to her offhand, with no real meaning.

She stepped up to the lake's edge and set the flower in the water. It floated slowly away from shore. Alice watched it, wishing her heartache could drift away as easily.

She'd leave early for Cavan on Saturday, and Sunday return early to the farm where she worked. She would make the walk on her own and maybe, in time, learn to push Isaac Dancy from her heart.

And on that thought, she watched Isaac's flower tip in the water and sink from sight.

Four

Alice didn't come to their meeting spot that Saturday, and neither did she meet him on Farnham road for the walk back. To Isaac's surprise, she didn't make an appearance the next weekend, either.

He had so many questions for her. Why, when he offered Miss Kilchrest another bouquet, one he thought was nice, didn't she seem any more enthusiastic than she'd been with the first one? Had Miss Kilchrest's collection of admirers diminished, or was he imagining it? Why did Mr. and Mrs. Kilchrest seem more inviting of late?

More important than any of the other questions, he wanted to know where Alice had gone, why she didn't walk with him anymore.

Late November gave way to earliest December, and still he didn't see Alice. She had to be avoiding him. They walked the same road twice a week. She knew exactly what time of day he'd be on that road. To not cross paths even once in weeks couldn't be a coincidence.

THE ROAD TO CAVAN TOWN

The maddening woman was clearly mad at him, though over *what* he couldn't say. They'd never had an argument in the months they'd known each other. They didn't always agree on everything, but those little disagreements never ended in anything other than smiles and continued friendship.

He hated that she had disappeared so entirely.

Walking down the streets of Cavan on the way to the Kilchrest home, Isaac stopped in his tracks. In the window of a small shop amongst a display of trinkets and jewelry and such sat a delicate lady's pin watch. Flowers of inlaid gold stood in contrast to the deep blue of the perfectly circular case. It hung on a bow-shaped pin leafed in matching gold.

Alice would love this. And, he thought with a smile, she'd not need to ask him for the time every weekend. He didn't know if Alice could read a watch, but he'd happily teach her how, especially if it meant seeing her again.

He slipped inside the shop and inquired after the price. 'Twas steep, more than he'd ever spent on a gift before. He made a comfortable living but wasn't rich by any means. The watch would set him back quite a bit.

I'd not have enough left to give Miss Kilchrest a Christmas gift. Not having a holiday offering for the lady he'd spent months courting made no sense whatsoever. And yet he wavered. Alice would love the watch. He knew she would.

He left the shop and the watch behind, but the question of Christmas gifts remained in his mind all the way to the Kilchrests' home. Odd that he knew precisely the present that would bring a smile to Alice's face, but couldn't begin to guess what Miss Kilchrest would like. He'd given her flowers on a few occasions, but the offerings hadn't made her gleeful by any means. He simply hadn't stumbled upon what she loved.

A stern-faced servant opened the Kilchrests' door. Isaac was not terribly accustomed to calling at a home where the owners didn't answer their own door.

"I'm Isaac Dancy. The Kilchrests invited me to call." He felt he ought to explain why he'd come, when, if truth be told, his position in the world was far more equal to that of a housekeeper than a master of the house.

He was ushered inside. Isaac had never been to the Kilchrest's home. He glanced about the entryway, with its fine furnishings and paintings and fresh-cut flowers. A great many flowers, in fact. 'Twas no wonder Miss Kilchrest hadn't been impressed with his offerings. She had no need of more flowers.

As he followed the housekeeper into the formal parlor, Isaac began to suspect that Miss Kilchrest was not in need of much of anything. The room was elegant, fancy even. His own home, in comparison, would seem run-down and plain to the point of being ugly. But that was one of the reasons he'd first began pursuing Miss Kilchrest. He had worked very hard for many years to make a success of his farm, despite the lingering shadow of The Great Hunger still clinging to the land. He wanted that bit of prosperity to be reflected in his home. He wanted his neighbors to receive a warm welcome there.

Who could do that better than a lady who'd grown up in refinement, learning from the cradle how to be sociable and genteel? The idea was a good one. He'd certainly spent enough months thinking on it.

Yet standing in the pristine parlor, his hat in his hands, Isaac felt very out of place. Elegance, he was discovering, was not always welcoming. Surely the version of refinement Miss Kilchrest would bring to his more modest home would be a bit less overwhelming.

The object of his matrimonial ambitions stepped inside a moment later. She wore the same smile she always did, content and calm.

"Welcome, Isaac." She motioned him to a white settee.

He brushed at his trousers, not entirely certain they

didn't yet bear dust from the road. White was not the most practical color for furnishings.

Mr. Kilchrest came inside and crossed to where he still stood.

"I hear you took in a good profit on your crop this year."

Isaac nodded. Prices had been good.

"Good, good." Mr. Kilchrest took up a seat nearby and opened a newspaper. That was to be the end of their conversation, it seemed.

Isaac didn't know if such behavior was normal for Mr. Kilchrest, or if he simply didn't have anything to say to him. He knew many of Miss Kilchrest's suitors had been invited to call on her family over the months, but he'd never been among their number. Where were the others? He didn't think the invitations were generally kept to one man at a time.

"Is there to be no one else?" he asked.

Miss Kilchrest's smile tightened a bit. "Not this time."

None of the others could come? Or none of the others would come? He didn't know where the uncharitable thought came from. He dismissed it immediately.

Isaac sat on the edge of the settee, still clutching his hat. A person was afraid to breathe in a room like that one. Everything looked breakable and clean as new. If any of the other men felt half as uncomfortable as he did in that moment, 'twas little wonder they weren't coming around any longer.

He attempted to match Miss Kilchrest's small talk but never had been one for conversations that felt pointless. She spoke of fashions and the weather and stories she'd heard about people Isaac didn't know. He tried to discuss improvements to his land or difficulties he had about his home, but she only put on that everyday smile of hers and nodded without comment.

They'd not had enough opportunities to become

acquainted. Isaac didn't think he'd do a very good job of it in her house. He simply couldn't feel at ease there.

Though he'd only been in the Kilchrests' home a quarter of an hour, Isaac was ready to be on his way. But he hadn't spent much time with Miss Kilchrest. He'd meant to further their connection, to make his case, to move closer to his goal of winning her regard.

"I'd be honored if I could walk ya home from church tomorrow," he said. An outdoor conversation would be far more enjoyable.

"Of course." *Of course you can*"? Or, "*Of course you would be honored to walk with me*"?

He stood and inched his way toward the door. "I'll wait for ya outside the church, then."

She only smiled. He'd simply have to wait and see what happened the next morning.

He was well on his way in a moment's time. The finer houses gave way to smaller, plainer ones. For the first time all evening, Isaac felt like he could breathe.

His feet carried him, not to his friend's house where he'd be spending the night, but down the street where Alice's grandparents lived. He wouldn't actually call on her. Alice had made quite plain that she didn't wish to see him. But he'd lost his footing at the Kilchrest home. He felt turned around and needed something familiar.

The sounds of laughter and music met him as he walked. He followed the noise to the side garden of a house two or three doors removed from where Alice spent her weekends. He wandered over to the low stone wall.

Quite a few people had gathered about, talking and playing music. There was chatting and dancing. Isaac smiled to see it. He'd attended many such gatherings as a child growing up in the countryside. His own neighbors gathered on occasion for traditional music and friendly chatter.

Just as he made to find the gate so he might ask to join them, his eyes fell on an achingly familiar face. Alice, her mouth turned up in a grin as broad as any he'd seen her wear, was dancing about the grassy area with the same man Isaac had seen her with several weeks earlier. Billy, she'd said his name was, and a "dear friend."

A dear friend.

A dear friend she was laughing with and dancing with. A dear friend she was smiling at. Isaac had enjoyed neither her laughter nor her smile in weeks. And he'd not ever danced with her.

Isaac spun about on the instant. The party held little appeal to him any longer. He'd wondered at Alice's absence, worried he'd offended her. All that time she'd simply found another whose company she preferred to his.

His steps echoed hard and fast around him as he trudged back to his friend's home. In all the months he'd watched Miss Kilchrest pay particular attention to any number of her suitors and not to him, he hadn't felt the deep, crushing disappointment he did in that moment.

Five

Billy Kettle did best when given tasks that were simple. Equally important to his success was a taskmaster who treated him with patience and understanding. Thus, when Alice learned he'd been retained to help serve at the Kilchrests' annual Christmastime party, she could not help a touch of anxiety. Mrs. Kilchrest didn't know Billy, didn't understand his struggles. Rumor had it the woman was a demanding employer.

Alice fretted over the situation throughout the week leading up to the party on Christmas Eve. She thought about it as she saw to her chores, as she lay on her cot in the tiny maid's room in the farmhouse where she worked. Isaac would have listened to her worries, would have sorted them out with her. But, she reminded herself, they weren't entirely talking to each other. Not that they'd sworn off each other's company. She simply couldn't face hearing him speak odes to Miss Kilchrest. So Alice avoided him. And he hadn't come by her grandparents' place, though he knew where they lived.

She'd simply have to find her own solution to the problem. By the time she arrived in Cavan late in the morning on Christmas Eve, she had settled on a course of action. She'd never warrant an invitation, and therefore couldn't keep a protective eye out for Billy that way. But she'd wager the Kilchrests could use an extra set of hands.

She spoke quickly with her cousin upon arriving in town then slipped over to the Kilchrests' home to offer her expertise. She knew better than to knock at the front door. A harried-looking housekeeper opened the back door, impatience written in every line of her face.

"I've no time for bothers just now," the woman warned.

"I'm not here to bother ya. I know ye've a party to put on tonight, and I came to see if ye're looking to hire more help for the day."

One of her eyebrows shot up even as her mouth pulled tighter. "Ya know how to work?"

Alice nodded. "I work at a large farm up the road toward Killeshandra during the week. I can cook, wash dishes, serve and clear tables—anything ye're in need of."

The housekeeper's eyes narrowed. "I'll pay ya a shilling for the day."

Alice managed not to roll her eyes. *An entire shilling?* The housekeeper gave new weight to the term "pinch purse." Still, Alice was taking the position so she could look after Billy, not to make her fortune.

"I'll take the work."

Without ceremony, Alice was ushered through the busy kitchen, up a flight of servants' stairs, and deposited in the formal drawing room.

"All the chairs and tables being brought in need polishing," the housekeeper said. "I trust I don't have to explain how that's done."

Alice shook her head. She didn't need the woman to hold her hand whilst she saw to basic household chores. In a moment's time she'd been provided with rags and polish and left to her work.

She'd not finished polishing a single chair before Billy came inside lugging a chair in each arm. He grinned when their eyes met.

"Are ya working here, Alice?" he whispered.

She nodded.

"I get to carry heavy things about tonight. Just like a regular footman, I'll be."

"Won't ya be a fancy servant, then?" Alice smiled at his eagerness. Just like a little boy anticipating a game of imagining things.

Billy set down his burden. "Da says I'm to wear m' fine Sunday clothes so I'll look respectable."

"Ye'll look fine, Billy. Right fine." She squeezed his arm.

His pout grew by the moment. "Fine clothes aren't very comfortable."

"No, they're not. *Necessary*, but not comfortable."

He nodded slowly and with great emphasis.

"You are not being paid to stand about talking."

Alice nearly jumped at the sudden voice, too refined to be any of the staff. She glanced toward the doorway. Mrs. Kilchrest stood there, looking at them with obvious disapproval.

"Yes'm." Alice gave a quick curtsey. To Billy's look of confusion, she added under her breath, "Best get back to work, Billy, and keep yer mind on yer chores."

Mrs. Kilchrest watched every step Billy took as he made his way from the room. Alice pretended not to notice, but set to her polishing again. Mrs. Kilchrest made a slow circle of the room, brushing a finger over chairs and tables, inspecting them for dust. Alice didn't voice her protest despite not having had a chance to polish anything in the room yet but the one chair.

No scolding was made. Either Mrs. Kilchrest realized

things hadn't been attended to yet, or she was too distracted by the arrival of her daughter.

"Must we do this every year, Mother? It is such a great deal of bother." Miss Kilchrest leaned unladylike against the window frame, looking out over the street below with such an expression of dissatisfaction as one might see on a petulant child.

"It is expected of us, Sophia. And you will behave."

Miss Kilchrest gave a dainty shrug of her shoulder, pulling back on the white lace curtain for the briefest of moments, before letting it fall back into place.

"Do not give me that dismissive face, young lady. This is the most sought-after invitation of the season, and I will not have you ruin it."

Miss Kilchrest crossed to a gilded mirror, turning her head about as she spoke. "We could serve them cold tea and stale cakes, and the entire county would still come in droves."

Mrs. Kilchrest tipped her chin upward, eying her daughter with reproof. Alice watched the exchange out of the corner of her eye, making a convincing display of polishing another chair.

"One too many servings of your sharp tongue have driven away all your most promising suitors." Mrs. Kilchrest speared her daughter with a scolding look. "Where have the wealthy suitors gone? What of those with influence and standing? They've seen your temper one too many times and have flown like birds before the winter. And what have you left now? Farmers and tradesmen."

Alice bristled at the distasteful tone with which Mrs. Kilchrest spoke of those "farmers." Isaac was among their number, after all. He didn't deserve to be spoken of so dismissively.

Miss Kilchrest smiled vaguely at her mother as she flitted toward the door. "They'll be back, Mother. They always come back."

Mrs. Kilchrest watched her daughter leave. 'Twas not an adoring look she wore.

And this is the family Isaac hopes to be part of? Alice shook her head. *He could do vastly better for himself.*

"Those chairs will not polish themselves." Mrs. Kilchrest's words snapped like a flag in a gale.

Alice rubbed harder at the legs of the chair and muttered a quick, "Yes'm."

She spent the afternoon bringing a collection of mismatched chairs to polished perfection, her thoughts full of Isaac, drat the man. His empty-headed, single-minded pursuit of Sophia Kilchrest frustrated her to no end. That he'd not been by to see her fully broke her heart. She ought to be mad at him, ought to be leaving him to his stubbornness. But she could not, *could not*, leave him to certain misery in such an unhappy household.

How, then, could she help him see what a mistake he was making?

Isaac slipped a finger under his collar, stretching his neck to fit better in his very best shirt. Perhaps it wasn't the sermons that made sitting in church so deucedly uncomfortable. The staid and formal party he stepped into at the Kilchrests' was worlds different from the cheerful, laughing gathering he'd spied on the weekend before.

Of course, at this gathering he'd not have to watch Alice smiling at another man. That sight had haunted him all week. Enough, in fact, that he'd gone by her grandparents' house that afternoon, fully intending to ask her . . . something. He didn't even fully know what he would have said to her. In the end, it hadn't mattered. Alice wasn't there, and wouldn't be back all day.

If he hadn't been expected at the Kilchrests' Christmas

celebration, he'd have simply sat himself down at the gate of Alice's family's home and waited. Questions about her and Billy had plagued him all week. He'd struggled to concentrate on his chores. He'd nearly forgotten to put his finest suit and shirt in his bundle, despite bringing it along every weekend for church. He'd walked the entire road from Killeshandra without noticing whether winter had stripped the trees bare, nor the color of the water. He'd thought only of Alice.

"Isaac." Miss Kilchrest greeted him when he reached her side. In that moment, the smile she always wore rubbed him wrong. 'Twas nothing like the brilliant smile Alice had given her *dear friend.* Miss Kilchrest's smiles had never been like Alice's.

"Good evening." His eagerness to be going rushed the words from him. "Thank ya for the invitation." *Now let me slip out.*

"Of course."

Her tone never changed, now that he thought on it. She always sounded as if she only half-listened to what he said, and as if his compliments were her due. Either he'd never noticed that about her before, or he was simply in a sour mood and attributing motives to her that she didn't deserve. Either way, 'twould be best for everyone if he simply went about his business for the night.

"Isaac, have you met Mr. Byrne?" Miss Kilchrest indicated a man obviously very near Isaac's age. The similarities ended there, though. Mr. Byrne's clothes were not made of homespun, nor did his shoes show signs of heavy use.

There were not many, in fact, in attendance who looked quite as humble as Isaac did. And not one of those from his walk of life, he further noted, was introduced as Mister *Anything.* 'Twas first names for the farmers and the tradesmen and the less affluent. Did they feel as out of place as he did?

He searched his mind for a quick and tidy means of excusing himself for the evening. As he'd been particularly invited, he wasn't certain such a thing could be accomplished without giving offense.

"What business are you in, Isaac?" Mr. Byrne asked, sounding at least a little genuine in his curiosity.

"I've a farm up near Killeshandra." Isaac pulled himself up. He was proud of all he'd accomplished. "I've two-hundred acres of decent soil, good crops, a few animals to my name."

Mr. Byrne nodded, seemingly impressed. Isaac would not have guessed that. "And how many tenants do you have on that two-hundred acres?" He looked over at Miss Kilchrest. "A man can make a very good living if he divides his land up amongst enough families." He held his lapels, chest thrust out. "Rents can make a man wealthy."

"I've no tenants," Isaac said firmly, eying the man's signs of wealth with growing dislike. "I'll not be the reason dozens of poor souls are forced onto plots of land too small to support them. I'll be responsible for their deaths if we've another potato blight."

Mr. Byrne looked him up and down dismissively. "Is that old tired tune still being played?"

Isaac set his shoulders. "Not by the dead, it's not. But those of us lucky enough to have lived don't intend to forget it soon. Nor will we forget those who grew wealthy on the backs of the dying."

To her credit, Miss Kilchrest looked a little uncomfortable, though whether she found Mr. Byrne's insensitivity or Isaac's proud determination more upsetting, he didn't know.

"Now, if ye'll—"

His words stopped on the instant. Across the room, Alice stood at the sideboard, setting out plates of teacakes, wearing the frill-edged aprons all the other maids wore.

She doesn't work here.

Then again, he felt certain there were a great many more servants there that night than on his previous visit. The Kilchrests had taken on temporary help.

Had Alice taken the position out of necessity? What could have happened to put her in such financial hardship?

Without a parting word to his hostess or her infuriating friend, Isaac took a step in Alice's direction. He got no further than that. A footman, tall and broad, stepped directly in front of him, holding a salver of champagne glasses. Isaac had never been one for anything but a strong mug of ale from the local pub, or perhaps a pint of home brew. Yet he found his eyes drifting back to the bubbling drink. The glasses were shaking enough to be worrisome.

He looked up at the footman and recognized him right off. 'Twas Alice's Billy. Was he trying to keep Isaac away from her? He'd have a fight on his hands if that was the case.

Isaac stood as tall as he could stretch, still not coming close to the man's height, and set his shoulders. But a closer look stopped any challenging words he might have tossed at Billy.

The man stood, watching his tray of glasses, biting at his lip, brow deeply creased. His gaze flicked briefly at Isaac. "I can't make 'em stop shaking 'round," he whispered.

Something was odd in the way he spoke, even the way he stood and held himself. Isaac couldn't put his finger on just what was unusual, but the combination deflated his temper on the instant.

The glasses trembled all the more. Billy looked more than nervous as he eyed his tray of drinks; he seemed actually fearful.

"Do ya need to set those down?" Isaac asked quietly but urgently.

Even Billy's head shake was a touch clumsy, almost like a child who still hadn't mastered the moving of his own body. "The housekeeper said I was to carry it 'til all the drinks was gone. They're not gone."

They'll be gone quick enough if ya drop them. Isaac looked to Miss Kilchrest. Surely she'd see the difficulty and give Billy permission to set down his load. She watched Billy and his tray with misgivings but made no move to intervene.

Alice seemed to have noticed the difficulty. She abandoned her teacakes and crossed toward them.

Isaac whispered quickly to Billy. "Set the glasses down. Better that then letting them slip."

Billy's hands only grew shakier. His face turned equal parts pale and red. "She's wearing her mean eyes."

Isaac, himself, took a step back at the hardness in Miss Kilchrest's expression.

"You bumbling fool," she hissed at Billy. "Anything you break will come out of your wages."

'Twas the first time Isaac had ever heard Miss Kilchrest speak sharply to anyone. Though he'd had more than a few uncharitable thoughts where Billy Kettle was concerned, he found he didn't at all like Miss Kilchrest's reprimand.

Billy's face crumbled. "I don't have money. I can't pay for it."

"Ya won't have to." Alice had arrived in time to carefully take the tray from Billy's hands. She set it on an obliging table without the tray shaking in the slightest.

Miss Kilchrest set her hands on her hips and waited not a single moment after Alice turned back before correcting her. "He'll not be paid for work someone else is doing for him."

Alice didn't flinch, didn't hesitate. "He was not hired to serve yer guests drinks. Yer housekeeper was told in detail of his limitations. If ya have objections to how he performed this duty that was not his own, ye'd best take it up with that bothersome woman."

Miss Kilchrest's face pulled tight.

"How dare you speak to me that way?" She spoke through clenched jaw. "I do not pay servants to be insolent."

Alice managed to look down her nose at Miss Kilchrest,

despite being shorter. "And the pitiful sum I'm being paid to be here tonight is not worth yer shrew's tongue. Good night to ya, Miss Kilchrest. Happy Christmas and all that."

Isaac knew a moment of pride hearing her speak with such strength of purpose. Alice was no wilting flower to shrivel at the slightest difficulty. A country lass, she was.

"Come, then, Billy. We'll take up the matter of yer wages with the magistrate if we must."

Billy's tall frame bent under what looked like embarrassment and disappointment. Alice took off her frilly apron and pressed it into Miss Kilchrest's hands before walking away with Billy, her hand resting on his back.

Isaac glanced back at Miss Kilchrest. Her gaze settled uncomfortably on Mr. Byrne. "I told Mother not to hire that man. He's *simple*, you know. That kind always bumbles everything."

Isaac made a quick bow, excusing himself without a great deal of grace. He couldn't abide Miss Kilchrest's company a moment longer.

He's simple. That kind always bumbles everything. That kind. The words repeated in his thoughts as he walked away from the Kilchrests' party. Many of his neighbors were simple people, though not in the same way. They were the very best Ireland had to offer, the salt of the earth. Would Miss Kilchrest hiss at and insult them for their simplicity? Would she turn his home into a place where none of his neighbors or family would feel welcome?

Miss Kilchrest had added to Billy's pain. Alice had come immediately to his rescue.

Miss Kilchrest hadn't cared in the least about the flowers he'd given her a few weeks back. Alice had smiled sweetly at the simple wild bloom he'd picked for her at the lake.

He'd spent four months trying to be the person Miss Kilchrest would notice and care for. In those same four months, he'd never needed to be anything but himself with Alice.

His walk through Cavan Town drove home two indisputable truths.

Pursuing Miss Kilchrest had been a mistake from the beginning.

And he'd been in love with Alice Wheatley for months, but had been too much of a fool to realize it.

Six

Alice hoped Miss Kilchrest's behavior had been enough to warn off Isaac. She'd been too upset, herself, to stay and talk sense into the man. That he'd come immediately to Billy's defense despite not understanding his circumstances only further endeared Isaac to her. He was a good man, no matter how misguided his matrimonial ambitions.

She packed her small satchel and pulled on her heavy woolen coat. 'Twas a cold Christmas morning, perfect for staying tucked in bed, curled up under the blankets. But 'twas also a Sunday, and Alice had no choice but to step out into the weather and make her trek back to the farm where she worked.

The hour was early, an approach she'd adopted weeks earlier after her falling-out with Isaac. Avoiding him was easier, kinder, on her too-tender heart. That morning there'd be no Billy to see her off. He'd been nearly in tears by the time she'd delivered him home. His da had thought it best to not wake him that morning, and not to find him work at the Kilchrests' again.

Alice slipped her satchel over her shoulder. She wound a thick scarf about her neck and tied her battered bonnet tight on her head. She couldn't hide in the warmth of her grandparents' house forever.

The air hung heavy and cold as she stepped out on to the streets of Cavan. A cold and lonely Christmas Day, indeed. If only men weren't so infernally blind and stubborn, she might have been spending her Christmas morning with Isaac at her side rather than missing him as she was.

Perhaps men weren't the only ones who clung to foolish notions.

'Twas something of a shame to mar the fresh, untouched layer of snow with her trudging footsteps. So few things in life worked out neat and tidy.

She passed the church where Isaac would be attending services.

And if I must be passed over for something, I suppose church on a Christmas morning isn't so bad a thing.

Alice turned her face into the light wind and continued on her way. The miles back toward Killeshandra would not be pleasant; that was quite sure and certain. Some other poor traveler was but a few streets ahead of her, braving the same elements.

She held her coat closer to her with her gloved hands. Perhaps if she thought hard on the blankets and the warm fire in the kitchen hearth in the farmhouse that waited at the end of that long road, she'd not feel the chill quite so deep and acute. If nothing else, the anticipation quickened her steps.

She quickly came even with her fellow traveler. He, apparently, hadn't sufficient imagination to push him onward.

Alice set her mind to offering him an encouraging smile and a Christmas greeting as she passed. A person ought to receive at least that when alone on a morning such as this one. No sooner had she reached the stranger's side than he spoke.

"Have ya a friend to walk around Lough Oughter with ya?"

Her gaze immediately jumped to his face. "Isaac?"

He didn't look at her but kept his eyes trained ahead. "Might I make the journey back with ya?"

She didn't answer right off, but continued walking in confused silence. She'd not at all expected to see him on the road.

"Why is it ye're not in church this morning? I've never known ya to miss services. And on Christmas Day of all days." 'Twas more shocking the longer she thought on it.

He finally looked at her, but his expression was one of apprehension. "I didn't know when ye'd be passing by, and I didn't dare risk missing ya. I've been out here some time already."

"Out here? In this weather?" *Heavens, the man must have been near frozen.*

Alice opened her satchel as they continued walking, digging through her meager belongings until she found the woolen scarf her cousin had knitted her. She'd kept it tucked away should she need more bundling during the walk home. But one look at Isaac's red nose and bare neck made up her mind on that score.

He was still clearly unsure of himself. Did he think she disliked him? That she didn't want him about? He'd been thick-headed and stubborn, but love doesn't fly away for such reasons as that.

"Come, then," she instructed, stopping and motioning him closer.

She began wrapping the scarf about his neck.

"I can't take yer scarf, Alice. Suppose ya need it yer own self?"

She shook her head. "I've a warm one on already. Now ya just take this, and don't make a great fuss over it."

He held quite still as she finished wrapping and tying. Alice's heart pounded clear into her fingertips. Except for the occasional moment when he helped her over a muddy bit of road or bumped against her on accident, they'd never really touched. Yet wrapping her scarf about his neck, her hands brushed against him. She felt the tiny moment of contact clear to her very soul. She gazed up to find his eyes locked with her own.

They stood there at the very edge of Cavan Town directly on the road leading away, simply looking at one another. Each breath they took fogged the air between them.

"I've been a fool, Alice," Isaac whispered.

"Have ya now?" Her voice emerged even quieter than his.

His hand lightly touched her cheek, just inside the brim of her bonnet. Such a look of sad regret weighed down his handsome face. "I'm too stubborn by half, ya know. And when my mind's set to something I don't always heed the world about me. I miss a great many important things that way."

For the first time in some weeks, Alice's heart smiled along with her lips. "Ya *are* terrible stubborn, Isaac Dancy."

His eyes traced her smiling face, and some of the heaviness left his expression. His hand slid from her face to her shoulder, down to her arm and took hold of her hand. "I hope, Alice, ye're every bit as forgiving as I am dimwitted."

"I'm a woman." She shrugged. "We've had to be forgiving since time began."

"Speaking of which . . ." He set something in her free hand.

What in heaven's name? She examined the little cloth-wrapped bundle. "What is it?"

"'Tis a present, it is. A Christmas gift."

"For me?" She'd not been expecting that.

"It's certainly not for Miss Kilchrest."

Alice shot him a look of warning at that. If the man truly wanted to get back in her good graces, he'd do well to leave a certain woman's name out of things.

Isaac looked immediately contrite, but with a hint of amusement in his eyes. Here was the banter she'd missed between them. Here was his silent, lighthearted laughter. She'd needed it these past weeks.

She untied the fabric and unwound the gift. After unlooping the fabric for a moment, she reached the center. 'Twas the most beautiful bit of jewelry she'd ever seen. Clearly it was a pin, but with a peg on the side. Alice pushed the peg in, and the round, blue and gold case opened.

"A watch." She'd always wanted a timepiece of her own, but never had she imagined one so beautiful.

"Ya need one, ya know," Isaac said. "Always pestering me to know the hour." He clicked his tongue and shook his head. "A man can only take so much aggravation."

"I don't know how to read it," she warned him.

His smile was kind and tender. "We've a long walk ahead of us. I'd be happy to show ya how."

Alice ran her finger over the delicate flowers on the deep blue watch case, inlaid with gold.

Beautiful.

"This must have come very dear." She knew he was not a wealthy man. He was not destitute, but he hardly had endless coffers at his disposal.

"It matches yer eyes, Alice. Matches quite perfectly. I couldn't pass it by."

Matches yer eyes. That he even knew the color of her eyes came as both a surprise and a comfort. Perhaps she'd not been so overlooked all those months. "Ya had to have purchased this before the party last night." Before Miss Kilchrest made her nature quite clear.

Isaac nodded. "I decided on a lot of things before last

night, though the evening firmed up my resolve on most of them."

How she hoped one of those decisions was to toss aside Miss Kilchrest in favor of her.

She pinned the watch to the front of her coat, careful to clasp it securely. "Will it do, do ya think?"

"Lovely." But he wasn't looking at the watch. "I don't know how I didn't see it before."

"Blinded by ambition, ya were."

He nodded solemnly. "And by my own stupidity."

"Aye. That, as well." She set a hand on his chest for balance as she stretched on her toes and placed a single, brief kiss on his cheek. "I thank ya for the fine Christmas present. I'll cherish it always."

"Will ya let me cherish *you*, Alice?" One of his arms wrapped around her, keeping her nearby. "Will ya at least let me prove to ya that I can, that I *will*? All these months, I've grown to care more for ya than any person I know. I tell ya my thoughts and worries. I trust ya with my concerns. I miss ya when ye're away and worry over ya when ye're not close by. All these months, and I never realized—"

"Ya talk too much, Isaac Dancy." She took hold of the scarf about his neck and pulled him within an inch of herself. "It's not words I'm needing just now."

His smile tipped a bit roguishly. "I'm most happy to oblige."

And he was. And did. His lips met hers in a caress so gentle at first, she hardly knew he'd begun kissing her. But his efforts quickly grew more urgent. Alice slid her arms around his neck and held fast to him.

Here was the affection she'd longed for from him, the reassurance that he cared for her just as she cared for him. 'Twas home.

Flakes of snow drifted softly and slowly down around them as they sealed quite a few unspoken promises with a fine bit of kissing on a peaceful Christmas morning on the road to Cavan Town.

A Christmas Promise

My mother named me Thomas, but everyone calls me Old Tom.

"Make us laugh, Old Tom," the other children often said as we'd lean against the gasworks wall, resting our legs from our childhood sport.

"What of the lad who chased after the banshee?" I've often been asked.

Or, "Tell us a tale of the wee folk."

The requests never changed, never stopped, even as I grew into the name they'd fashioned for me.

"His eyes are old," 'twas always said of me. "Old eyes speak of an old soul." Then they would ask me to tell them a story. And I did. Every time. Tellers of tales are not *born* in Ireland; we are *made*.

"I've a mind to hear something sad," said the man dispensing pints in the pub, dangling before me the promise of something for wetting my thirst if only I'd weave a tale.

And I obliged him, as is the custom in these parts. Kilkenny is an aged city, its people more ancient still. We tuck our souls into the spaces between the words of the stories we tell, feeling them safely hidden away there. We care not that a story be true, only that it be well told.

This one, though, is true *and* real. 'Twas not in my time, nor in yours, but it was in someone's time just the same . . .

One

Ireland, Late 1820s

Not all roots take hold in County Mayo. For that reason, a certain Sean Kirkpatrick, his feet unsuited for firmly planting in the western lands, set those feet eastward on the promise of a position as a stable hand at Kilkenny Castle. He'd been challenged to prove his worth by driving a team of high-spirited nags from Dublin to Kilkenny in a given amount of time with not a scratch nor hair missing on either of the beasts. Arriving in one piece himself was not a requirement.

Sean had in his possession a map of questionable authenticity but no other thing to aid him in finding his destination. He might as well have tossed a length of yarn on the seat beside him and obeyed its twists and turns for all the good the map was doing. He felt certain he'd passed the same outcropping of rocks a half-dozen times, and the trees seemed to be mocking him at every turn.

"A fine lot you are," he muttered at them. "Couldn't give me so much as a hint, could you, say a branch pointing me in the right direction?"

Winter had arrived weeks earlier, though the branches were not yet bare. Somehow their refusal to act as divining rods made their half-emptied state all the more dispiriting. If he had to be lost in the vast circular mess that was the road to Kilkenny, he felt Mother Ireland ought to at least have given him a bit of color to enjoy.

Those were days of poverty, they were. Want and desperation had led many a man to do far worse than speak harshly to trees. And, though it would seem otherwise at first glance, Sean was not, in fact, mad. Lost, yes. Frustrated, decidedly. But he'd not entirely lost his mind.

Rain had fallen cold and steady all that morning, and, it now being quite firmly the afternoon, the effects of a wet morning were felt everywhere: the dripping trees, the muddy road, the wet state of Sean's backside. He was none too happy to have not yet reached Kilkenny as he ought to have. How easily he'd pictured himself arriving at the stables a day ahead, horses in fine feathers, himself not looking the least shabby. But rain and roads had conspired against him.

Don't you go about thinking that the Irish are a superstitious people. We *are*, of course, but I'd rather you didn't think it. Still, honesty compels me to admit that Sean Kirkpatrick, upon passing the same collection of very large rocks for the seventh time in a single day, felt he'd best turn off the road and follow the rocks, seven being a lucky number and he being Irish and, therefore, not one to take chances with luck. Call that superstitious if you will. We prefer *cautious*.

The path he guided his cart along led past one field after another, each divided from the next by low walls made of stone. Buildings dotted the landscape now and then, rough stone structures no doubt housing hay or animals. He thought he even saw, a great distance off, a thatched-roof cottage with a river-rock chimney and yet another rock-made wall. Ireland rather specializes in rocks.

Sean continued on for a full Irish mile, a distance far shorter than an actual mile but long enough for calling it a mile when sharing the story later and wishing to make things sound more desperate than they truly were. He saw no people, no animals even. He'd stumbled upon a great deal of nothing—another Irish specialty—but he'd not yet found the road to Kilkenny.

He came upon a hay barn filled nearly to the rafters, a rare enough sight during a time when the only thing most families had up to the rafters were children. Sean slowed his horses as he passed, watching for signs of life inside. There were none.

'Twas little point continuing down a path that could only end in muddy disappointment. He turned off and drove a bit past the hay barn, meaning to turn his cart around when he could find a bit of space to do it.

He urged the horses to the left and leaned himself a bit as well in anticipation of the turn of his vehicle. Anticipation, however, does not always prove reality. The horses moved, but the cart did not.

The horses made valiant efforts to move along, tugging and pulling and glancing back at him as if in blame. The cart was utterly stuck.

Now, most men, no matter how stubborn and hardheaded, recognize the futility of continuing when a pursuit has proven impossible. But the promise of wages when one has none can override sense with the greatest of ease. Sean, operating under this particular flavor of desperation, hopped from his perch and strode, as much as one can stride through thick mud, to the horses' heads.

He eyed the pair of them with as fearsome a look as ever his mother had produced when he'd caused mischief as a lad. He knew the look well. "Are you not eager to reach your new home, then? You'd rather play about in the mud than keep on?"

Sean swore that the beasts rolled their eyes at his scolding as if to point out that he, and not they, had been the one harebrained enough to drive into a muddy field in the first place.

"Well, you might've warned me, you might." He pulled off his sodden hat and slapped it against his thigh, sending droplets of water in all directions, punctuated by the very Irish disposition for colorful and detailed cursing.

He pointed a warning finger at the horses in turn. "Don't you go letting anyone steal you away, now. I've a job waiting, and it depends on you two bein' here when I return. Do a lad a favor and don't go wandering about with any strangers."

A nicker was all he received in response. That'd have to do, he supposed.

He trudged back along the short path he'd taken past the tall hay barn, knowing that doing so would put him back on the road he'd been on before, the one that led through the fields and past the distant buildings. If he could make his way to the cottage, someone there might lend him a hand, and, in doing so, save his neck.

Admitting he'd clearly taken a wrong turn in his attempt to find Kilkenny, that he'd been unable to find it at all, would be embarrassing, to say the least. Adding to that the confession that he'd managed to get his cart stuck in the mud, and it was enough to make him consider simply turning around and walking back to Mayo.

As he walked around the barn, a bark so loud and deep that it echoed through him in stomach-turning vibrations destroyed what little peace he still felt. He knew of only one dog with such an enormous voice: the Irish wolfhound, a breed so large, not another dog in all of creation stood as tall or as menacing. And he, apparently, was about to encounter one.

Sean searched his brains, trying to remember who was the patron saint of "not being devoured by a man-eating dog." A second bark rumbled through the air, overlapped by another and then another.

Three dogs. They bounded around the corner and directly at him, a hungry gleam in their ferocious eyes.

And that is what comes of traveling in Ireland without a reliable map.

Two

Here in the Emerald Isle, we've a great many terms for a woman so beautiful that the entire island sits up and takes notice every time she leaves her house: Irish Rose. The Gem of Ireland's Crown. If a man is wise: my wife. But we lag far behind in universal terms for women who are quite pretty but who don't stop the earth's rotation simply by arriving somewhere. Were there such a term, Maeve Butler could have adopted it as another given name.

She was lovely; all who saw her could confirm as much. Her eyes were fine, her hair dark and thick, and her smile filled with laughter. But those who took time to meet her learned quickly that her best feature was her quick wit. The woman was, in a word, clever.

Thus, she needed only an instant to realize that her dogs had caught a scent. The beasts had bolted, raising such a racket their barks must've bothered the Marquess and his family clear up at the castle. She further sorted out, by virtue of the beasts' overwhelming enthusiasm, that whatever they'd taken to chasing was a bigger prize than a rabbit or bird. That left two possibilities: an unfamiliar dog or an unfamiliar person.

She'd not seen anyone pass the hay barn, where she'd been inspecting the stacks after the day's rain. But then, she'd been clear in the back.

Maeve pulled her scarf more snuggly around her neck and slipped out of the barn, whistling a jaunty tune. She'd always enjoyed the first cold days of the year, when harvest was over but the bone-chilling air of winter wasn't biting her yet.

She spotted her dogs quickly; they were roughly the size of small horses, after all. And standing on a tall rock in the midst of the barking beasts was a man. Even from that distance, she could tell he wasn't someone known to her. Not many people wandered up to the farm. Those who did were familiar, so much so that the family could generally identify them by their coats alone.

One time, Finley Donaghue had come visiting in a new coat of which he was quite proud, and Maeve's brother Kieran had nearly shot him, thinking he'd come upon a stranger bent on robbing them rather than their nearest neighbor.

The man on the rock wore an entirely unfamiliar coat.

"*Fág é!*" She called. The dogs backed off at once, still eying the stranger but no longer "hunting" him. "*Anseo.*" All three dogs returned to her at once. They were large and intimidating—the very reason her brothers insisted she keep them nearby—but they were also intelligent and well trained. And they only responded to commands issued in Irish, which marked them as far superior to dogs who preferred English.

Maeve moved near enough to be heard by the stranger, who still stood on his rock but remained at enough of a distance to let him know she didn't entirely trust him. Too many years of want and hunger had left Ireland's people wary of strangers.

"Are you so fond of rocks, then, that you go about standing on them whenever possible?" she asked.

"I'm trying to avoid being your dogs' next meal."

She scratched behind one of the dogs' ears. "These little lambs? They'd not hurt a fly."

"Perhaps, but I'm not a fly, now, am I?"

Like any true Irishwoman, Maeve Butler held decided opinions about every topic, even those she'd not yet heard of.

She was, for example, a firm believer in not cursing in church or walking heavy-footed through a graveyard. She also believed that a man ought to be quick-witted if he could at all help it. And this man seemed to be just that.

"Have you a name, stranger, or do we simply call you 'He Who Stands on Rocks'?"

He stepped onto the ground but without letting his wary gaze move the slightest from Maeve's protectors. Her loyal companions flanked her, not looking away from the trespasser. They wouldn't attack, however, unless she told them to or unless He Who Stands on Rocks did something foolish like rush at them.

"I'm Sean Kirkpatrick," he said. "And I'm a bit turned about. I'm trying to reach Kilkenny."

"You're close," she said, "but you've turned off the main road. This here's a farm, not a thoroughfare."

He looked about as if surprised. "I thought it seemed a touch too quiet."

Miss Maeve Butler had a soft spot for smart men, 'tis true enough, but if a man also had a fine sense of humor and a bit of a handsome face, she was lost. Fortunately, she had a knack for keeping a disinterested expression on her face when her heart was leaping about. Being the only sister in a house with two brothers made it a necessary skill.

"I'll not say you're as sparkly clean as a king lazing about on his throne, but you're not dirty enough to have been walking the roads on such a wet day." He must've had a horse or cart or something somewhere nearby, but she didn't spy one.

"My team and cart are stuck in the muddy road on the other side of your barn."

She glanced in the direction he indicated. "Muddy *road*? That, my friend, is a field."

"Yes, well, my map wasn't terribly helpful."

"I'd say not." She gave him a quick nod. "Best of luck to you." To the dogs, she called, "*Tar liom!*" They followed obediently at her side as she walked in the direction of the curing shed.

"Hold up there a moment, lass. You'll not be leaving me stuck, will you?" He caught up to her quickly.

Rufus, the largest of her hounds, objected—loudly. Sean jumped backward.

"*Buachaill maith*," she told Rufus, pointing for him to back down. She eyed the newcomer a moment. "I suppose it'll not do to let your horses suffer." Maeve pretended to deeply ponder the horses' well-being. "That does it then. I'll send my brothers back with a few draft horses and a strong length of rope. They'll have your cart out, but they'll rib you something fierce. If you've any bits of your ego left intact, best tuck them firmly away. Your pride's about to take a beating."

He pulled his coat more firmly around himself. "If they'll help me get my team to the castle stables in one piece, I'll gladly serve as the fodder for whatever jokes they choose to make at my expense."

Maeve was an expert at letting a smile form slowly enough that anyone seeing it couldn't mistake its significance. An odd talent, perhaps, but a useful one. "Once they've pulled you free of the mud and you've endured their humor, let me know if you're as 'glad' about it as you expect to be."

"They're that bad, are they?"

Telling silences are also a talent of some rarity. Maeve, in addition to being clever, was rare.

She left Sean to ponder the mess in which he'd landed himself. She was doing a fine bit of pondering as well. Pondering a witty conversation. Pondering a man with terrible taste in coats but an impressive lack of arrogance. Pondering what it would take to convince her brothers to let her make a trip to Kilkenny if Sean Kirkpatrick meant to be there long, though she'd not mention that last part to them.

Lest it seem Maeve Butler was a woman of weakness, too timid to stand up to the dictatorship of her brothers, hers was not a concern about obtaining their permission so much as not wishing them to tag along, scaring Sean off with their relentless, if playful, tormenting. She loved her brothers, but like any sister worth her salt, Maeve found them tiresome.

She came across Liam not far down the road and waved him over. "We've a stranger on the land. He's managed to get a cart stuck in the mud of the fallow field just beyond the hay barn."

"What's your man doing driving a cart through a field in the first place?"

The Irish have a few quirks in the language, quirks of which we're rightly proud. One of these is the tendency to refer to a person as "your man" when we've no intention of making any real claim on a fellow. Maeve knew this. Liam knew this, and he hadn't meant to inspire in his sister any kind of connection to this stranger who had such a poor sense of direction.

Yet his words did just that.

Fortunately, for Maeve more than anyone, she truly was as smart as the neighborhood gave her credit for being. Smart enough not to fancy herself in love with a man she didn't even know.

And smart enough not to dismiss him entirely.

Three

Liam and Kieran Butler hadn't stopped laughing since introducing themselves. Sean attempted to take their teasing in stride. Attempting doesn't always mean succeeding.

"Do all lads from Mayo not know the difference between a field and a road?" Liam, the ginger one with at least a stone's worth of muscle on his brother, had latched on first thing to Sean's home county.

"And what was it, Sean from Mayo, that convinced you to lead these beasts into the mud?" Kieran had also made a point of mentioning Sean's home in nearly every sentence.

"It didn't seem so terrible an idea on the map," Sean muttered, hands thrust into his coat pockets.

The men's identical grins only widened.

"And do you always let a map do your thinking for you?" Liam asked. "Or only on rainy days?"

"Around here," Kieran jumped in, "every day's a rainy day."

"Meaning," Liam added, "he's somethin' of a muttonhead every day."

Sean ought to have been rewarded with a fancy title, or at least an estate, for the forbearance he showed that afternoon. Having his intelligence called into question again and again pushed his endurance to its limit.

But these two jesters had brought with them three very large draft horses, likely about the only thing that'd get Sean's cart free of the mud and, in so doing, save his hide. So he kept his mouth shut. Never let it be said the Irish haven't a knack for strategizing.

"Seems less than proper, though, leavin' these fine animals stranded this way," Kieran said. "Seems we ought to do something about them."

"Seems." Liam nodded, as if pondering deeply.

"I assumed that was the reason you brought the horses along." Sean indicated them with a jerk of his thumb.

"Oh, not at all," Liam insisted. "They're fine company, they are, tell the best jokes. There's this one about a muttonhead who gets his cart stuck in the mud. It's hilarious, I tell you."

"Now, I've a difficult time believing that, brother," Kieran said. "Not the bit about the talkin' horses. *That* I could imagine happening. But a fella driving a cart into a muddy field? That seems unlikely."

Sean shook his head at their nonsense. "Your sister told me that the pair of you would rib me over this. I think she made rather light of it."

"Well, but she didn't let her dogs eat you," Liam pointed out. "That tells us there's more to you than a stick in the mud." He turned to his brother, grin growing. "*Stick in the mud*. The *mud*. That wasn't half bad, now, was it?"

"I'll tell you what *is* half bad: this cart." Kieran gave it a firm tap with the toe of his boot. "He's managed to sink this thing deep. We'll not be pulling it out on our own."

"Again, I figured that was why you brought the horses," Sean said.

The brothers laughed, and, though Sean still wasn't enjoying being the recipient of their teasing, he found that he could smile along with them.

"We could try pulling the cart out with these beasties." Liam patted one of the very large horses they'd brought. "But I fear it's too stuck for that and would only splinter."

Sean shook his head. "Can't let that happen, lads. The cart's not mine. It belongs to the castle, as the horses do."

"Fortunately, *they're* not stuck," Liam said. "We can take them to the barn to warm up and get a bit to eat. Then I suppose we had better send for Donaghue and the up road Butlers and dig out the Marquess's cart." He looked at Sean. "Did you know that the owner of the castle was recently made a fine Marquess? I'd wager he'd be none too happy to hear that his new stable hand went and broke a cart."

Sean's day hadn't been a great one; that declaration didn't help. "The cart and animals have to be to Kilkenny stables by tomorrow at nightfall. I'd hoped to arrive early to impress a few important people. You see, I need this job the way crops need the sun—desperately."

Much of the humor in the brothers' faces eased into an optimism tempered with concern, an expression one often sees on faces in Ireland. Even when we know there's little reason to expect a happy ending, we expect it anyway. Some might blame that on the Guinness. But truth be known, 'tis nothing more nor less than being raised to believe in better things to come. We've had to make that way of seeing the word a choice, as there's been precious little these past centuries to be hopeful about.

Yet hope arrived for Sean Kirkpatrick in the form of a burly farmer by the name of Finley Donaghue and another pair of brothers with the surname of Butler, though with the added distinction of being "up road" Butlers. It was the custom in days gone by for people to adopt the same surname as the nearest family of distinction. That, in Kilkenny, was the Butler family of Kilkenny Castle. And, thus, the countryside for many miles in all directions was littered with Butlers who had no more claim on the imposing structure than they did on Dublin Castle. But Butlers they were just the same.

The six of them were digging out Sean's cart until past nightfall, a time that comes early in winter, long before anyone is truly ready to retire to his bed. Sean's cart emerged a bit worse for the experience, but in the course of that muddy undertaking, he made his first friends in this new county. Liam and Kieran invited the lot of them to take supper up at the cottage.

"Won't your sister have something to say about that?" Sean had learned from his own sainted mother that a man who valued his continued existence didn't spring guests upon a woman without warning.

"Oh, Maeve'll be expecting us," Kieran insisted.

"Give the lass our regrets," one of the up road Butlers said. "We've a few chores yet to see to, and we mean to do them before the night grows too cold."

Sean shook their hands firmly, hoping to communicate that he wasn't an utter idiot despite the predicament they'd found him in upon first meeting. "I thank you again for your help."

"You're in Kilkenny now," up road Butler the second said. "We look after one another."

"I'm appreciative."

A few more firm nods split the group. Sean, Liam, Kieran, and Finley Donaghue made their way to the cottage.

"You're certain Miss Maeve'll not mind us dropping in for supper?" Sean asked.

"She'll not mind," Liam said.

"And how is it you're so confident of that? Have you the second sight?"

"If I had, I'd've locked the gate this morning to keep

troublesome lads from Mayo off our land, now wouldn't I?"

They'd only just reached the door of the cottage—precisely like every other cottage one generally sees in the countryside, from its thatched roof and white walls to its red door and small windows. It isn't that we aren't a creative people; we're simply limited by the materials on hand and by the somewhat crushing weight of not ever having any money.

Irish cuisine is about as varied as Irish country architecture. Had Sean been asked to hazard a guess as to the menu Miss Maeve Butler had concocted, he'd likely've hit quite close to the mark. He knew in an instant, as does every Irishman, the aroma of colcannon and soda bread, and that was precisely what he smelled the moment they stepped inside.

"You're late, lads," came the greeting from just out of sight around a corner. "I've kept your meal warm, but if I hear a word of complaint about it bein' over cooked, I'll skin the lot of you and serve you to my hounds for breakfast." Maeve stepped into sight, offered them all a brilliant smile and added, "Dinner's on, then."

There's hardly a soul who's not heard of love at first sight. Yet, more often than not, 'tis a good dozen or so sights before a heart begins to realize it's in danger of never being quite whole again. Sean needed neither one nor twelve sightings of Maeve Butler to begin falling rather irreparably into the first stages of love with her, the first being something along the lines of, "that fine lass has caught my attention, and I'm wishing to know her better." Sean needed only two sightings to reach that starting place.

The first sighting had mostly been about her dogs and his horses. But the second one, *this* moment, with Maeve standing there, her apron dirtied with dinner, her hair hanging every which way, her large wooden spoon aimed at them all like a queen making a royal accusation—that moment did it for him.

He was well and truly gone, or at least pointed in that general direction.

Four

Different lands have their own unique ideas about those things that make a man attractive to a woman. In Scotland, they put a great deal of importance on kilts and tossing tree-sized logs about. In England 'tis of great importance for a man to sport particularly clean clothes and fine manners. No one quite knows what to make of the Americans' approach to almost anything.

But in Ireland, a man coming in from the fields, smelling of earth and fresh air, invigorated with the satisfaction of a job well done, and glowing with pride of ownership is . . . not terribly realistic. Most men newly returned from the fields smell of things far less pleasant and shine with nothing so much as a heavy sheen of sweat. I'd not say *that* is the key to an Irishwoman's heart. But a man who won't work hard or is too dainty to dirty his hands won't get far in the countryside.

Sean arrived in Maeve's home, smelling and looking like he'd been rolling about in a mixture of mud and wet dog fur.

She ought to have been entirely put off on the man, yet something about the filthy smelliness of him had quite the opposite effect. Seeing proof of his hard work, and a smile on his face despite the struggle he'd had that afternoon, couldn't help but inspire admiration. And if a man can earn a woman's admiration, the task of earning her affection becomes far more feasible.

"You were planning to wash before sitting at my table, weren't you?" she asked him.

He took up her dry tone of teasing. "Indeed. But I couldn't imagine your brothers' having any idea where I might accomplish that, so I thought I'd best ask you."

"Sorted them out straight off, did you?" She laughed at her brothers' looks of feigned offense. "There's a well a few yards back of the house. You can wash up there. And the rest of you, as well. I'll not have you turning my kitchen into a muddy field."

"We had best avoid that," Liam agreed, "else Sean'll likely get himself stuck in here as well."

Sean took the ribbing in stride. "And do the two of you intend to let me fall in this well of yours, stumbling about as I will be in the dark?"

"You'll have to take your chances." Kieran slapped a hand on Sean's back.

The lads were outside in a moment. Though she ought to have set herself to the task of placing bowls and cups and such on the table, Maeve's mind had followed the men out the door.

That Sean Kirkpatrick is a handsome man, mud and all. And quick-witted. And not easily offended. Now to discover if he turned his nose up at simple country fare. For if a man can't stomach a woman's cooking, 'tis best for all concerned that he not come around at mealtimes. And if he'll not be around at mealtimes, there's little point in him being around the rest of the day, either.

But Sean quite heartily approved of her cooking, both in

words and in his very enthusiastic devouring of the meal. Indeed, he referenced a good number of saints as well as the heavens themselves between bites.

"You'd best not praise her too highly, Kirkpatrick," Liam said, wiping the last of his colcannon from his bowl with a slice of soda bread. "She'll get it into her head to go work at the kitchens up at the castle, and we'll lose our cook and our sister all in one go."

'Twas Finley who responded, the first word he'd said since arriving for supper. "You'd not up and leave us, would you, Maeve?"

Where the Butler boys were rather expert at teasing, Finley Donaghue was of a more sober mien. His question was asked in absolute earnest, the kind of earnest that either endears a person or makes the entire room a touch uncomfortable. In that room, with that question, 'twas something of an endearing discomfort.

Maeve took another quick bite before answering Finley's question. "Seems to me, seeking one's fortune up at the castle is becoming quite the fashionable thing." She allowed the quickest glance in Sean's direction. "And *I* actually know how to get to Kilkenny."

"Perhaps you'd accompany me there, Miss Maeve, to make certain I don't lose my way again." A slow smile tugged at Sean's lips. "'Twould be a shame if I drove into another field."

Liam spoke before Maeve could manage even the quickest of answers. "You'll not be driving anywhere tonight." Liam, being oldest, tended to make declarations for other people as if he were the law. "But come morning, Maeve and one of her hounds could take you up the road."

"If *I* choose to." Maeve, being the much-put-upon younger sister, tended to correct Liam's declarations as a reminder that he was not, in fact, the law.

"And *do* you choose to?" Sean held her gaze.

Maeve had never been one to let her heart override her

head. But now and then the struggle between those two parts of herself proved a close-run thing. Sean's question set her insides flipping about. Did he *want* her to go with him? A bubble of wonderment formed deep inside, growing as his gaze remained steady on her.

"I suppose Rufus and I could spare some time in the morning to see to it that you don't get yourself lost again." She took a bite and half-shrugged. "If you're needing me to, that is."

"I do believe I most decidedly need you to." His smile tipped a bit even as a laugh entered his eyes. "Though I could do without Rufus coming along."

"Rufus is going," Liam added with the firmness of an older brother when a near stranger proposes walking out with his younger sister without a chaperone. And Rufus was a fine chaperone. The hound wouldn't stop at simply shooing away a suitor making advances; Rufus would likely *eat* him.

"Good," Sean said, much to Maeve's surprise. "He can help pull the cart."

A sense of humor he had, to be certain. Maeve found herself very much looking forward to joining Sean Kirkpatrick on his way to Kilkenny in the morning. Indeed, it might be worth her while to get him a little bit lost and prolong the outing.

"It has occurred to me, Miss Maeve, that you may be of a mind to misdirect me so as to steal a few extra minutes with me." Sean kept driving his cart as though the remark wasn't the least bit remarkable.

Maeve knew otherwise. The man had all but read her thoughts the night before. She didn't truly intend to mislead him, but she'd most certainly given it some consideration. "If

I'd wanted a few extra minutes of your time, I'd've made you help wash dishes last evening instead of allowing you to seek your bed first thing."

"I'd've helped, you know." He expertly guided his team around a bend in the road. "Your brothers, however, saw me as a wounded sparrow in need of tucking safely in a nest."

Maeve laughed long and hard, for she knew far better what her brothers had seen him as. Not a bird in the nest, but a fox in the henhouse. If not for Rufus running alongside the cart, standing nearly as tall as the horses themselves—and the admittedly short distance to Kilkenny—she'd have been the one tucked "safely" away at home.

"And have you a knack for washing dishes?" She threaded her fingers through each other.

"I'm almost as good at it as I am at reading a map." He wiggled his dark eyebrows in the way that's meant to indicate one is aware of how idiotic one is being, all while pretending to not be idiotic at all.

"Well, what does your map tell you is up in the distance?"

"Kilkenny?" He let his doubt show. "But we've only been driving a quarter of an hour."

"I did tell you you were close, now, didn't I?" Her laughter died out when she saw the tightening of his lips and jaw.

"A quarter of an hour?" he repeated, tension in his tone. "I was a mere fifteen minutes away?"

Would the mild-mannered Sean Kirkpatrick show himself to be a man with a violent temper? She could abide a great many faults in a man, but an overly hot disposition was not one of them.

"Saints, I could've walked that far."

Maeve shook her head. "Not in the dark, you couldn't have. 'Twas only a sliver of a moon last night. And we know full well the unreliable nature of your sense of direction."

His head turned slowly toward her. She watched for any

signs of an explosion. Even Rufus slowed his trot a bit to come up more evenly with her.

"Are you meaning to goad me over that for the rest of m' life?" His eyes, thank the heavens, had begun to dance. Not a jig, necessarily, but not a dirge, either.

"Are you saying you mean to keep my acquaintance for the rest of your life?" She was likely being too bold, but Maeve never had been one to err on the side of bashfulness.

He only smiled and focused once more on the road. Maeve allowed her own smile to blossom. How was it that having known him only since the previous afternoon, that she was already turning about inside at the thought of seeing him again and again? Perhaps she wasn't so levelheaded as she liked to believe. But levelheadedness, in general, is rather overrated. 'Tis a fine thing to be a wee bit mad now and then.

"Am I needing to make any crucial turns, Miss Maeve?" Sean asked.

"This road'll lead you directly past the castle, Mr. Sean," she answered.

"*Mr. Sean?*" He clearly objected to her choice of name for him. But, then, she was finding herself objecting to *his* choice of name for *her*.

"*Miss Maeve,*" she pointed out.

He shook his head quite firmly. "I'm being entirely too forward as it is, having you accompany me on only the second day of our acquaintance, and with only a dog along for propriety."

"Are we so very fine and fancy now?" She sat up quite straight and proper, adopting her best English accent, which wasn't very good at all. "Why, Mr. Kirkpatrick, how very bold you are, sir. Why, I shall swoon straight off if you do not assume a bit more indifference."

Far from indifferent, Sean laughed long and hard. His booming enjoyment even startled the horses and brought Rufus's eyes around to him, a look of suspicion in their depths.

"What'd it be like living in England, do you think?" He talked through his continued chuckles. "Having to be so stiff and proper all the miserable time?"

"The English are likely not quite the way we imagine them." 'Twas a more generous statement than most in Ireland made about their less-than-congenial neighbors to the east. History had tainted the two people's views of each other. Centuries of hatred tend to do that. "Just as we're not the mindless animals they so often claim we are," she added.

"Do you think, Miss Maeve, that Ireland will ever be a real country, free to rule herself?" Contemplation sat heavy on Sean's posture and expression. An earnest question, then, not idle conversation.

It was saying something for two people to be comfortable enough for perplexing topics when they'd only just met.

"If the Americans can manage it," she answered him, "anyone can."

That brought another round of laughter, from Sean and Maeve both. The two made quite a pair riding together, smiling and quite at ease in each other's company. The castle came into view in the next moment, something that happens quickly upon the approach to Kilkenny.

"There's a sight for your sore eyes, I'd imagine." Maeve indicated the imposing structure. "The stables are just across from the castle." She motioned in that direction.

Sean whistled appreciatively. "Those're stables? The house I grew up in could fit inside them one hundred times over."

"Indeed. It is a bit showy, for sure, but it also makes the town seem a tad more fancy. And it's a fine-looking structure. Nothing to be ashamed of, at least." Maeve took a moment to be amazed at how many ways she'd found to compliment a stable.

"I've only realized—you have no means of returning home." 'Twas an admirable quality in a man to be concerned over a woman without being overbearing about it.

"As you said yourself only a moment ago, I live an easy distance from Kilkenny. And today's my market day, anyway. We make this walk quite often, Rufus and I."

"Quite often, you say? And do you make this 'quite often' walk past the Kilkenny stables every time?"

She smiled up at him. "If I choose to."

He pulled the cart directly in front of the stables. "This is my stop, Miss Maeve."

"Do you think you could find your way to calling me Maeve?"

"I think I could manage." He held the horses' reins as she climbed down from the low cart. He tipped his hat. "A fine good morning to you, Maeve."

"And to you, Sean." If he could use her Christian name, certainly she could use his. She'd gone but one step when he called out to her.

"Do you, then?"

She looked back over her shoulder at him. "Do I *what*?"

"Choose to walk past the stables when you come to market from now on?"

This was an invitation she knew herself incapable of resisting, but he needn't know that. Not yet. "You keep a weather eye out, Sean Kirkpatrick, and see if I do."

Five

Sean kept a weather eye out. And a sharp eye, a keen eye, and every other kind of very watchful eye but didn't see Maeve Butler even once over the following days. He hadn't the luxury of time away from his duties. The stable master allowed him only enough time away on Sundays to attend mass. He was to prove himself a tireless and uncomplaining worker during his first week on the job, he was told. Then, and only then, would he be permitted time of his own.

Though he didn't see Maeve, he thought of her often. For some, a head of golden hair or of fiery red is quite the end all of beauty. Sean had always had a particular weakness for hair of the darker variety. And he'd always been unable to resist a laughing smile. Wit went a long way in capturing his attention as well. Maeve was all those things, but she was something more as well. She was . . . He had no idea what she was, which was precisely why he wanted to see her again. But the confounded colleen never showed her lovely face.

Late in the afternoon of a mild Wednesday—"mild" by comparison, of course, meaning rain had fallen all the day long with a fierce wind that bit through even tightly knit sweaters and thick, woolen coats—a man's voice sounded through the castle stables.

"I'm needing to borrow one o' your stable hands, Desmond."

Sean leaned around the stable door, straining to catch sight of Liam Butler. Even with the comings and goings of a large staff and a great many animals, he thought he might manage to find the man. Gingers generally stand out in a crowd.

"You'll not be convincing me that you and Kieran can't manage your animals." Desmond was the stable master and never let a soul forget it. "And I know perfectly well that sister of yours can keep her hounds in line."

"'Tis the sister we're needing help with," Liam answered.

Worries for Maeve flooded over Sean as he stood in that stall, his task forgotten, dirtied straw stuck to the end of his abandoned pitchfork.

"Nonsense," Desmond grumbled. "That lass is tougher than the both of you combined."

"Don't I know it." Liam looked about the place. He didn't appear at all like a brother worried over the welfare of his sister, but rather one plotting very nearly against her. "Have you a place where we might talk without being overheard?"

Desmond gave a silent nod. Before stepping away, he looked over the stalls and the many hands working there. "Back to your chores, lads," he barked out. "You're not bein' paid to stand about."

Sean set back to his task on the instant. He knew better than to ignore a dictate from Desmond. The man ruled with an iron fist right up until the work was done for the day, when he turned into precisely the sort of fellow one liked to run into at the pub. Days were long and grueling at the castle stables, but the evenings were a regular romp. Still, Sean couldn't quite lose himself in the merriment. His thoughts were a quarter of an hour down the road.

All those things considered, when Desmond relieved Sean of his duties a full hour before usual and even went so far as to give him the evening off, he didn't utter so much as a word of complaint. "I'm much obliged to you."

"Don't be." Desmond was a tough old bird. "I'm letting you go on an assignment, not as any kind of favor to you."

"An assignment?"

"There's a family just outside Kilkenny in need of a bit of help."

Ah, yes. Liam's visit. "The Butlers?"

Desmond's eyes narrowed. "And how is it you knew that?"

"I understand there are a great many Butlers hereabout. I figured 'twas a likely guess." A wee falsehood could be excused when one doesn't wish to play one's hand where a woman is concerned.

Desmond didn't seem terribly impressed with Sean's logic. But then, Desmond wasn't often impressed. "They do happen to be Butlers, in fact. Fifteen, perhaps twenty minutes along this road. You're looking for the six boulders Butlers. If you reach the up road Butlers, you've gone too far."

It's identifiers such as these, "six boulders" and "up road" and such, that contribute to Ireland's reputation for bein' a bit adorably simple. What we're not given credit for is how very ingenious such a system truly is when nearly everyone for miles around has the same surname.

"What sort of work am I to do there?" Sean had overheard enough of Desmond and Liam's conversation to be fully curious.

"It's not for you to turn it down, so there's little point in asking. On your way, lad."

He was on his way, as instructed, his way being directly back to the same pile of rocks where he'd made his fateful turn off the main road a week or so earlier. He recognized it easily and found that, though he'd been walking for a good bit of time, knowing Maeve Butler was up the way had put a spring back in his step.

He meant to ask why it was she'd never come to see him and whether he'd imagined the connection between them, perhaps even discover where he'd gone wrong. Though men don't generally like to let on that we worry over such things, we most certainly do. And Sean *had* been worrying a bit.

He reached the familiar red door and lifted his fist to knock, but a voice stopped him.

"Have you come, then, Sean?" Kieran was even then approaching the same spot. "Liam thought you might, though Maeve's despairing of it."

"She's expected me?" That seemed encouraging, though with women one couldn't always tell.

Kieran nodded. "We let her know that old Desmond wasn't likely to allow you any time of your own this first week or two, but she kept right on hoping."

Encouraging news, to be sure. "Why did she not drop by the stables and give me a wave? She said she might."

"And she might have if not for an unfortunate tumble off the ladder." Kieran scratched at his stubbly chin. "Fortunately 'twas only a rung or two. Well, it might've been six. Eight at the very most."

"Saints above." Sean grabbed the handle and pushed the door open.

He found his Maeve in an instant, sitting in a rocking chair at the hearth, her head dropped into one upturned hand. At her side sat Finley Donaghue going on about sheep and acreage. Other than seeming rather bored out of her mind, she appeared well. Relief pulled a sigh from the very depths of Sean.

A CHRISTMAS PROMISE

Maeve looked up at the sound. On the instant, a grin split her face. "Why, Sean Kirkpatrick! Aren't you a sight?"

"A fine sight, or a horror?" he pressed with a smile of his own.

"Why've you not come sooner?"

He crossed directly to her and hunched down before her. If Finley was surprised at the interruption, he didn't say anything, and Sean was too intent on looking at Maeve to bother eying the other fellow to see his reaction.

"Desmond won't allow his stable hands any time of their own during the first few weeks in his employ. 'Tis his way of breaking us the way some would break a horse."

"I told you so," Liam called from the kitchen.

"You've not taken French leave, have you? I'll not allow you to lose your position on account of visiting me."

He slipped his hands around hers. "Desmond gave me permission. But what's this I hear, lass, about your falling near to your death?"

"'Twasn't so bad as all that. I turned my ankle a touch and haven't been able to leave this house on account of I don't walk terribly well yet."

He rubbed at her hand with his. "How long've you been cooped up in here?"

"A week." Those two words told Sean all he needed to know.

"An entire week? Why, you must be climbing the walls."

Kieran answered before she could. "Not with that ankle, she isn't."

Maeve threw her brother a look of ill-amused scolding. For the sake of family harmony, Sean thought it best to wander off with Maeve for a time. Family harmony being quite important and all.

"Have you a riding horse?" he asked Kieran. "Or a carriage or wagon of some kind?"

"We've a hay cart," Kieran said.

That'd do. Sean returned his gaze to Maeve's lovely dark

eyes. "Would you care to go for a quick ride with me in a very fine and fancy hay cart?"

"I'd be in your debt for ever and ever, Sean Kirkpatrick, if you could find a way to get me out of this house for even a moment."

He raised her hand to his lips and pressed a kiss to her fingers. "Consider it done, lass."

He stood once more and turned to face the Butler brothers, who were standing a piece behind Finley Donaghue, whom he'd nearly forgotten about. The company of a good woman can do that to a man—make him forget everyone around him.

"Point me in the direction of your barn, men. I've a cart and horse to make acquaintance with."

Liam didn't agree to the very reasonable request. "You stay here and keep our sister company—*honorable* company—and the three of us'll bring the cart 'round."

"Three?" Finley looked up at the man as though he'd marched his brain clear out of his head. "Why would it take three people to do something so simple?"

Kieran slipped a hand under Finley's arm and pulled him out of his chair. "What we've undertaken, man, isn't simple in the least."

The two brothers all but marched their neighbor from the cottage.

"It seems Liam and Kieran have it in their minds to play matchmaker, Maeve." Sean looked back at her, half expecting a look of horror. What he saw was pondering—deep and uncertain pondering.

"Does that frighten you?" she asked quietly.

"It does a bit," he admitted. "But not enough to send me running back to Kilkenny."

Maeve shrugged. "You'd likely get lost if you tried."

"Troublesome woman," he muttered.

"Admit you love the ribbing."

He didn't bother hiding his grin. "I'm beginning to."

Some women blush elegantly and adorably, with perfect pink patches bringing a rosy hue to their complexion. Other women blush in a way that vaguely resembles the measles and makes a fellow worry that something's terribly the matter. Maeve, for all her prettiness, did not fall in the first category.

"Where do you keep your coat and warm blankets?" Sean asked. "'Tis a mighty cold evening out there."

"Blankets are in the chest against that wall." She pointed across the room. "My coat is hanging on a nail in my bedroom."

When Liam peeked his head inside once more, she had her coat on and the blankets were at the ready. "Your cart awaits," he announced. "And we've a lantern for you. The evening's growing dark already."

Sean turned back to Maeve. "Can you walk at all, or do you need me to carry you?"

"I can walk a bit, but not far and not for long."

"Well, then, if your brother hasn't any objections, I'll carry you out to the cart."

Liam motioned for him to go ahead, something that, frankly, surprised Sean. He had two sisters of his own, and he and his brothers had been quite protective of them, perhaps overly so.

"You seem to have decided I'm trustworthy," Sean said.

Right on cue a deep, rumbling bark sounded from just outside the door. "Rufus is going along," Liam said.

So perhaps the Butler boys weren't entirely decided on the matter of Sean's worthiness. Still, they were allowing him to ride with their sister.

"Why is it only old Rufus is sent out as chaperone?" Sean asked. "I recall with perfect clarity that you've a few other hounds equally as large lurking about the place."

Maeve's slow-forming smile spoke of amusement. "Rufus is the meanest of the lot, but only when he's alone. If all three came along, you might manage a bit of mischief before it's noticed."

"I doubt that. I've attempted to outrun them, you'll remember."

She shrugged a single shoulder. "I did say you would manage only 'a bit' of mischief."

Sean bent down, slipping an arm under Maeve's knees and another behind her back. She slid an arm around his neck, holding fast to him. After standing and making a few adjustments, he carried her to the door and outside to the waiting cart.

Blankets were situated. The lantern was hung on the cart's hook. Rufus took up his position directly beside the cart, eyes narrowed at Sean.

"Where would you like to go?" Sean asked Maeve. "This outing is for you, after all."

She thought a moment. "Could we just drive about for a time? I'm nearly desperate to see something other than the walls of this house."

"I'll go anywhere you like, Maeve Butler."

It often happens that a man is caught quite by surprise when he realizes he's grown unexpectedly attached to a woman.

Sean Kilpatrick was no exception. And mingled with that surprise was just a tiny bit of fear. For once a man begins to love a woman, his life is never quite whole again without her.

Six

"Seems to me Desmond is something of a dictator." Maeve didn't at all like the idea of any person trying to "break" Sean. Anyone could see he was strong and independent. She liked him that way. She liked him very much, indeed.

Sean didn't seem overly concerned, though. "He'll ease off in time. 'Tis his way of weeding out those who aren't willing to work."

There wasn't much to be seen as they drove along the paths that wove through the family farm. The sun had set, and the land was dark. But she was warm in her coat under the blanket he'd provided, and she was grateful for the fresh air and the joy of Sean's company. Finley, though he was a dear family friend, hadn't Sean's knack for conversation nor his quick wit.

"Have you had a good first week at the stables?" she asked. "Or has it been terrible?"

"It's been grand, actually. Such fine animals and the stables, Maeve." He whistled appreciatively. "They're quite the finest stables I've ever seen."

"So is it the stables you like best or the horses?"

"The horses, to be sure. I've always liked animals. Except, perhaps, for Rufus there," he added with a chuckle.

Upon hearing his name, Rufus let out a quick bark.

"I think Rufus likes *you*," Maeve said.

"Oh, certainly. He'd like me for supper, is what he'd like."

Maeve moved a bit closer to Sean, and not entirely because the night was growing colder. A week she'd been watching for him, hoping he'd come. And here he was, directly beside her, laughing and talking and lifting her spirits. Little wonder her heart was spinning about inside her.

"Which of the horses is your favorite?" she asked.

He glanced at her. "You don't truly want to hear about my boring job, do you?"

"Why wouldn't I?"

"I worked at a stable in Mayo, and m' sisters never did want to hear a single word about what I did."

She shook her head at his rather thickheaded logic. "They're sisters. And sisters are quite different from"—she wasn't sure what to call herself at that point—"from not-sisters."

"Well, then, *not-sister*, I'd have to say that my favorite horse is a chestnut the Marquess has named Chestnut."

She laughed silently. "The Marquess is not particularly creative, it would seem. Now, why is it Chestnut is your favorite?"

They rode on that way for long, enjoyable minutes, the night growing darker and chillier. She learned about the animals in his care, about the family he'd left behind in Mayo. He asked after her work and her joys. He wished to know of her late parents and her childhood.

Theirs was such an easy and natural conversation that one might be excused for thinking they benefited from a long acquaintance. And, seeing how they slowly inched closer and closer together as they drove along, even they began to feel that there was more to the evening than two near-strangers getting acquainted.

Ireland, you must understand, is peopled first and foremost by dreamers. We'll fight when we must, and we're not entirely without brains. But the trait that most defines us is the heart of a poet, and it shows most in quiet moments like that one, when a hopeful sort of love is born.

⁂

The next week, Sean came by for Sunday supper, and again the week after that and the week after that. Desmond, it seemed, felt he'd earned one night a week to himself. The change might've also had something to do with the scones Maeve brought to old Desmond whilst emitting a few heartfelt sighs of regret over never being able to see her fine lad. Desmond was a tyrant—there was no denying that. But he was also a man without a wife and in firm possession of a sweet tooth, something Maeve had managed to discover by means of endless questioning of Liam, who had known the man for many years.

Whatever the reason for the hard-nosed stable master's softening toward his newest stable hand, Maeve saw a great deal of Sean Kirkpatrick as Christmas approached. He came every Sunday without fail, no matter how miserable the weather, and she found herself watching the front windows all the day long, praying he'd come a bit early.

On his sixth Sunday visiting, when the other lads moved from the small kitchen, Sean remained behind. "I can't promise to be very good at it, but I'm hoping to help with the dishes."

"You're *hoping*? Were you thinking I'd say no?" Even if he proved an absolute dolt at washing dishes, she wasn't about to turn him away.

"I warn you, I've little experience with it."

"I'd wager you're a fast learner." She tossed a large, dry rag in his direction. "I'll wash. You dry."

He was a natural-born dryer, which was rather like saying one was a natural-born breather. Drying dishes didn't require much skill.

"Donaghue is here every week, I've noticed," he said as he dried a pewter plate. "Does he come around often?"

"Finley's been visiting since he was a lad, back when all of our parents were yet living."

"An old friend, then?" Sean slid the dried dish into the age-worn cabinet.

"Quite old."

Sean raised an ebony eyebrow. "He's my age, you realize. That's not so very old."

She scrubbed a bit of potato off the large serving pot in which she'd made the night's coddle. "He was always Liam's friend. I suppose that makes him seem older. Almost like another brother."

"Is that what he is to you?"

In that moment, with an intuition most women are born with, Maeve pieced something together. Despite all of the time they'd spent together, despite her tendency to snuggle close to him when he drove her about in the cart, and despite the rather obvious cow eyes she made at him across the table every Sunday evening, Sean was jealous.

Of Finley Donaghue, of all people.

The kind thing to do would have been to put his mind at ease, to swear reassurances and speak sweet words of tenderness. But the *wise* thing was to let him discover her feelings for himself. If their pattern became her having to swear up and down to her feelings anytime life gave him reason to wonder even a little bit, 'twould be a long and tiresome life indeed.

She let him chew on his thoughts as they finished the last of the washing. Sean didn't grow angry or demand answers. He made no further comment, really, only stood with a furrowed brow and a downturn to his lips that clearly said, *I'm pondering where I stand with a woman, and I'm not terribly keen on the answers I'm formulating.*

So Maeve, being a font of compassion as well as a believer in the importance of a bit of humor, decided to help him along a bit. "Did you know that Finley has nearly five hundred head of sheep, a surprising number of which have black wool? Did you further know that he's at his wit's end over a particular weed growing in his back pasture? His wit's end, Sean."

His confusion only grew. She managed not to laugh, but 'twas a close-run thing.

"And can you guess how it is that I know he's at his wit's end over the weeds in his back pasture?" she pressed. "Because he told me. He has, in fact, told me several times a week for the past three years. Weeds, Sean. *Weeds.* For three years." She took the rag from him and hung it over the back of a chair. "What was the last topic you and I chose to talk about?"

"We've covered so many in just the past quarter-hour."

Maeve stepped closer to him and set her hands on both of his arms. "Precisely, you daft man. You are the one I enjoy talking with, the one who stays behind to help me rather than taking his leisure at the fire with my brothers." She slid her hands up his arms and to his shoulders. "You are the one for whom I brave cold winter nights simply to snatch a moment of your company. Finley comes around often, as he's a neighbor and a good friend of Liam's. But you, Sean Kirkpatrick"—she wrapped her arms around his neck—"are the one *I* watch for and wait for and hope will someday come by more often than once a week."

His arms slid around her waist, and he pulled her close against him. "I'd be here every day if Desmond allowed it."

"Because you like me?"

"Because Finley, apparently, needs help with his weeds."

She leaned her head on his shoulder, settling into the warmth of his embrace. A woman could grow quite used to such a thing. "Christmas is this week."

"Is it? Didn't we just have Christmas a year ago?" His hand rubbed a slow, lazy circle on her back.

"Will Desmond be allowing you the day, or are you to be slaving away on Christmas, as well?"

His head rested atop of hers. Her heart leaped about. She held more tightly to him.

"We're to have Christmas evening to ourselves," he said.

Just what she'd hoped he would say. "Will you come have Christmas supper with us?"

"I'd love to."

She pulled back the tiniest bit, looking into his face. "Do you promise?"

His lopsided smile made another appearance. "When have you ever known me to turn down a meal?"

But she wasn't teasing in that moment. "Do you promise to come for Christmas? It's all I want, the only gift I'm hoping for. If you promise you'll come, I know you will. You'd never go back on your word, not to me."

His eyes filled with sincerity. "I solemnly swear to you, I'll be here."

"I'll be watching at the window."

Sean lowered his head. Instinct told her she was about to be kissed. And kissing instincts are seldom wrong.

Their lips drew ever closer. And closer. Her pulse pounded in her ears and neck. Another inch, perhaps less, and his lips would be on hers.

A rumbling bark filled the kitchen. Maeve and Sean both froze on the spot.

"What is Rufus doing inside the house?" she asked.

"Exactly what he's supposed to do," Liam called from the other room.

Sean grinned. "I believe that means the time's come for me to go."

Disappointment swept over her, tempered only by the knowledge that he'd be back in only a few days. As she watched him disappear into the cold, dark night, she reminded herself of that. She would see him again on Christmas Day.

He'd promised.

Seven

Christmas Day is rather less than joyful when one is working for the privileged upper classes. For, no matter the promises made of half-days and minimal duties, should the family one works for decide that Christmas Day would be utterly perfect for an unplanned jaunt through the countryside, someone must remain behind to receive the return of the carriage and horses. And that someone is then forced to spend his Christmas afternoon and evening pacing the length of the stable yard, contemplating the hurt and disappointment no doubt felt by a certain Irishwoman down the road.

I promised her. I solemnly swore. And Sean, being a decent sort of fellow, didn't care to be breaking a promise to any person, least of all his Maeve. But what could he do? Leaving would have cost him his job. Losing his job would have meant leaving Kilkenny and Maeve entirely.

There was no way of telling Maeve what had happened. She would think he'd broken his word.

"If you promise you'll come, I know you will," she'd said.

"You'd never go back on your word," she'd said.

"I never want to see you again," she'd say next.

He couldn't bear the thought. But what could he do? He was every bit as stuck as he'd been the day they'd first met. He paced back to the arched entryway to the stable yard and set his eyes on the castle across the way.

How many of the Marquess's servants were required to spend their Christmas away from loved ones? Likely quite a few. They had an advantage over him, however. He was spending his Christmas with a stable full of horses, not another person in sight. They, at least, had each other.

He stuffed his hands in his coat pockets and trudged his way past a long row of horse stalls, eyes focused on the floor ahead of him. "Maeve will have my neck, assuming she agrees to see me again."

Sean wasn't an entirely unreasonable man, and the more logical part of him knew he was likely making more of his Christmas absence than need be. But he was also a man in love, which has a tendency to override one's ability to think clearly. He didn't want to disappoint Maeve, and neither did he wish to spend the holiday away from her. Indeed, he was growing ever more convinced that he never wanted to spend another day away from her.

I might even get around to telling her that, if I'm ever allowed to leave this stable, that is. Grumbling, one must understand, is quite the most productive way to pass an evening. If nothing else, it makes a soul feel the tiniest bit better. Kicking at stray bits of straw helps as well.

Beyond the stables, voices raised in laughter and song echoed from the village. People were celebrating together, happy and contented. He, alone, was . . . alone.

It being Christmas and a holy day, he limited himself to only the mildest of curses, nothing that would make a priest call him in for confession, but he was none too happy.

Stepping back out to the stable yard, he shot a wary eye heavenward. Not a flake of snow fell, something Maeve might have blamed his absence on other than himself.

She was likely sitting at the window, watching for him to come. Or had been for a time until she'd given up on him.

The bells at St. Canice's had long since rung the call to evening mass. The sun had set. He couldn't help wondering if the Marquess's family meant to return that evening. They'd set off to visit friends who had a country home near Castlecomer. 'Twas entirely possible they'd opted to remain for the night. One benefit of being fine and fancy was the ability to cause inconvenience without consequence, at least not to one's fine and fancy self.

And so Sean sat on a stool in the empty stable yard, a weight in his stomach and on his heart. "'Twas all she wanted for Christmas," he informed the unhelpful heavens. "A visit, the chance to sit at each other's side, to talk as we always do. 'Twas all she wanted, and I promised her. I *promised* her."

He leaned his elbows on his legs and rested his head in his hands. He'd planned to tell her that he loved her. A man doesn't build up the courage to do so easily, which made the night's events all the more tragic. 'Twould have been quite a perfect Christmas.

But sometimes all one needs for perfection is an added measure of patience.

A mere moment after Sean had chastised the heavens, the sound of approaching hooves pulled his head up out of his hands. The family, it seemed, had returned. He'd be terribly late getting to the Butlers' cottage, but he would get there just the same. He would knock at the door for hours if necessary until Maeve allowed him to explain and apologize.

He rushed to his expected position, just inside the entry arch, and stood at respectful attention. Into the stable yard came not a fine carriage pulled by a high-stepping team, but a humble and rickety old hay cart, pulled by two draft horses and driven by a ginger farmer, with a dark-haired beauty beside him, and a tall, stick of a man behind.

'Twasn't the Butlers of Kilkenny Castle nor the up road Butlers, but the six boulders family, his Butlers. And his Maeve.

Liam pulled the cart to a stop in the middle of the yard. Sean stood in shock, frozen at the unexpected sight. His Maeve.

True to the feisty colleen she'd proven herself to be, Maeve hopped from the cart without waiting for anyone's assistance, then came directly toward him.

"I am so very sorry, Maeve. I'd not meant to—" He managed nothing beyond that.

"We've brought supper, Sean. Will Desmond pitch a fit if we eat it here with you, do you think?"

"Supper?" His thoughts swam too swiftly for making complete sense of her words.

"When you didn't arrive, I assumed you'd been made to stay here rather than being given the evening to yourself."

He nodded, his worry still too great for a verbal response.

"So we brought Christmas supper to you."

He took her hand, his own trembling with uncertainty. Did this mean she'd not lost faith in him? "I have to wait for the castle family to return with their carriage and team. I'm the newest hand, so the lot fell to me." The glove she wore was cold. Her hand beneath must have been near to freezing. "You shouldn't have come so far in the cold, love. You'll catch your death."

She reached up and touched his face. "I'd've gone clear to Mayo if need be."

"You aren't angry with me for disappointing you?"

Hers was a soft and alluring smile. "You've not disappointed me."

"Kiss the lass, already," Kieran called from the hay cart. "We've a Christmas supper to eat."

"There are empty stalls at the end of the row," Sean said. "Your animals'll be warm there."

Liam smirked a bit. "Trying to shoo away your audience, are you?"

"That is precisely what I'm doing. Now off with you."

They obliged.

Sean turned every ounce of his attention back to Maeve. He pulled her fully into his arms.

"I was so afraid you'd be boilin', love. I broke m' word to you. You gave me your trust, and I broke it."

"You've not broken my trust in you, Sean. I trust you enough to have never doubted all the day long that you'd've come if you could."

He lightly brushed his lips against her forehead. "I don't deserve you."

"No, you don't." She wrapped her arms around his neck. "But you come close enough, that I'll not hold it against you."

He kissed her temple, then her cheek. Heavens, but he adored this woman. "Maeve, darlin' Maeve. I've nothing to give you for Christmas. I haven't money for a fine gift, and I didn't make it out to see you today." He cupped her face in his hands. "But I give you what I have, love. I give you my devotion and my caring, and I give you my love, all of it, every beat of my heart and every breath that fills my body."

He meant to seal the promise with a fervent kiss. She, however, was quicker than he was. She rose up on her toes and kissed him, her lips to his, making a promise without words that matched his spoken vow.

A promise of days and months and Christmases yet to come. A promise of love.

A CHRISTMAS PROMISE

That Christmas was not in my time, nor in yours, but it was in someone's time just the same. Sean and Maeve shared many a supper, both at the castle stables and at the six boulders Butlers' cottage. One might say their courtship was undertaken along the very road that first brought Sean Kirkpatrick to that fateful muddy field.

He'd taken a wrong turn, made a mistake. And what a grand mistake it turned out to be. By their second Christmas, the two were happily married. In time they were blessed with a daughter, who had a daughter, who had a son.

She named her son Thomas, but everyone calls me Old Tom.

Dream of a Glorious Season

London, 1810

Miss Elizabeth Gillerford counted amongst her most notable realizations one she had at the very wise age of eight and three quarters. She came to the irrefutable understanding that her heart would forever belong to the twelve-year-old boy to whom her sister had already pledged a life of devotion: their neighbor, Julian Broadwood.

Falling desperately in love was painful enough for any eight-year-old girl, but having a heart so fickle as to devote itself to the object of the deepest longing of one's sister added another layer of acute discomfort. Thus Elizabeth spent the next ten years in various stages of misery and heartbreak.

Mary, her older sister, had made her first bows to Society two years earlier, and, seeing as Julian had made very few appearances, Mary remained unhappily unattached but determined to wring a proposal out of Julian. Unfortunately, their parents were sticklers for the strictest versions of social etiquette, so until Mary wed, Elizabeth simply had to wait for her own debut in Society. At nearly nineteen, she was quickly growing embarrassingly old to have not made her bows.

"Society doesn't entirely forbid a younger sister from being out before her older sister is married," Elizabeth argued to her parents a week before the Season was set to truly begin once more. "Especially if the older sister doesn't seem to be making progress and the younger sister is more than old enough to have a Season."

Her father was already shaking his head, the movement setting his jowls flopping about. "Some may be willing to flaunt expectations willy-nilly, but the Gillerfords are stalwart. We do not bend to—"

"—the fickle winds of ever-changing opinion," Elizabeth said under her breath in perfect unison with her father's declaration. She had long ago learned a deep appreciation for his opposition to fickle winds. In full voice once more, she argued, "I am nearly nineteen, Father, and will soon be so firmly lodged on the shelf that I may as well be a book in the darkest corners of a lending library."

Mother chose that exact moment to wander inside. "Oh, dear. You haven't been frequenting the lending library, have you? People will begin to form the wrong idea of you."

"They might think I read?" Elizabeth asked dryly.

"Precisely." Mother emphasized the declaration with a widening of her eyes and a desperate nod of her head. "A girl should read, of course; she simply shouldn't make a point of doing so. The ladies will think you a touch too blue for their company, and the gentlemen will think you a vast deal too educated for theirs."

This was an old argument that Elizabeth knew far too well. "Gregory does not think me too educated for *his* company."

Mother waved that off. "Brothers are supposed to overlook their sisters' faults."

Faults. Lovely.

"What of Julian Broadwood?" Elizabeth asked. "He has never shown any disgust at my refusal to hide my literacy."

Mother had no immediate answer. Father filled in the gap.

"He is meant for Mary," he said. "No doubt he already views you quite as his own sister, and therefore has joined Gregory in turning a blind eye to your oddities."

"Has he at last declared his intention to court Mary, then?" She tried to ask the question casually. But how does one lackadaisically ask if one's heart is about to be crushed to a fine powder and sent adrift on, as her father would have called it, the fickle winds of change?

"Our family and the Broadwoods have always understood that young Julian and our dear Mary would make a match of it," Father said in a tone of scolding. "He needn't come to make a formal declaration."

"Well, if he means to marry her, I wish he would hurry and do so." Oddly enough, she very nearly meant it. "If she were engaged, I could make my bows and find myself a husband, since no one in the neighborhood bothered to conveniently produce a son for me to marry."

She refused to admit to anyone that, as far as she was concerned, Julian fit that description. She preferred to do her suffering in secret.

Mother dropped onto her chaise longue, pressing her fingers elegantly to her temples. "You do give me such headaches with all of your nonsense, Elizabeth."

"I know, Mother. I know." She left her parents in the sitting room and walked out of sight down the corridor before sighing aloud in frustration.

A girl should read, of course, she simply shouldn't make a point of doing so.

She had endured such ridiculousness for nearly nineteen years. She couldn't do so much longer. Heaven help her, if she was left on the shelf and had to live out her life in her parents' house, she would go mad.

Two

Julian stood beside his best friend, Damion, on the walk outside the Gillerfords' London home, attempting to convince himself to go inside. As an old friend of the family, he couldn't very well not make an appearance at their ball. More pressing even than that, his mother would summon him to Broadwood House before breakfast had even cooled the next morning to ring a peal over his head if he didn't spend at least a full hour at the Gillerfords' ball, dancing and socializing and generally pretending he was happy to be there.

"Don't turn lily-livered on me now, old boy," Damion, insisted. "You've ducked out of nearly every social obligation these past two years. I'll not keep making excuses for you."

Julian groaned and dragged himself forward.

"I doubt Miss Gillerford will be waiting on the other side of the door with a vicar and a license," Damion reassured him. "You'll be obligated to a single set with her. You've courage enough for that, surely."

"Dancing with her is like a prisoner tying the knot in his own noose."

Julian plastered a smile on his face as they stepped into the front foyer. There stood his row of anxious executioners: Mr. and Mrs. Gillerford grinned with glee at seeing him. Mary's eyes took on that eerie aura of possessiveness she'd first adopted when she was ten and he almost twelve. He liked it even less now than he had then.

He made his bows as quickly as possible without being rude. Mary opened her mouth to say something. Julian spoke first. "I do not see Miss Elizabeth."

Mrs. Gillerford hit him playfully with her fan. "You know full well that she is not out in Society yet."

He did, indeed, know, and it bothered him to no end. "But she is quite of an age to be so."

Mr. Gillerford's brow furrowed with indignation. "She'll have her come out when it is proper."

In all truth, the "proper" time had come and gone. Beth ought to have made her bows the year before. He could easily picture her upstairs, watching the carriages arrive and quite eloquently decrying the ridiculousness of her exclusion from it all.

He found her absence trying as well. She, along with her brother, who avoided London as one would a den of hungry wolves, were the only members of that family with whom he enjoyed spending time, Beth being preferable even to Gregory. She conversed with intelligence. Her sense of humor displayed her innate wit. She didn't flaunt her wealth or beauty the way her mother and sister insisted on doing. In short, she was pleasant company, a rare enough thing in Society. He'd always liked her.

"You will be pleased to know that our Mary has her supper dance open," Mrs. Gillerford said.

Julian was far too adept at side stepping such things to fall into that trap. "I shall be certain tomorrow to ask my mother what fortunate gentleman was granted the privilege of claiming her supper dance." He took a step closer to the ballroom. "Forgive me for holding up the reception line so long."

With that, he made good his escape.

"Excellently done," Damion said, slapping him on the back. "Does Wellington know your knack for stratagems?"

"I have had several years of practice." He glanced back at the reception line, barely holding back a shudder. "The Gillerfords have it firmly in their heads that I am destined to be their son-in-law. *I* am firmly convinced that they would take a supper dance, or an overly long glance, or my willingness to be in the same room as their older daughter as tantamount to a declaration. They'd have our announcement in the papers by morning."

They stepped into the ballroom with its din of voices. He and Damion cringed in unison. Together they'd survived more than their share of Society functions.

"Time for the 'two in a row'?" Damion asked the question to which they both knew the answer.

"I'll meet you at the punch bowl in an hour," Julian said. "Make certain to greet enough matrons to warrant whispers over tea tomorrow. If we're forced to be here, we may as well receive credit for it."

They set off in opposite directions, in search of two young ladies they could ask to dance. Experience had shown them that two sets within two hours, plus a few well placed "Good evenings" gave the impression they had spent far more time at a ball than they actually had.

Julian had made a point of choosing for his two-in-a-row partners young ladies who didn't seem likely to have any other partners. Those ladies relegated to the lonely corners were often neglected and ignored. They deserved to be treated with kindness. And he generally found they were finer company than the belles of the ball.

Out of the corner of his eye, he spotted a silhouette in an unused doorway. He couldn't say just how he knew, but he identified her in an instant. Did Beth always spy on her parents' balls, or was today a special occasion? He intended to ask her, though doing so meant abandoning his efforts at securing a partner for the first set of dances.

Damion'll have my neck. Still, he moved quickly in the direction of Beth's hiding place. He might manage to fit in two sets after speaking with her. But time or no time, he wanted to see his old friend.

Just as he reached the doorway, she disappeared into the darkness. With a quick look around to make certain no one in the ballroom saw him, he slipped out and stepped into the room beyond.

Only moonlight spilling through French doors illuminated the space at all—Mr. Gillerford's library, by the looks of it.

"I know you're in here, Beth," he whispered.

"If you give me away, so help me . . ."

He turned back in the direction of her voice and found her watching him from beside the door, arms folded defiantly across her chest. She'd always been firmly independent. That was one of the greatest things about her. Julian snatched up her hand and pulled her over to the French doors.

"Where are we going?" she asked.

"Outside," he explained. "If we're found in here, I'll have to run myself through with my own sword."

"Rather than be forced to marry me, is that it?"

Being caught alone meant not merely a forced marriage, but also leaving her reputation in ruins, painting himself as a cad, and destroying their friendship. So, yes. He'd rather they not be found out. He shrugged, keeping to the more casual tone they'd thus far employed. "More or less."

A few people wandered about on the terrace. Julian slipped Beth's arm through his. "Pretend that this is commonplace," he whispered. "We'd best not attract too much notice."

"No amount of pretending will change the fact that I'm not dressed for a ball."

He hadn't noted her attire until that moment. Her dress was decidedly plain, but at least she wasn't in her nightrail or anything equally scandalous. They kept to the edges of the small, lantern-lit garden. Poor Beth looked deucedly uncomfortable. He wouldn't keep her but a moment.

"What is this nonsense I hear about you not having a Season again this year?"

"Didn't you know, Jules?" she answered dryly. "The Gillerfords are stalwart and cling stubbornly to even the most archaic of notions."

"That makes me wonder if you're actually a foundling."

Beth had more sense in her smallest toe than her entire family did combined. "What half-witted notion is your father clinging to this time?"

She picked a flower from an obliging bush. "He won't allow me a Season until Mary is married."

Julian eyed her sidelong. "Has he met your sister? You'll never get a Season."

"Believe me, I am fully aware of that." She spun the little yellow flower in her fingers. "I am hatching a plot to abduct an unsuspecting gentleman and force him to wed her."

He stopped right in the middle of the path. "Is that what this is? You're walking me to my matrimonial demise?"

"Don't be dramatic." She kept walking, leaving him behind.

He hurriedly caught up to her. "You didn't pick me for Mary?" He was busy enough disabusing *Mary* of that idea without Beth taking up the same notion.

"Good gracious, no," she answered. "If you ever set your cap at Mary, I'll—"

"—run me through with my own sword?" he finished for her.

She shrugged. "More or less."

Lands, Beth was always vastly fun to spend time with.

She deserved her share of Society and diversions.

"Your banishment must be remedied," he said firmly.

"It's not banishment so much as forced hermitry." She sighed, though without any of the theatrics so many young ladies employed. "At times I feel trapped in this house."

"What would you do if you had London at your feet and the freedom of being out in Society?" He was honestly curious.

"Hatchard's. Hyde Park. Balls, dinner parties. At this point, I would settle for anything other than these corridors and this back garden." She held her hands up in helplessness. "I said 'hermitry,' and 'hermitry' it is."

"We must find a way of getting you out of this house." There had to be a solution.

Beth tossed him a lopsided smile. "Are you volunteering to sacrifice one of your friends for Mary's cause?" Her auburn eyebrow arched doubtfully.

"I have far too few friends to risk losing one in such a drastic fashion. They would all abandon me after that." He took her hand in his and met her gaze. "I *will* think of something, Beth. I swear to you, I will."

"I'll hold you to that," she warned.

He pressed a kiss to the back of her hand. "Now, sneak back in and up to your room. I'll return to the ball after I'm certain you haven't been spotted." No point working on her entry into Society if he'd ruined her reputation beforehand. "Dream of a glorious Season, my friend."

"Or Mary's untimely demise," she said.

He grinned. "Whichever brings you the greatest satisfaction."

He kept to the gardens for a long moment after she slipped away and around the back of the house. It was utterly unfair that she was denied Society and all its enjoyments simply because her older sister was too wretched to be courted.

"I will find a way to help her," he vowed. "I will."

Three

Since Elizabeth was destined to die a lonely old maid with a vast deal too many cats, the ten minutes she had spent with Julian at the ball were likely to be the highlight of her rather pathetic existence. He'd laughed with her, listened to her, swapped ridiculous observations on the absurdities of life. That had been their way for years. It was little wonder, really, that she was so fully in love with the thick-headed man. They were wonderful together, but he thought of her only as little Beth, with whom he'd grown up.

She sat on the window seat in her bedchamber, her stitching lying untouched on her lap. Sewing was possibly her least favorite occupation. She'd much rather read, but Father's Town library was severely lacking in anything with even the slightest appeal.

Mary stepped abruptly inside. "I need your green bonnet."

Elizabeth had long since stopped expecting her sister to

ask for anything, let alone ask kindly. "You have boxes and boxes of lovely bonnets."

Mary rolled her eyes and sighed loudly. "But none of them are green. I cannot be seen in my cream carriage dress without a green bonnet. Now, where is it?" she demanded with a stomp of her foot.

I am going to die alone.

Fanny, the lady's maid whom Mary and Elizabeth shared, rushed in. "Miss Gillerford! Miss Gillerford! Mr. Broadwood is here to fetch you already."

That brought a look of near panic to Mary's face. "The bonnet, Elizabeth. Give it to me."

"Mr. Broadwood is insisting that Miss Elizabeth come as well," Fanny said.

"Elizabeth? Come along on *my* carriage ride?" Mary's shout likely carried across the Channel. She flew from the room in an instant.

Elizabeth met Fanny's eyes. "Has he really invited me along with him?"

She nodded. "And he told Mrs. Gillerford that he'd not take Miss Gillerford unless you came as well. Your mother is in quite a state, I tell you."

Dear, sweet Julian. "It seems to me that, for the sake of my mother's health, I had best dress for a carriage ride."

Fanny was a step ahead; she had Elizabeth's carriage dress out of the wardrobe already and laid out on the bed. "If we are really quick, you can be downstairs before Miss Gillerford reaches the end of her tantrum."

"Excellent."

They had a speed borne of years spent helping Elizabeth dress during the rare few moments Mary wasn't demanding her maid's presence. Elizabeth hurried down the stairs just as Mary was storming up them.

"I don't know how you managed this," she hissed, "but do not embarrass me."

Elizabeth ignored the all-too-familiar warning and

continued to the front entryway. Julian stood there, gloves still on, hat in his hands. He looked up as she approached, and his perturbed expression melted into a friendly smile.

"I see word has reached you," he said.

"To quote my beloved sister, 'I don't know how you managed this.'" She accepted her wrap from the maid at the front door.

"I simply chose to be stubborn about it," Julian said. "You being in a carriage with your sister and me—an old family friend—along with a maid, would be quite unexceptional. It isn't quite a Society function, but at least you will have left the house."

She tightened the ribbon under her chin. "When I inevitably join a convent, I will make certain to submit your name for sainthood."

His adorable smile surfaced on the instant. "You? In a convent?" He shook his head and chuckled. "The vow of silence alone would see you expelled."

Elizabeth shrugged. "Then I suppose you'll simply have to kidnap a husband for me."

"I thought we were forcing someone to wed *Mary*."

"Did I hear my name?" Mary was practically running down the stairs. She held her blue bonnet on her head with one hand and clutched her skirt with the other. "I am ready. We can be on our way now."

Mary stopped directly beside Julian, perhaps a touch too close for propriety. He held himself stiffly but quite civilly.

"How lovely it will be to make a turn about Hyde Park during the fashionable hour," Mary said. "Why, simply everyone will be there!" Her eyes darted to Elizabeth, and she added, under her breath, "And I do mean *everyone*, even those who aren't wanted."

Elizabeth ignored her sister. This was her one chance at escape, and she wasn't going to miss it. She waited patiently at the door, watching Julian expectantly. He flashed her the briefest of smiles, enough to set her heart fluttering about—a sensation she went to great lengths to keep hidden.

"Ladies," he invited, motioning to the door. "The park awaits."

A dark-blue landau with black trim sat in front of the house, its folding top down to reveal fine grey leather upholstery. A driver, in livery that perfectly coordinated with the vehicle, was already in position. Julian clearly didn't wish to prolong the outing any longer than absolutely necessary. She could appreciate that—Mary's company grew tedious after a matter of moments—but, for her sake, Elizabeth wished the ride could last all afternoon.

I will simply have to savor it.

Julian handed Mary up first. She sat on the forward-facing seat, directly in the middle. Elizabeth was handed up next. As she moved to sit rear facing, Julian spoke up.

"Do make room for your sister, Miss Gillerford," he said. "Surely you would not insist she ride rear-facing. Such a thing would be unforgivably rude."

To give someone a forward facing seat was an indication of their importance, or in the matter of gentlemen and ladies, it was an act of chivalry for him to give up that seat to her. Mary clearly would not countenance her younger sister being given as much consideration as herself, lest the two be viewed as equals. Elizabeth knew her sister too well to expect otherwise.

Mary sputtered a moment whilst Elizabeth stood on the top step, unsure where she ought to sit. "But my maid has a sad tendency to grow ill in a carriage if riding rear-facing." Formulating schemes and half-truths at a moment's notice was one of Mary's particular skills. "So Elizabeth simply cannot sit here."

Mary's brow assumed a triumphant arch.

But, then, so did Julian's. What had left him so decidedly pleased?

"I would hate for your maid to be ill," he said. "Miss Elizabeth, would you kindly assume the rear-facing seat?"

She did. She would have ridden up beside the driver if it meant a few moments out of the house.

Just as gallantly as he'd handed up Elizabeth and her sister, Julian offered Fanny his assistance and saw her situated beside Mary. "That leaves me the place beside Miss Elizabeth. I hope you do not mind."

"Not in the least." She managed the response in a tone of only casual interest despite the laughter begging to be released at the sight of Mary's thunderous expression. She would wager that her sister had only just realized how her fabricated story had cost her the opportunity to sit beside the object of her matrimonial ambitions.

But Mary never was long discouraged. "We may just as easily—I daresay *more* easily—make this outing without Elizabeth." Somehow the dismissive remark was made in a tone of utmost sweetness and innocence.

"Perhaps." Julian took the seat beside Elizabeth and motioned for the driver to set the horses in motion. "But her presence will prevent any unwanted whispers."

"Whispers?" Mary smiled and swatted in his direction with her hand. "Why, you silly man. What whispers could there possibly be? Our families are neighbors, and our connection is quite well established."

"Perhaps, but we are *not* actually related. I would hate for Society to take any notions into their heads that are neither accurate nor welcome."

Mary shrugged a dainty shoulder. "No one would ever suspect us of anything untoward."

"I am far more concerned that they would suspect us of courting."

Mary's coy smile dropped off quickly, and her demeanor grew more than a touch icy. But she did stop talking, which, Elizabeth would wager, was a welcome change for everyone present. She had never seen anyone handle Mary as neatly as Julian just had. She felt a real urge to applaud.

"Have you ever been in the park during the daily crush?" Julian asked Elizabeth.

"I haven't, but I have heard a great deal about it. Is the spectacle as ridiculous as I suspect?"

A laugh rumbled deep in his chest. She'd always liked his laugh, even when they were young and it had been more of a giggle. "There is a great deal of the ridiculous about the ritual. Once we reach the park, the carriage will all but come to a stop, perhaps inching forward now and then. Completing a full circuit will require vast swaths of time, far more than it ought."

"Perhaps the horses should be permitted a brief nap between the sixth and seventh hour," Elizabeth suggested. "Or a moment's respite for dinner."

Again his laugh filled the space between them. A lady could happily spend the rest of her days listening to the sound.

"Does everyone simply arrive at the park, come to a standstill, and then, once darkness falls, inch their way back home?" she asked.

"Nothing as painless as all that, I'm afraid." His brown eyes lit with mirth. "We will be required to bid good day to every person who passes by—at least to those we ought to consider not too far below our notice."

"And how does one know which are too lowly or ill-mannered to be acknowledged? Do they wear signs?"

"Signs?" Mary sputtered her way into the conversation at last. "How utterly ridiculous. Little wonder you have never had a Season. You wouldn't have the first idea how to go about it."

Julian gave Elizabeth a dry look. "Oh, there are signs, Beth. Irrefutable signs."

"You are going to make me laugh, and then I will be lectured about being properly demure, and that will ruin this entire outing."

"Who could possibly disapprove of seeing you laugh?" he asked.

Elizabeth rolled her eyes in perfect unison with Mary's huff of disapproval before she said, "If you are trying to make me jealous, Julian, you will have to flirt with someone other than Elizabeth. No one could possibly believe a gentleman of your standing would be interested in her."

Her sister's barbs had long ago stopped wounding. Julian, however, did not seem immune to the shock of her vitriol.

"And why wouldn't a gentleman be absolutely enthralled with Miss Elizabeth?" he demanded.

Mary smiled lightly, as though she truly thought Julian's question was an ironic one. "Even at the slow pace of the park, we'd not have time enough to list all the reasons, now would we?"

The barbs might not have wounded Elizabeth any longer, but she still didn't enjoy them. "I have complete confidence, dearest sister, in your ability to rattle off as much of the list as you possibly can during the course of this excursion."

That, apparently, served as an invitation enough for Mary. "You are here as a guest," she said firmly. "Inserting yourself into the conversation is rather ill-mannered."

"Reason number one," Elizabeth mouthed to Julian, holding up a single finger.

"And whispering is rude as well," Mary added.

Elizabeth added a second finger to the first. Julian seemed to only just hold back a grin. He looked away from them all, waving to someone familiar he saw not far off.

"Here comes Mr. Carson," Mary said. "He has four thousand a year and is related to some of the first families of England." She hissed under her breath to Elizabeth. "Do not—"

"—embarrass you," Elizabeth finished for her. "I know the rules, Mary."

"You know them, but you do not follow them."

Elizabeth caught Julian's eye once more. She held up three fingers, not bothering to hide her amusement.

"We are making remarkable progress, aren't we?" he whispered. Then, at full voice, he greeted a young gentleman who had just ridden up alongside the carriage. "Damion, I would like to introduce you to someone."

With a look that could only be described as approaching panic, Mr. Damion Carson said, "I have already made Miss Gillerford's acquaintance." He eyed Mary as if she were an owl and he a helpless rodent. It seemed that he really did know Mary.

"I wish to make you known to Miss *Elizabeth* Gillerford." Julian proceeded without hesitation. "She has not made her official bows yet, but I assure you, her acquaintance is well worth making."

Mr. Carson offered a proper inclination of his head. "Miss Elizabeth, it is an honor to meet you at last."

"At last?" That was an unexpected phrase to hear tagged onto the end of a sentence uttered by a gentleman she did not at all know.

"Julian has mentioned you many times before," he explained.

He had spoken of her to his friend? Her heart picked up at the thought. Perhaps her adoration of him was not so entirely one-sided.

"I understand you two grew up together," Mr. Carson added.

And with that her heart dropped once more. Had Julian said nothing more about her than merely the fact that they'd grown up together?

"We all grew up together," Mary interjected.

Mr. Carson kept his gaze on Elizabeth and Julian. "Yes, I understood that as well. And" —he actually seemed to be speaking to Elizabeth now—"I am told you are fond of books and have a similar taste in literature as Julian. I confess that histories and treatises are not entirely to my liking, though I have enjoyed a few."

So that was the topic of discussion with which she was concerned: her taste in books. How lowering.

"I do read other things, of course." She had always been plucky, something for which she was particularly thankful at the moment. "I simply have limited to access to anything else. Mr. Broadwood occasionally lends me volumes from his family's library, but he is often engaged elsewhere during the Season and no longer has time for his childhood friend, more's the pity."

Mr. Carson smiled broadly. He struck her as a genuinely happy person, and she was glad of it. Julian would do well having such a friend in his life. "I have seen our Mr. Broadwood at any number of Society events during the Season, and I assure you his time would be far better spent perusing the shelves of a library than inexpertly navigating the social whirl."

"I look forward to one day watching his ineptitude in action," Elizabeth said.

"It is a sight to behold. And I hope that when you do have your Season, you will allow me to dance with you, as I find I would very much like to continue building our acquaintance."

Elizabeth blushed so immediately and so deeply that no one in all of Hyde Park could have failed to notice. "I would like that as well."

Mr. Carson looked past her at Julian. "Thank you for making this fortuitous introduction."

"My pleasure," Julian muttered, sounding as though it had been anything other than a pleasure.

What has come over him so suddenly?

"Miss Elizabeth." Mr. Carson bowed over her hand. "It has truly been a joy speaking with you." He looked over at Mary. "Miss Gillerford, it has been . . . as it always is."

Elizabeth watched Mr. Carson as he set his horse to a

slow trot away from the carriage and disappeared into the press of people gathering in the park. She liked him. He had a sense of humor quite similar to Julian's and a kindness about him that she admired. For a moment she imagined Mr. Carson, married, and calling on her and Julian in their home, an abiding friendship growing between all of them.

She'd entertained daydreams of that sort for years, even during that long-ago time when she'd thought the only obstacle to her imagined happiness was Mary. She'd realized in more recent years that Julian had as little interest in courting Mary as he did in courting *her*. She hadn't lost her dearest love to her sister; she'd simply never had his *love* in the first place.

◈◈

"I am firmly on the verge of throttling Mary Gillerford." Julian paced once more the length of his sister's sitting room.

"You have been on the verge of throttling her for ten years, Julian," Helene reminded him.

"Yes, but now she has gone beyond simply leeching the life out of me. She is attacking Beth, and doing so in public." He stopped at the mantle, tapping his finger on its edge. "Mary insulted her on the way to the park yesterday. She made sly comments about her to nearly every person we spoke with. And, as if she'd not done a thorough enough job of it, she spent a full quarter of an hour afterward criticizing Beth's conduct, her dress, her conversation, everything she could think of."

Helene set her sewing on her lap. "Mary's unkindness is the reason she has not had a single suitor despite being in her third Season. She, of course, insists that the real reason is being already promised to you."

Julian's jaw tensed on the instant. "I do not know what our parents were thinking, encouraging that idea all of these years. I have certainly never been in favor of it. Intelligent men dream of more noble deaths than being nagged into an early grave."

"That, we do." His brother-in-law, Robert Pinnelle, stepped inside at that exact moment. "And we choose our wives accordingly." He greeted Helene with an affectionate kiss on the cheek then sat beside her.

"I am so pleased you've come in," she said, "as I have had an absolutely brilliant idea and need you to extol its virtues shamelessly."

"What is this brilliant idea?"

"As you well know, I have not hosted a dinner party in weeks."

"Do I know that?" He clearly didn't.

"Of course you do, love. After the last one, you told me, whilst you were kissing me, how much you'd enjoyed the evening."

That was a touch more information than Julian had bargained for.

"I remember the kissing part," Robert said.

Helene continued as though Robert were keeping up perfectly. "I must have guests over again. I am simply bereft of company."

"I know it is my duty to agree with you wholeheartedly," Robert said. "And yet I can't help feeling a little insulted."

"You know perfectly well what I meant. You do not always attend functions with me, and you are so often gone during the day doing your important things. This house—indeed, this city—is so lonely without you."

Julian jumped in once more. "That is quite a boon to your pride, old man. All of London is not companion enough for her without you."

"As I said, an intelligent gentleman chooses his wife wisely."

Helene tossed them both looks of sorely tried patience.

"Neither of you is allowing me to share my brilliant idea, and I think it is very badly done of you."

"My apologies, dearest," Robert said. "Do tell us your idea."

Apparently mollified, Helene continued. "I mean to invite the Gillerfords for a small dinner gathering, and I mean to insist that Miss Elizabeth Gillerford be included in the invitation."

Brilliant indeed! Julian's heart lightened at the thought. Beth would have reason to leave her house once more, even if she was required to do so in the company of her irksome family.

"Gillerford?" Robert's brow drew in. "The family who are neighbors of your family in Surrey?"

"The very same," Helene confirmed.

"Hold a moment." Robert held up a hand. "Isn't their daughter the one with the crazed look in her eyes?"

"I do not believe I have ever heard Mary described so precisely." After taking a moment to ponder that fitting turn of phrase a little more deeply, Helene continued her explanation. "Mary, the older sister, is the frenzied one whom everybody avoids like an eel pie on a hot summer's day. Miss Elizabeth is the younger sister, and is a lovely person with very civilized eyes."

Robert's ponderous gaze landed on Julian. "Aren't you supposed to marry one of these sisters? I am certain your mother said something about that."

Julian shook his head in disbelief and took up pacing once again. He ought to simply flee Town before Mary's claws were lodged even further into him. But that would mean abandoning Beth to her family's unkindness.

"Mrs. Carson told me that her son met Miss Elizabeth just yesterday and mentioned her quite a few times last evening," Helene said. "I believe young Mr. Carson is near enough to family to be included in the dinner." A matchmaking gleam filled her gaze. "I believe they would get on quite famously."

"Beth is not yet out," Julian quickly pointed out.

Helene didn't seem the least bothered by that information. "But she is of an age. After all, one need not have a Season to be courted."

"Courted?" He nearly choked on the word. "How have we jumped that far already?"

Robert eyed him with blatant curiosity. "What has you wound so tightly? Carson's your friend, as is Miss Elizabeth."

"I simply do not think that they would suit each other." He was pacing again. Something about the suggestion of Beth and Damion making a match of it did not sit well in his mind.

"Nonsense. They would be perfect together." Helene met her husband's eyes. "They really would be."

"It is settled then." Robert lifted his wife's hand to his lips. "Extend your invitation to the Gillerfords and Mr. Carson, and let my secretary know the date of your party so I can make absolutely certain I do not miss it."

Helene hopped to her feet, her eyes brimming with anticipation. "I shall make my list immediately."

"I am on that list as well, aren't I?" Julian called after her. He received no answer.

I had better be on that list.

Four

Elizabeth watched out the carriage windows as one grand house after another passed by. Helene's invitation had been nothing short of a godsend.

"But why should Elizabeth be asked?" Mary demanded to know for the hundredth time. "She is not yet out. First the park, and now this. It is utter nonsense."

Mother patted Mary's hand. "Mr. Pinnelle is a man of tremendous importance; your father told me as much, though he was unaccountably vague about the reasons for Mr. Pinnelle's consequence. We must make a good impression on him, as I do not believe he has taken much notice of our family."

"Besides all that," Mother continued, "Helene has known Elizabeth all her life and likely feels some obligation to include her, even if she would not normally do so."

Elizabeth didn't care if Helene *had* sent for her out of pity, and was simply grateful for yet another temporary escape from her imprisonment. Julian, no doubt, had found a way to make this evening happen.

"Do you suppose Pinnelle House has a library?" she asked no one in particular.

"I certainly hope you do not mean to embarrass the family while we are there," Mother said. "Reading when you are supposed to be socializing with the other guests."

"But then, she is not out," Mary said. "Perhaps it would be best if she didn't socialize."

The carriage pulled up at just that moment. They had arrived. Elizabeth bit back a grin of delight. A single evening's entertainment was not precisely a dream come true, but it was a taste of freedom. The anticipation of it was nearly her undoing. Somehow she maintained her composure right up until the moment Julian himself met them at the front door.

"Ladies," he greeted.

Mother and Mary executed perfect curtsies.

Elizabeth clapped her hands together and exclaimed, "Oh, Julian, this is the most wonderful thing."

He smiled at her antics, as always.

Mother, also as always, was horrified. "Elizabeth! I certainly hope you know better than to address a gentleman so intimately."

"I have called him by his Christian name all his life." Yes, she was in the wrong, but the promise of the evening had made her rather bold.

Julian stepped near her side. "Actually, I believe you generally called me Jules during our childhoods."

"Mother would simply love that, now wouldn't she?" Elizabeth said.

He lowered his voice, his gaze lingering a moment on her face. "*I* would love that, which ought to count for something."

Something in his expression, in his closeness, left her

quite upended. She covered her confusion with a quick change of topics. "Did you arrange for all of this?"

"It was Helene's idea." He motioned toward the doorway through which they were all to step. "But I will happily take credit. I did promise to help you escape your imprisonment, after all."

"You did, and I expect you to make my evening away as pleasant as possible."

Her teasing didn't have its usual effect. Rather than meet her jest for jest, he simply watched her more closely. He looked as though he was searching for the answer to some unspoken question.

Helene approached them, arms outstretched to take Elizabeth's hands. "My dear, old friend," she said. "I am so pleased you were able to come this evening. I feel as though we have not seen each other in ages."

"Thank you for the invitation."

Helene shook her head. "None of that. We are nearly family, after all." She hooked her arm around Elizabeth's and, without ceremony, walked with her further into the elegant drawing room. Almost as an afterthought, she glanced over her shoulder at Mother and Mary. "And you are, of course, most welcome as well."

"We always feel most welcome amongst your family." Mary latched onto the words like a terrier pulling a fox from its den. Her eyes quickly turned to Julian. "We are practically family, as your sister said. Or soon will be, at least."

Elizabeth fought to keep her expression neutral. If she laughed, her family would make her life a misery for the rest of the evening and beyond. That would be a shame and a waste of a once in a lifetime—she very much feared *lifetime* wasn't an exaggeration—opportunity.

Julian kept a noticeable distance without being outright rude. "I see Mr. Gillerford was not able to join us this evening. Is he . . . at his club?"

"Father is indisposed this evening," Elizabeth said. "Gout being the persistent monster that it is."

"Elizabeth Mildred." Mother looked horrified. "A lady does not use the word 'gout' in public."

"At least I didn't say 'Jules,'" she muttered.

If the sudden combination of coughing and clearing his throat was any indication, Julian overheard.

Helene invited Elizabeth to the settee near the low-burning fire. Despite not being the coldest part of the year, the weather had been unfortunately damp and overly cool. Helene had ever been kind, but there seemed to be a pointedness to her attentions.

Julian saw Mother and Mary seated in the sofa facing the settee, and then, to Mary's obvious shock, he chose to sit beside Elizabeth.

"This is not the way to win Mary's affection," she warned.

"Is it not?" He didn't look worried. "What is the way, then?"

"The key, my friend, is opera."

Julian eyed her questioningly. "She will fall madly in love with me if I attend the opera with her?"

Elizabeth shook her head solemnly. "She will fall hopelessly and irrevocably in love with you if you *sing* opera to her. All the time. No words, only singing."

He leaned a touch nearer. "You have heard me sing, Beth."

She pretended to think deeply about that. "Actually, I believe I meant that if you sing to her every day you will *prevent* her from falling in love with you. Yes. That's what I meant."

"Excellent. I will never *speak* to her again." He sat up straight once more. "Helene's dinner will be ruined and that, my dear Beth, will make my evening an utter delight."

"I will do my utmost not to embarrass you or her."

"That sounds like Mary talking, and I will not stand for

it." His was not an entirely joking tone. "You have never embarrassed me, not even when you were little and followed my friends and me all over the neighborhood while we were home on school holiday. Not then. Not now."

Not being embarrassed by her was a few too many steps away from loving her, but it was at least inching in the right direction.

A quick knock at the door announced the arrival of another guest. Elizabeth knew only that it would not be her brother, as Gregory was in the country, enjoying a quiet stay at the family's estate.

"Who else has Helene invited?" she asked Julian.

"Damion," he said.

"Your friend from the park? But why have you not gone to greet him as you did us?"

He folded his arms across his chest. "Damion is a grown man. He can find his own way inside."

Julian seemed to have been seized by a case of the doldrums. It had often been her task to tease him out of a difficult mood. So she took it upon herself to do so again.

"Are you calling me an incapable infant?"

He didn't take the bait. Instead, he watched his friend's entrance with precisely the look Elizabeth had always imagined Hamlet had given his uncle after piecing together the older man's role in the late king's death.

"What has Mr. Carson done to earn your wrath?" she asked.

Julian slumped a bit lower on the settee. "He accepted Helene's invitation to come tonight."

Damion, having stepped inside, seemed to sense Julian's glare of death, and, oddly enough, appeared surprised by it. Whatever complaint Julian had with his friend, the feeling was not mutual. As Damion made his bows to the ladies and Mr. Pinnelle, his gaze continually returned to Julian. After a moment, he came and stood near the settee.

"Miss Elizabeth, a pleasure to see you again."

"And you, Mr. Carson." Though Elizabeth didn't think of herself as slow-witted, she did have an unfortunate tendency to let her mouth run away at times when she ought to hold her tongue. "Perhaps, sir, you would be so good as to tell me why our friend here"—she indicated Julian with a brief wave of her hand—"is in such a sour mood this evening."

"Elizabeth," Mother hissed.

But Damion did not appear shocked by her lack of demureness. "I would wager his mood was perfectly pleasant whilst only the two of you were conversing." The devilish glint in his eye brought a smile to her face.

"Very perceptive, Mr. Carson. Though that means *you* are the culprit behind his disgruntlement."

"It would appear so." He made a bow to Julian. "Am I to expect pistols at dawn?"

Julian allowed the smallest softening of his expression. "I haven't decided yet."

Elizabeth was happy to see something of his usual cheeriness return, but she didn't like to see him act so unlike himself. She set a hand on his. "Are you feeling unwell, Jules?"

Mary quite suddenly appeared at her side. "Take a turn about the room with me, dearest sister." The request was made through clenched teeth; Elizabeth knew better than to deny her in such cases.

Mary pulled Elizabeth's arm through hers and dragged her away. They'd only moved a handful of steps from the group before Mary launched into a harshly whispered rebuke. "You are acting far too familiar with the gentlemen, Elizabeth. You are embarrassing us all."

Julian had said quite the opposite.

Mary squeezed her arm harder, and a little painfully. "If this is the way you behave in Society, it is little wonder you've not been given a Season."

"I rather think *you* are demonstrating the reason far more clearly than I am."

Mary's steps fumbled a moment. "I suspect I should be offended."

"Never mind." Elizabeth had no desire to spend her one and only dinner party arguing with her sister. "I will do my utmost to be well behaved."

"See that you do." Mary's possessive gaze settled on Julian. "I believe Julian means to press his suit tonight."

"Do you?"

"Why else would he be acting so skittish? The dear man is nervous."

Elizabeth was certain that Mary was not at all the reason for his behavior, though she couldn't quite decipher the real one. Perhaps Julian had realized Mary's expectations for the evening and was unhappy at the prospect of spending the night dodging her efforts to force a courtship. That very well might be precisely the cause of his sour mood. Fortunately, Elizabeth could help with that predicament. She'd acted as a buffer between her sister and Julian many times over the years; she could certainly do so again.

"I believe I will further my acquaintance with Mr. Carson," Mary said firmly, pulling them both back in the direction of the other guests. "Being on friendly terms with the closest friend of one's intended is crucial, after all."

Poor Damion. "Will you not be stretched a bit thin, paying attention to two gentlemen? And you would do well to not neglect your hostess, either."

That brought Mary's glare back around. "Do not presume to tell me how to conduct myself in Society. I know more of it than you ever will."

"Something I have you to thank for," she muttered.

"I beg your pardon?" It was a rhetorical question if ever Elizabeth had heard one. "Do not act as though *I* am the reason for your lack of opportunities. You, Elizabeth, would never make a splash in Society. You are too plain, too unrefined. You are in the shadows not because of me but because that is where you best fit. Enjoy this evening away from your books; it is likely the last you will have. Few people will take pity on you the way Helene and Julian have."

Mary could cut deep when she chose to, tonight piercing even Elizabeth's fortified armor.

They were but a step from the other guests. Mary took a moment to add one more jab under her breath. "Do not monopolize Julian's time the way you always do. It was sweet when you were ten, but you are no longer a child, and he cannot be expected to continue enduring you."

Enduring.

Certainly Julian more than merely *endured* her. They were friends, good ones. Had he not vowed to help her have some enjoyment in London? Had he not taken her for a carriage ride despite the inconvenience of Mary's company?

Still, the word seeped into her, filling the most vulnerable cracks in her heart.

But, if Elizabeth could but endure Mary, she could spend a nice evening away from home and in Julian's company. That would be worth all of the barbs and angry glares.

"Dearest Helene," Mary said, approaching their hostess with an overdone look of worry. "I am afraid my sister is not feeling well. She is too shy to say so herself; indeed, I fully expect her to deny the state of her health, but she is doing poorly."

Quick as that, Mary had brought Elizabeth's evening to an end. Mary had even circumvented any attempt Elizabeth might make to reveal the deception.

Mother jumped in, putting the final nail in the coffin. "She did feel under the weather earlier today," she insisted. "I knew she should have remained at home."

Helene didn't look entirely convinced. And yet, manners didn't allow her to contradict her guests, especially when one of the bold-faced liars was a mother speaking on behalf of a daughter who was not yet out.

Helene gave Elizabeth an unmistakably apologetic look. "I suppose there is little for it but to call up the carriage and see to it that you are returned home."

"I suppose not." Elizabeth was too disappointed, too frustrated, too angry to say more. She spun on her heel and marched from the room. She might be forced to leave, but she would do so alone and without the feigned attentions of uncaring family members.

She stood in the entryway for several long minutes, waiting for the carriage to be brought around. The driver had likely only just finished unhitching the team for the evening. Mary never did care who she inconvenienced.

One of the maids stepped into the entryway, buttoned in a light coat.

"Have you been commissioned to accompany me home?" Elizabeth asked.

"Yes, miss." The maid offered a curtsey.

"I hope doing so does not cause you too much inconvenience."

"No, miss." Any well-trained servant would say as much, whether or not it was true.

"And what if it causes *me* too much inconvenience?" Julian asked from a few feet away. The butler handed him his outer coat.

"Are you coming along, as well?" Her heart skipped about in hope.

"No gently bred young lady should be forced to traverse London entirely unprotected." He winked at her. "A great number of questionable areas of Town lie between here and your home, you realize."

There weren't any, actually.

"Why do I get the feeling you are using this as an excuse to flee a certain matrimonially minded lady?"

DREAM OF A GLORIOUS SEASON

"Because you know me better than anyone."
And yet, you *know so little of* me.

Five

Throughout the ride, Elizabeth was pale and withdrawn. Even Jane, the maid Helene had sent along for propriety's sake, watched Elizabeth closely. Though Julian hadn't overheard the sisters' conversation, he knew enough of the older sister to be certain that her words hadn't been kind.

The carriage arrived and a footman handed them all out. Julian followed in Elizabeth's wake as she made her way up the front walk and stayed near her after she stepped inside. Jane, at the housekeeper's invitation, went down to the kitchens for a warm posset.

Upon reaching the front entryway, Elizabeth did not quite look him in the eye. "Thank you for seeing me home," she said quietly. "I hope the dinner is lovely." She turned and walked up the stairs.

Watching her slow ascent—shoulders slumped, head a bit bowed—Julian ached for her. She so seldom let Mary's unkindness affect her, but clearly it had injured her this time. He took the stairs two at a time and caught up with her in the corridor.

"Beth. Wait, please."

She stopped but didn't look back.

He stepped around to face her. "I'm sorry that Mary—" His words ended abruptly. Tears hovered on her lashes even as one escaped in a trickle down her cheek. "You're crying."

"Only a little." She pushed out a deep breath.

He motioned for her to slip into the sitting room. He knew that Beth severely disliked showing emotions; she would be mortified if any of the staff came upon her while she was tearing up. She took the handkerchief he offered and wiped away the tears hovering at the corners of her eyes.

"Was Mary particularly vicious?" he asked.

She sighed. "She said I will never escape the shadows because I'm too inferior to belong anywhere else."

"Did she?" What an utter termagant Mary was.

"And that I'm plain and poor company. That no one other than my books would ever wish to spend an evening with me." She'd put on a brave face, but the slight quiver of her chin betrayed her upended emotions.

"Mary never was terribly bright." He set a reassuring hand on her arm, watching her for any signs of recovery. That her own sister could be so cruel was heartbreaking. "Her lies are so transparent, one can only assume she realizes that were your parents to come to their senses and allow you a Season, you would cast her into a shadow from which she would likely never emerge."

"You are saying that only to make me feel better."

"No, Beth. Truly." She needed to know the truth of her worth. "You are lovely, and your company and conversation would be coveted by everyone with whom you'd interact during the social whirl. You would be in demand in a way Mary never has been, and that frightens her."

She shook her head. "You are obligated to say nice things like that; you're practically my brother."

Brother. That word carried a flavor he could not like. They'd always been something a bit deeper than mere friends, but *brother* didn't hit the mark at all.

He reached out and took her hand. That simple, familiar touch had always carried with it a feeling of comfort and peace, almost as if he'd returned home.

"Your sister will be wondering what is keeping you," she said. "And, as Mary pointed out, only my books are missing me. I should really get back to them." She pulled her hand from his. "Thank you for arranging this evening, even if it didn't work out quite as I'd hoped. The gesture meant a great deal."

A moment later, he was alone in the sitting room. He missed her the instant she was gone. It had ever been that way with Beth. Yet, there was something more to his longing for her this time. He ached for her to return, could hardly countenance climbing back inside the lonely carriage without her.

He returned to Helene's home every bit as lonely as he had been upon leaving Elizabeth. Dinner had been held for him, but he had no appetite for it. He merely picked at the food whilst thoughts spun and collided in his mind.

Upon the gentlemen rejoining the ladies after port, Damion launched directly into the topic foremost in Julian's mind.

"It is a shame Miss Elizabeth could not remain this evening," he said. "I was hoping to make her better acquaintance."

I wager you were. Julian sat a little apart from the others, eyeing his friend with growing suspicion. Was Damion the real reason Elizabeth was so distraught at missing the dinner?

"Yes, a shame." Mary's sincerity was nonexistent.

Helene patted Damion's arm as she passed. "We'll have Miss Elizabeth over again sometime and will be sure to invite you as well."

Julian did not like that idea at all. Helene sat beside him and turned her head toward him, a triumphant gleam in her eye. The rest of the room took up individual conversations.

"Is this not remarkable?" Helene said. "Damion is quite smitten with Elizabeth, I can tell."

"How could any gentleman not be?" His compliment was likely clouded by the monumental pout he couldn't seem to wipe from his face.

Helene apparently noticed. "Are you not happy for your friend? He and Beth got on famously."

Julian slumped lower in his chair. "I plan to toast their happiness at the first possible opportunity," he muttered.

"You are in a sour mood this evening." She eyed him scoldingly. "Are you jealous?"

He sputtered. "Jealous? Of Damion?"

Helene shrugged a shoulder. "He seems happy. Perhaps you would like to be happy as well."

"I am happy. Very happy. Deliriously happy."

Helene's eyebrows arched. "Your dry tone and dead eyes are truly convincing, Julian."

He pushed out a puff of air. "I don't even know why I am feeling so ill-tempered tonight. Although you did serve lamb this evening, and you know I prefer beef. Perhaps that is the reason for my bad mood."

"You like lamb well enough, Julian. My menu is not to blame." Her gaze narrowed on him. "Now that I reflect back on dinner, you weren't glaring at your plate, but at Damion. Have the two of you come to blows over something?"

The answer that first jumped into his head was *"Not yet,"* but that made absolutely no sense, so when he spoke, he amended it to a simple, "No."

Helene made a sound of pondering even as her gaze took in the rest of the guests. "It is a shame Elizabeth couldn't stay. She is such a delight, far more so than her mother or sister."

"It was a lie, you realize. She wasn't actually ill."

"Of course it was a lie. Mary cannot bear the fact that her younger sister outshines her at every turn. But what could I do?" Helene always had possessed the kindest of hearts. "We may simply have to kidnap Elizabeth and sneak her into a ball or two."

Dancing with Beth at a ball. The idea was surprisingly pleasant, not that he'd ever thought that dancing with her would be *un*pleasant. He was remarkably confused.

"I have known Elizabeth and Damion for many years now," Helene said. "I cannot believe that I didn't realize sooner how utterly perfect they are for one another. Did you?" There was something a little too pointed in the question, as if Helene wasn't actually asking the question she'd voiced aloud.

"I never would have put the two of them together if you hadn't," he said. "Why did you, by the way?"

The question appeared to surprise her. "Is there some reason why I shouldn't have? Damion is young and unattached. He has a lovely little estate and a tidy income. And he is a fine gentleman. Elizabeth is also young and unattached. She comes from a good family with more than respectable connections. And she is a simply lovely person. How could I not encourage a match?"

"Because they—because I—" He couldn't seem to come up with a good reason. At least not a logical one. "They wouldn't suit."

"I had my suspicions, but this confirms it." A sudden smile lit her face. "Oh, heavens, Julian. Good heavens."

"Good heavens *what*?"

She pressed a hand over her mouth, looking at him wide-eyed.

"I do not like that look." He'd seen it too often growing

up, usually preceding either tears or a scheme that later got him into tremendous amounts of trouble.

"I had hoped, but now I know," she said from behind her hand. Helene often failed to get to her point.

"Know *what*?"

She patted his hand. Her brow furrowed in something very much like pity. "That you are in love with her."

Julian nearly choked, despite not having anything in his mouth or throat. "I am not in love with her," he insisted under his breath. "She's Beth. She's a friend."

Helene was already shaking her head. "She *is* Beth, though only you call her that, and she *is* your friend, but she is far more than that as well. There's such a fondness in your eyes when you look at her, a fondness that has grown considerably of late. And newly arrived in the picture is a surprisingly murderous glint when you look at Damion. The puzzle is not difficult to piece together, dearest brother."

Julian opened his mouth to object but was silenced by his own thoughts. His heart had broken for her. His temper had risen on the instant in response to her family's unkindness. Even before that evening's events, he'd thought about her when they were apart. His day improved on the instant when he was with her. He was happier in her company than in that of any other person he knew.

But that wasn't love.

"Tell me, Julian, what would you do if Damion were to come over here right now and declare himself madly in love with her? If he were to insist upon riding to her home and declaring his passion, kissing her senseless, and pleading with her to marry him with all possible haste?"

Julian didn't have to think about it. "I'd kill him."

"Why?" Helene asked on a laugh. "You like them both, and Elizabeth is, by your own declaration, only a friend."

"Beth is *my* . . . friend. She's my Beth. Damion doesn't know her the way I do. He doesn't understand her or cherish her like I do. He doesn't—" His words ended as the realization of what he was saying truly settled on him.

"He doesn't love her like you do?" Helene finished for him. "Ponder on that, Julian. Your mind and your heart have not been listening to each other. I, for one, think it is about time they start."

"I haven't the slightest idea what you wish me to tell you." Elizabeth looked from each of her parents to the other several times. "I am sorry for Mary that Julian didn't press his suit last evening, but I am not privy to his thoughts or intentions."

"She said something to him on the drive home, I am certain of it." Mary sent her a look of such hatred that it nearly stole Elizabeth's breath. Mary had disliked her more and more over the past few years, but had never been so openly hostile. "What did you say in the carriage that changed his mind?"

"We didn't say anything. You can ask the maid Helene sent along. It was a silent drive."

"Then what did you say *after* the drive?" Say what one might about the state of Mary's compassion, there was no denying the quickness of her mind.

Elizabeth chose to be honest, if incomplete, in her

response. "He asked if I needed anything before he left, and said he was sorry I wasn't able to remain for dinner." She shrugged as though his words, his touch, from the night before hadn't been equally heavenly and torturous. "Then he left. It was nothing of significance." How she hoped that wasn't truly the case.

"Elizabeth," Father said, using the stern voice reserved exclusively for her, "Julian Broadwood has been dragging his feet where Mary is concerned. You ought to be doing everything in your power to help convince him that the time has come to fulfill the expectations he created."

"Expectations *he* created? What has *he* ever done to convince you that he had any intentions?" Her temper had been piqued, and she couldn't seem to calm it. Julian did not deserve such besmirching. "Does he call regularly? Insist on claiming her for every supper dance? Has he declared himself in any capacity?"

"That is quite enough, young lady." Mother's lips all but disappeared. "Do not speak so boldly of matters about which you know so little."

"And how much do *you* truly know of it?" Her indignation sent her to her feet, too agitated and upset to sit any longer. "While the three of you have spent the past decade scheming and planning and assuming, *I* have spent those years coming to know the object of your designs. Julian Broadwood is decisive and determined, without being unfeeling. He would never allow a decision of this importance to be made without him, but neither would he lash out at anyone attempting to force it on him. He is a good man, and you" —she turned to Mary—"do not deserve him."

"How dare—" Mary stopped quite suddenly. Her narrowed eyes widened. "Oh." Her shock turned to disgust as she uttered the word again. "Oh. You are in love with him. You. Plain little Elizabeth, whom he has likely not given a second thought, are in love with him."

"That is not at all what this is about."

Mary's gaze grew calculating. "I notice you don't deny it." She turned to their parents. "Now we know the truth of it."

"Have you been sabotaging your sister's courtship?" Father demanded. "Is that the reason Julian hasn't offered yet?"

"Of course not," she said. No one was truly listening to her any longer.

"How long have you been nursing this ridiculous *tendre*?" Mary laughed through the words. "Look at the way she blushes, Mother. There is no question; she is in love with him."

Now they were both laughing, and Father was watching her quite as though she were a stranger to him.

"Does Julian have any idea of this, do you think?" Mary asked Mother, both ladies grinning as if they'd never heard anything so amusing in all their lives.

Mother gave it a moment's thought. "It may explain why he has been reluctant to undertake his suit; he fears hurting her feelings. Bookish girls always are the most easily overset, being too little acquainted with the world."

Mary nodded her agreement. "I think we had best send her to stay with Gregory in the country." Mary's triumphant look in Elizabeth's direction told her, in no uncertain terms, that her sister knew such a thing was hardly necessary, but she didn't mean to pass up the opportunity. "We do not wish to risk a repeat of this outburst when others are present."

As if on cue, the drawing room doors opened, and the butler stepped inside. "Mr. Julian Broadwood," he announced.

Elizabeth had never before wished to simply sink into the ground, but in that moment she would have happily procured a spade from the gardener and dug her way straight to the center of the earth. "Please, Mary," she quietly pleaded. "Do not spill your speculations into his ears."

But Mary stepped past Elizabeth and closer to the door. "Why, Julian, how wonderful to see you."

"And you, Miss Gillerford."

Elizabeth turned enough to watch Mary lead him farther into the room. *Please don't say anything, Mary. Please.*

"Do sit with us," Mary invited, indicating a seat very near the one she then lowered herself onto.

He didn't take the chair, however, first stopping to offer his bows to Mother and Father, and then he turned to face Elizabeth. "Miss Elizabeth." He offered her a bow as well.

She somehow managed the appropriate response despite her heart being firmly lodged in her throat. Mary looked far too pleased with herself for Elizabeth's peace of mind.

Julian was watching her a touch too closely. "You are pale," he said. "Is anything the matter?"

She looked quickly in Mary's direction, rather desperately hoping that her sister had softened. If anything, Mary seemed even more jubilant. The worst, Elizabeth was quite certain, was yet to come.

"Beth?" Julian whispered. "What is wrong?"

"Julian," Mary cooed. "We have been having the most diverting conversation. Your arrival could not have been better timed."

He didn't look back at Mary but kept his searching gaze on Elizabeth—on *her*. She had no doubt he could see the abject misery in her eyes. Mary wouldn't hesitate to humiliate her.

"Please don't do this, Mary." Begging wasn't likely to prevent humiliation, but Elizabeth had to try.

"Do what, sister? I simply wish to include our dear friend in our very enjoyable discussion." As innocent as a viper, she was.

Elizabeth stepped closer to her sister. "I will stay with Gregory for the remainder of the Season, if that is what you wish. I will stay there until your future is firmly decided, if need be. Only, please, do not do this."

Mary simply arched an eyebrow. Elizabeth looked to her parents but could see that she would get no help from that quarter. Too many years they'd spent making plans for Mary and Julian; Elizabeth's concerns had never been as important to any of them, and not always even to herself.

"Do you know what we discovered this afternoon?" Mary said, obviously addressing Julian.

"Please don't," Elizabeth whispered.

"My dear little sister is in love. How very quaint, don't you think?" There was a viciousness in Mary's declaration that robbed it of any degree of sweetness.

Elizabeth's heart shattered.

"Is she?" Julian didn't sound amused. He didn't even sound convinced.

"Oh, yes," Mother said. "She certainly is." Her voice added to the declaration would make it more convincing. "But I suppose every girl must have her hopeless fantasy. It is certainly nothing for the family to be ashamed of."

It was always about the family.

Don't read in public, Elizabeth, you'll embarrass us.

You can't have a Season until your sister is married; how would it look for us?

Keep to your quiet corner, Elizabeth, where no one will eye us sidelong upon hearing your impertinent questions.

"Would you care to hazard a guess who it is she fancies?" Mary offered to Julian.

Elizabeth couldn't bear it. She fled the room, not caring that doing so would only add fuel to her family's complaints about her lack of manners. She wasn't quite fast enough to miss Mary's next words.

"It's *you*, Julian. How adorably ridiculous is that? She is in love with *you*."

Whether he believed Mary's declaration, Elizabeth didn't know. It didn't matter. The next time he saw her, he would see the truth of it in her eyes. He would see how hopelessly she loved him.

And he would either find her ridiculous or pitiful.

She couldn't bear either one.

Seven

For a moment, Julian couldn't even think. He'd come to Elizabeth's home on the hope that she might take a turn about the garden with him, or sit a moment in the sitting room. Something. Anything. He'd wrestled with the realization that Helene's conversation had proffered him and had, in the quiet hours of morning, realized his sister was right.

He did love Elizabeth, with a steady and deep love built on years of friendship. He'd thought his distaste for Mary was the result of her undesirable company and little more. How wrong he'd been. Elizabeth had claimed his heart, and he hadn't even realized it.

"Did you hear me, Julian?" Mary interrupted his thoughts. "Elizabeth, quiet, bookish Elizabeth, fancies herself quite in love with you. Is that not the most diverting thing?"

He met her victorious gaze. "Why are you like this,

Mary? You inflict pain with glee. You didn't used to be this way."

Her smile disappeared on the instant. "I only meant to share something amusing. Do you not find it funny?"

"Not in the least. For though I cannot approve of the way you went about it, hearing that there is even a chance that Miss Elizabeth might care for me is, perhaps, the most encouraging thing I have heard in this home these past three years."

Shock began to give way to panic in Mary's face.

He eyed Mrs. Gillerford but found himself with nothing to say to the lady. She'd allowed her younger daughter to be mistreated and hurt again and again, never protecting her, and never seeming to care. At times, she'd even participated in the cruelty.

"Mr. Gillerford, under the circumstances I feel I should tell you that I am in love with your daughter. Not this one." He motioned to Mary. "And should I be so fortunate as to earn her regard in return, I would very much like to have a conversation with you in the near future."

Mr. Gillerford's heavily creased brow pulled deeper. "We are speaking of *Elizabeth*?" He clearly didn't think that possible.

She deserved so much better than this family.

"If you will all excuse me," he said, addressing them as a whole, "somewhere nearby, the lady I adore is hurting, and that is a circumstance I cannot allow to continue." He sketched a quick bow and turned to go.

"Julian, wait." Mary caught up to him with alarming speed. "If I have offended you—"

"The one you ought to be apologizing to is your sister. And then, may I suggest you search inside yourself for the kindhearted girl you were when we were children. She got lost somewhere along the way, and you would do well to find her again."

For once, Mary was speechless.

"Good day, Miss Gillerford." He left her there with no more than that.

A short distance down the corridor, he came upon the housemaid who had accompanied them on the drive through Hyde Park. "I am looking for Miss Elizabeth."

"She's stepped outside, into the back gardens, sir."

"Thank you."

That is precisely where he found her, on a bench in a lonely corner of the manicured gardens, with her head in her hands and her shoulders shaking as she cried. She didn't look up as he approached, though she must have heard his footsteps.

He sat beside her, unsure what to say.

She spoke first, her voice tremulous. "Can we please pretend this day never happened?"

But the day had been a revelation for him. For his part, he could not wish it undone. He set his arm about her and gently nudged her toward him. After a moment's uncertainty, she accepted the unspoken offer and turned into his embrace, her face buried in his waistcoat.

Julian rested his head atop hers, marveling that he'd not sooner realized his feelings for Beth. He'd embraced her and held her hand and sat near her before, and always he'd experienced a rare and almost magical sense of belonging. But each time, he'd dismissed the feeling as nothing more than the result of their longstanding friendship. How blind he had been.

"I missed you last evening, Beth." He surprised himself with his own candor. Mary's words had given him hope and courage. "I am never as happy in anyone's company as I am in yours. I wish you could have stayed for dinner."

"Mary ruined that as well," she said from within his arms.

"What else has Mary ruined, dear? Her words were meant to wound, but they missed their mark." He stroked her back, wishing she wasn't so miserable. A gentleman didn't often pour his heart out. Doing so whilst his lady love was weeping added an element of worry to the undertaking. "Do you remember last evening when you asked Damion why I was in such a sour mood?"

She nodded against his chest, still not showing her face.

"Helene invited him with the hope that you and he would develop a fondness for each other." He still flinched at the idea, despite having reason to believe that Helene's efforts had been in vain. "*That* is why I was unhappy."

"I don't understand."

Nothing for it but to make a full confession. "Your sister made a declaration just now. And while I don't know the truth of it, I should like to make one of my own, if you will allow it."

She pulled a bit away, enough to look up into his eyes. So much pain, so much misery on her beloved face.

"Do you still have the handkerchief I gave you yesterday?" he asked.

She shook her head. "Not with me."

With a bit of maneuvering, he managed to fetch a square of linen from his coat pocket without fully releasing her. He gave it to her and allowed her to dab as necessary. Her gaze didn't leave his face.

"What is it you want to confess, Jules?" She looked equal parts hopeful and worried, no doubt matching his own expression.

He brushed away a lingering tear from her face with the pad of his thumb. "I love you, Beth," he said, diving right to the heart of the matter. "I cannot say with any certainty how long I've felt this way. It came on gradually, with the natural progression of our friendship."

Beth seemed to be holding her breath.

"Was Mary being truthful? Did she have the right of it?" Now it was his turn to hold his breath.

Her voice was quiet when she answered at last. "I have loved you since I was eight years old. But you have always been meant for Mary. Even when it became apparent that you didn't share her expectations, it hardly mattered. I didn't know who had your devotion, only that your heart would never be mine."

He cupped her face, his pulse leaping inside him. "Oh, Beth. It was *always* yours. I was simply too thickheaded to realize it sooner."

She closed her eyes, breathing what could only be described as a sigh of relief.

He kissed her, slowly, savoring a moment which had, unbeknownst to him, been a very long time in coming. His Beth, his dear, wonderful Beth. How had he not realized the true state of his heart?

They sat there for a long moment, she in his embrace, as he inwardly shook his head at his own stupidity. How fortunate he'd been that his idiocy hadn't cost him her love. What if she'd grown weary of waiting on him? What if someone else had captured her heart after he'd inadvertently broken it again and again for years?

"Mary will be unbearable now." Beth leaned more heavily against him. "Do you suppose she would ever find me if I simply refused to leave the garden?"

He hadn't thought much about the repercussions of his declaration on her home life. "I'd wager your entire family will be impossible."

She wrapped her arms around him. "Let's stay out here forever so I never have to face them."

"I have an even better idea. Let us go pay a call on Helene. I'd wager she'd require little convincing to invite you to stay with her for a few weeks, perhaps even until the end of the Season."

"Do you think she would?"

He kissed the top of Beth's head. "I am certain of it. And I could come for Helene's at-homes, and awkwardly take tea, and attempt to catch your eye. Robert, I am certain, would enjoy playing the overprotective guardian, demanding to know my intentions and insisting I return you unharmed from every ride in the park."

He could feel her laugh, and it did his heart good. She'd been unhappy enough that day for a lifetime.

"It will not, perhaps, be a true debut as you deserve," he said, "but I hope it will make up for, in a small way, your lack of a Season."

"Promise to steal a kiss now and then, despite the watchful eye of my overprotective guardian, and I will consider myself well compensated." She pressed a kiss to his cheek then settled into his arms. "You are the only reason I came to London these past three years. I wanted to see you."

"I was so unforgivably blind, Beth." He held her ever closer. "But I will atone for it. I promise you, I will."

Eight

All of London had likely heard Mary's tantrum after Julian had announced that Elizabeth would be spending the remainder of the Season with his sister. While Elizabeth had taken no satisfaction in the display, she'd seen it as an insight to her sister's character. Mary had always been given everything she'd ever wanted without question, and usually without delay. Julian had been firmly on her list of intended acquisitions, but he had chosen Elizabeth.

The passage of a month had neither lessened her memory of Mary's anger nor left her in any less a degree of awe at Julian's affection for her. That he loved her, she was absolutely certain. His devotion could not have been more evident. He held her hand at every opportunity and never bid her farewell without a kiss, however protracted, given Helene's vigilant presence.

Elizabeth's parents had still not given their approval for

her to have a true Season, so her days were spent as something of a companion to Helene, accompanying her on shopping expeditions, sitting quietly nearby during her at-homes. She didn't accompany the Pinnelles to the theatre or musicales or balls. But Julian came for dinner every evening before the social whirl began to spend a precious hour or two with her before propriety required that he leave. She loved those brief moments with him but longed to have the right to be with him always.

Four weeks to the day of Elizabeth's departure from her parents' home, Helene held a dinner party. The guest list matched precisely that of the previous dinner Elizabeth had been forced to quit early. As the appointed time came and went, however, she could not help a feeling of disappointment. Julian had not yet arrived.

Mary did not wear the smug look Elizabeth might have expected. Indeed, she noted something quieter and more ponderous in her sister's expression than Elizabeth had ever seen. She didn't know at all what to make of it.

Just as she began to wonder if Julian meant to come at all, she heard the arrival of a carriage. As it always did, her heart lightened simply knowing that he was nearby. A moment later, the butler stepped into the drawing room.

"Mr. Broadwood and Mr. Gregory Gillerford."

Her brother had come? From Surrey?

Only Helene, Mr. Pinnelle, and Julian did not appear surprised. Elizabeth's gaze darted from Julian to Gregory and back again. Her brother made a quick succession of *good evening* to their parents and Mary before turning an enormous grin to Elizabeth.

"Haven't you an embrace for your favorite brother?" he teased.

She adored him; she always had. Eagerly taking his invitation, she embraced him for a long, drawn-out moment.

"I do wish you had come to London with us. I've missed you ever so much."

"And I wish you'd stayed in Surrey. The old pile of rocks isn't the same without you." He released her, still smiling all the while. "Julian here insisted I make the journey to Town. It seems he has some scheme up his sleeve."

She turned her attention to her dearest love once more. "A scheme? Dare I ask what it is?"

"I had meant to wait until after dinner, but seeing as everyone is here, and staring at me, I suppose I would do well to jump straight to the heart of the matter."

What was he hinting at?

He took her hand, holding it both gently and earnestly, and led her to where her father stood watching in confusion.

"Mr. Gillerford," Julian began. "It will come as no surprise to you, seeing as I told you as much only a few short weeks ago that I love your daughter. I have loved her for a very long time, and my feelings have only grown. She is the dearest person to me in all the world."

She'd once worried that he merely endured her. But he'd declared her the dearest person in the world to him, and he'd said it without hesitation or qualification. The dearest. *His* dearest.

"As she was not permitted a proper Season, I have not been able to court her in the manner she deserves. The chaperonage of my sister and brother-in-law has allowed me to call on her, and I have done what I could to press my suit. I have cherished every moment of her company this past month. But I find I can no longer be content with mere snatches of her time."

Elizabeth had to remind herself to breathe. She knew what he was saying, the declaration he was building toward. She had imagined this moment so many times and wondered if, perhaps, she was dreaming yet.

"Our families are well enough known to one another that I need not make you acquainted with my social standing or financial situation," Julian continued, still addressing Father. "Further, you have known that I was courting your daughter these past weeks yet made no objection, so I do not believe you are opposed to the idea."

Father shook his head firmly. "I long ago decided you'd be a good match for my daughter, though I'd assumed you would court a different one. Everyone assumed that."

For a moment she allowed her father's words and her family's lack of enthusiasm to dampen her happiness. But for *only* a moment. They might not be happy for her, but how could she be anything but overjoyed?

"I, for one, think this match is brilliant," Gregory tossed in. Little wonder he was her favorite, if her only, brother.

Julian turned and faced Elizabeth, taking her hands in his and holding her gaze. "Dearest, dearest Beth. I have cherished these past weeks with you, but I can no longer bear being limited to mere snatches of your time. I do not wish to take dinner with you and then say goodbye. I do not want to spend week after week counting the hours until I may see you again. I want to be able to simply turn around, and there you are. I want to be able to call you *my* Beth, and to be *your* Jules."

How was it possible that a person could smile and tear up at the same time? She didn't know whether to throw her arms around his neck or keep still and quiet so he would continue declaring his love for her. She'd waited ten years to hear these words.

"Please, Beth, do me the honor of becoming my wife so we need never be apart again, my dearest, most darling friend. I cannot promise to never be as thickheaded as I have hitherto been, but I solemnly vow to love you with every breath and every thought and every beat of my heart for the rest of my life. Will you marry me, Elizabeth Mildred Gillerford?"

She couldn't speak. She didn't have the breath left in her to do so.

Gregory moved ever so slightly closer and loudly

whispered, "The word you are searching for, Elizabeth, is 'yes.'"

She laughed through her amazement and bubbling emotions. "Yes. Of course I will, Jules. *My* Jules. My darling friend. Of course I will."

Despite the audience and her mother's gasp of surprise, Julian kissed her quite thoroughly, holding her to him as if he meant never to let her go. He held her even after ending their kiss, smiling at her, his eyes filled with unmistakable love.

"I've been waiting for this since I was eight years old," she said. "I've known since then that this was what I wanted."

"I hope, my love, that you will tell me everything else you've ever wanted." He pressed a kiss to her forehead then rested his head against hers. "I mean to make all of your dreams come true. Every last one."

In that moment, she believed that even the most impossible of dreams could, indeed, come true.

A Lesson in Love

One

London, 1813

Lucy Stanthorpe had every intention of taking London entirely by storm. She was returning in triumph, having survived two Seasons as a debutante and ultimately securing for herself a husband any lady would be proud to call her own. She had her darling Reed to go with her to balls and musicales, and to drive her about Hyde Park during the fashionable hour. She wouldn't spend the entire Season sitting alone in the parlor, or unclaimed for dance after dance at the fashionable balls. She could go to every event with her husband at her side. And she would love every elegant minute.

This Season would be simply wonderful.

"I wonder what will be playing at the Theatre Royal," Lucy said as the carriage rolled over the cobblestones toward their London home. *Her* London home. It was a wonderful thing to have a place of her own, one she and Reed would come to every year, where she could host her own at-homes and balls, where they would one day have children in the nursery and years of memories. "Lady Parvell will, I am certain, host her annual musicale. And I have missed the British Museum. We must visit it this summer."

Reed nodded as he flipped a page of the newspaper. "I understand the Egyptian collection has been recently expanded."

The first thing they'd found in common was their love of history and the museum. She wouldn't have to spend the Season begging her father to take her to see the exhibits.

"Ooh, and Gunter's for ices." Lucy grinned at the reminder of one of London's greatest treats. "And Hyde Park during the fashionable hour." Reed had taken her for a drive in the park more than once in the final days of their courtship. She'd come to love going to the park with him for company.

Reed gave her a quick smile. She hoped that smile of his would always make her a little giddy.

The carriage pulled to a stop in front of the tall, columned Stanthorpe family London residence. Reed's mother was spending the Season in the country with her sister, so they would have the house entirely to themselves.

"Welcome home, darling," Reed said, leaning in to press a quick kiss to her lips. One corner of his mouth twitched upward, his eyes twinkling. "What I wouldn't have given to say that to you this time last year."

She shook her head at his comment. "We didn't know each other yet this time last year."

"Oh, I assure you, I knew exactly who you were long before we were formally introduced."

That was a bouncer if ever she'd heard one. The Stanthorpes sat on a more elevated rung of Society than her family could claim. She doubted Reed had taken even a passing notice of her before being all but forced to dance with her at the Parvells' ball the Season before.

Lucy gave his shoulder a playful shove. "You are an unrepentant flirt, my dear."

"I speak only the truth."

The carriage door opened. The footman put down the step. Reed folded his paper and tucked it under his arm then stepped out of the carriage. He turned back once his feet were on the walk and held his hand out for her. He never failed to offer her that courtesy, just as he always offered his arm when they walked together and kissed her farewell every time they parted. Was it any wonder she adored this thoughtful, loving man?

Reed pulled her arm through his and walked with her up the front steps, where the butler held the door for their arrival. "Welcome home, Mr. and Mrs. Stanthorpe."

Lucy only just held back a giggle. Even after seven months, she still loved to hear herself addressed as Mrs. Stanthorpe.

"We are most happy to be back in Town again, Taylor," Reed said. "I trust our rooms are ready for us?"

"Of course, sir."

"Perfect. Would you send word to the kitchens to have our dinner brought to Mrs. Stanthorpe's sitting room?"

"Of course, sir."

She and Reed walked up the elegant front staircase. "Oh, darling," she said. "This will be the very best Season I have ever spent in London. I am certain of it."

He lifted her hand to his lips and pressed a light kiss to her knuckles. "Indeed. I find myself looking forward to the next few months, something I don't usually feel at this time of year."

Musicales. Balls. Soirees. The theater. Her mind simply spun with all of the wonderful things they would see and do. And they would see and do them together.

It would all be perfect. Positively perfect.

Reed Stanthorpe couldn't imagine a better prospect for a London Season. Days at his club. Afternoons at Gentleman Jackson's Boxing Salon. Quiet evenings at home. Heaven knew he'd spent more than his share of Seasons forced into the social whirl. If there'd been any other way of undertaking a courtship, he'd have jumped at the opportunity.

But he was a married man now. No longer would he have to run from one social engagement to another, or stay up until all hours of the night, or drag himself through the interminable evenings at Almack's. He wouldn't need to endure the tiresome company of Society every single evening. He'd have Lucy's companionship, which was all he really wanted. Most everyone else grew tedious after a few encounters.

"What do you think of this gown, dearest?" Lucy leaned closer to him. They sat side by side on the sofa in her sitting room, having finished the fine meal Cook sent up for them. Lucy pointed to a sketch of a gown in her copy of *La Belle Assemblée*. "This style is a bit bolder than any I've worn before, but I'm a married woman now, so I'm permitted more options."

Reed didn't know much about ladies' fashion and couldn't say what exactly was different about the gown she pointed out from those she'd worn before. "I think it's lovely."

"So do I."

He adored the way her eyes danced about when she was excited. Society had such a dampening effect on the natural exuberance of a debutante. He'd seen that in her face when they'd been introduced. She was bubbling over with life and enthusiasm. He'd known from that moment on that he simply had to know her better—that the woman behind those dancing eyes was worth the aggravation of endless social calls and balls and trips to the theatre.

"And, thank the heavens, I am no longer confined to pastels." Lucy groaned dramatically, as if her previous color palette had been a most excruciating form of torture. "I have decided I absolutely must have a dress in a vibrant shade of blue."

Reed nodded his approval. Though he knew little about fashion, his lovely wife already had a dressing gown of blue. When she wore that shade, her eyes looked like sapphires, and her hair shone like gold.

"I am sorely tempted to buy myself a matching silk turban with a very tall feather to wear at balls," she declared firmly.

"Good gracious, no."

His immediate objection brought a wide-eyed look of surprise to her face.

"Darling," he said. "Only the oldest and dreariest of matrons wear feathered turbans."

"Doesn't your mother wear one?"

"Yes, which is—" He stopped short at the overly innocent look in her eyes. She was funning him, the little minx. Two could play at that game. "Which is, come to think of it, actually a very convincing argument. A feathered turban, yes, but don't neglect a powdered wig to complete the ensemble."

Her smile spread until her dimples reappeared. "A powdered wig for you as well, my dear. And knee breeches and heeled dancing slippers with great gold buckles."

"And shall I sport yards and yards of lace as well?" he asked.

"Of course." She looked ready to burst with laughter. "We will be quite the fashionable couple amongst the older set."

He slipped his arm around her shoulder and pulled her

closer to him. "As much as I complain about the ridiculously close cut of today's jackets and the tedious nature of having my cravat tied in the latest style, I do not for one moment wish to trade that for the cumbersome fashions of our parents' generation."

Lucy set her magazine on the seat beside her and shifted so she knelt on the cushion facing him. She reached up and touched his face. "Even in the most ridiculous fashions, you would be the most handsome gentleman I've ever known."

"Flattery, my love?"

"I speak only the truth," she said, repeating the declaration he'd made in the carriage earlier. Her teasing tone indicated she'd chosen the response on purpose.

Reed kissed her well and deeply before pulling her fully into his arms. Yes, a Season spent quietly at home, away from the hustle and bustle of Society. Just the two of them. The perfect London Season.

Two

"Reed." Lucy stood in the doorway of Reed's bedchamber, looking with dismay on her husband in his shirtsleeves, his cravat tossed aside, and his feet shoeless. "You cannot go out dressed the way you are."

Though none of her new, fashionable gowns had arrived from the *modiste*, she had chosen the most modish of her older gowns to wear that night. Her abigail had threaded ribbons through her hair and quite artfully tucked tiny white flowers throughout. And Lucy had chosen to wear the amber necklace Reed had given her at Christmas. She'd taken great pains in her preparations, and there Reed sat in his shirtsleeves.

He kept his gaze on the paper held unfolded in front of him. "I mean to stay in tonight."

Lucy stepped inside. Surely Reed was teasing. He'd required prodding each evening since their arrival in

London, but tonight was different. They were scheduled to attend the Parvells' ball, the event at which they had first been introduced the year before. On that night a year earlier, she'd arrived nervous and unsettled, so afraid of spending the evening as a wallflower. But then she'd met him, and everything in both of their lives had changed for the better. The Parvells' ball would always be special to the two of them.

Lucy stepped inside. "Tonight is the *Parvells' ball*, dearest," she reminded him.

"We have been out every evening this week," he said. "I am too weary to go out again."

They had indeed attended several functions over the past few nights, but Reed had insisted on returning home long before the events were over. They'd not been out late; neither had they attended more than one function in any given evening. Furthermore, he'd spent the day at his club. How could he be too tired for a ball, especially *this* one? This was their special anniversary.

"We replied to the invitation already, Reed. The Parvells are expecting us."

"The ball will be exceptionally crowded." He turned a page of the paper, slumping down in his chair a little more. He was the very picture of a gentleman settling in for a long, leisurely read. "The Parvells will not notice our absence, nor will they care."

"I will care," she answered. "I have been looking forward to this evening. And I am already dressed to go."

"But, as you pointed out," he said, "I am not."

"I cannot go without you," she said, her voice quieter than before. Married women had more freedom than unmarried, but to attend a ball without her husband when they were only newly married would be not only noted, but fodder for the gossips. More than that, she *wanted* him to go with her. "We needn't stay beyond the supper dance."

He lowered his paper and looked at her over it, his expression one of near exasperation. "The supper dance isn't until one o'clock in the morning. I have no desire to be out that late."

"But we would be out together. And we could dance with each other."

"We have been out almost every night since arriving in Town."

She stepped to his chair, unsure what to make of the annoyance in his face. "Have you not enjoyed the Season thus far?"

"I would enjoy the Season far more if I were permitted to spend it in peace and quiet." His sincerity could not have been more apparent. He didn't seem angry, simply determined to remain home.

Lucy held back the immediate protest that sprang to her lips. Perhaps he really was tired. He had objected the evening before, and she'd pleaded with him until he agreed, just as she had the evening before that and the one before that. She didn't want to argue with him again. If he didn't wish to go to their special anniversary ball, she wouldn't press him to.

"I won't pester you to go. There will certainly be other balls." She managed a bit of a smile.

"Yes, there are always other balls," he said dryly, a touch of a smile on his face.

Lucy pondered that a moment, even after Reed raised his paper once more. He'd always seemed to enjoy balls while he was courting her. Not only balls; he'd eagerly sought her out at musicales and soirees, and he'd visited her family box at the theatre every time she was in attendance.

So why was he chafing so much at the social whirl now? While they were yet unwed, he could only have enjoyed her company for the brief moments allotted a couple with no understanding between them. But now married, they would have each other's company the entire night at whatever event they attended.

Perhaps that is the difficulty. He has grown weary of me.

Lucy refused to ponder that idea more deeply. "I'll leave

you to your paper, then." She leaned down and kissed his cheek.

He gave her a fleeting smile then returned to his reading once more. She returned to her room. There was no need to tug the bell pull; her lady's maid hadn't left yet.

"Were you needing something else, ma'am?" The maid's look of confusion was more than understandable.

"There's been a change of plans," Lucy said, keeping her expression and tone light. "We will be staying in tonight."

And they stayed in the next night, and the night after that. For an entire fortnight, the pattern repeated. She dressed for the evening's engagement then attempted to convince him to join her. Sometimes he did. Most times he did not.

The night of her dearest friend Fanny Alistair's ball, Lucy stepped into Reed's room once more, a feeling of dread settling on her shoulders. She'd lived this moment so many times over the past weeks, never sure if Reed would agree to an evening out. He'd not once agreed to attend a ball.

Her heart dropped at finding her husband in his usual nightly state of half-dress. They'd spoken only that morning at breakfast of Fanny's ball and Lucy's desire to attend. He couldn't have forgotten.

"Reed?"

He looked up. She could see in his eyes that he knew immediately what she'd come to ask. "I suppose this means you don't wish to stay in tonight?"

"Tonight is Fanny's ball," she reminded him. "I have longed to attend a ball."

His shoulders slumped. "There will always be others. We needn't to go to all of them."

"*All* of them? We haven't gone to any of them."

"But balls are so tedious. Wouldn't you rather have a quiet evening—"

"A quiet evening at home?" She repeated the phrase she'd heard from him more than any other the past two weeks. "There wasn't a single Society function last Season you didn't seem to make an appearance at," Lucy said. "You danced with me at every ball, sat beside me at every musicale."

Reed rose from his chair and crossed to the doorway. "Of course I did, Lucy. Every unmarried gentleman knows what is required of him. We dance that dance because we must."

"I don't understand."

He took her hands in his. That familiar gesture set her thoughts more at ease. No matter their different preferences of late, he was ever tender and kind. She disliked feeling at odds with him.

"I attended the balls and soirees and everything else last Season because you were there," Reed said. "I was courting you, dear. A suitor is required to do all those things. A husband is not."

A husband is not. The pieces began to fall into place. "Now that you've secured yourself a wife, you aren't obligated to squire her about to all those 'tedious' affairs."

"No, thank the heavens." He smiled as if being excused from accompanying her to those same entertainments they had once enjoyed was the greatest of escapes. Had he feigned his pleasure the Season before? Or did he simply not wish to be bothered to take her about?

"You don't wish to go to Fanny's ball tonight?"

He slipped a hand beneath her chin and gave her a quick kiss on the lips. "No gentleman ever wishes to go to a ball. We only go when we absolutely have to, but once that obligation has passed we happily leave the chore to those gentlemen still neck-deep in the Marriage Mart." He gave her a lopsided smile then walked back to his chair.

This was her future then. She would either be forced to attend balls alone and be a wallflower as she'd feared during her time as an unwed young lady, or she would spend her nights in Town gazing out windows, wishing her husband had enjoyed dancing with her as much as he'd pretended to.

A suitor is required to do all those things. A husband is not.

She had been worth the effort of a courtship before they married. Now that he'd secured her hand, going about with her was seen as a chore, a distasteful bit of effort he'd rather not make.

Lucy returned to her bedchamber as she had so many times over the past two weeks. Her maid had taken to simply waiting for her. In silence, she helped Lucy undress then pulled the many pins from her hair.

Why did I even bother?

She felt rather like an old pair of slippers. She wanted to be worth the effort to him again. She wanted the feeling of being cherished and treasured, the joy of dancing with him, of watching for him to appear at her theatre box. She wanted him to do all those things, not because courtship *required* it of him, but because he wished for her company.

Her "perfect" Season had crumbled. She had looked forward to the coming months with eager anticipation. Then Reed declared going about with her a "chore." Her heartache began to give way to frustration then a surge of determination.

Perhaps it is time Reed discovered what life is like without his comfortable old slippers.

Three

Lucy occasionally took a breakfast tray in her room, so Reed thought little of it when she didn't join him for the morning meal. He spent a leisurely few hours at his club then an invigorating afternoon at Gentleman Jackson's. He fully expected to find Lucy up and about when he arrived home. The sitting room, drawing room and back gardens, however, were empty.

Lucy wasn't in her rooms or his. He made a quick check of the guest bedchambers and nursery, on the off chance she might be there. But in the end, he returned to his wife's bedchamber baffled.

Perhaps she was out making morning calls. The hour was only a bit late for that. She might simply be on her way back.

He moved toward the door, intending to spend some time in his book room, catching up on a few matters of business. He stopped, however, before stepping out of Lucy's bedchamber. Reed looked back at the room. Something about it was different, odd. But what?

The furniture was all the same and in the same places. He didn't think the curtains were different or the coverlet on Lucy's bed changed.

Where are her perfume bottles and her hairbrush?

Lucy kept more knickknacks on her dressing table than anyone Reed had ever known. But the dressing table was empty. Utterly. He pulled open the doors of her wardrobe and found it as empty as her dressing table. His wife and all her belongings had vanished.

What in heaven's name? Reed tugged on the bell pull. Someone in the house had to have seen her that day. Someone must know what had happened.

A moment later, one of the chambermaids stepped inside.

"I had hoped to speak with Mrs. Stanthorpe's abigail," Reed said.

"Begging your pardon, sir, but she's gone with Mrs. Stanthorpe."

Ah. Someone did know something. "And where did Mrs. Stanthorpe go?"

"I don't rightly know, sir. But she left in the carriage."

The driver would know where he'd taken Lucy. "Thank you," Reed said.

She gave a quick curtsey and scurried from the room. Reed waited but the briefest of moments before walking to the entryway. After inquiring of the footman whether or not the carriage had returned and learning that it had, Reed sent word to the stables that he wished the carriage brought around.

While he waited, Reed had ample time to ponder the odd turn of events, as he couldn't make sense of it. Where could Lucy possibly have gone, and why would she have taken her clothes, perfume, and jewelry with her?

With the precision Reed had come to expect from ever-efficient Taylor, the butler arrived at the front door in time to open it just as the carriage came to a stop in front of the house.

"What instructions do you wish me to convey to John Coachman, Mr. Stanthorpe?"

"Ask him to take me to the same destination he took Mrs. Stanthorpe earlier today."

"Very good, sir."

Reed settled into the carriage, his curiosity growing by leaps and bounds. He couldn't make heads nor tails of Lucy's departure, especially with her belongings missing, but felt certain the mystery would be clear soon enough.

The carriage wheels rolled over the cobbled streets, keeping to the finer areas of Town. At least Lucy hadn't wandered into dangerous corners. He recognized the house where the carriage at last stopped.

Why would Lucy bring all her belongings to her parents' home?

Reed climbed out of the carriage and made his way to the door. A moment later, the very proper butler welcomed him inside. As a member of the family, Reed wouldn't be required to stand on ceremony the way a visitor would.

"Good afternoon, Graves." Reed gave the butler a quick nod of acknowledgement.

"If you would, please, sir, your calling card." Graves held his hand out, his bearing as haughty as any proper butler's ought to be, but with the smallest hint of apology in his eyes.

Reed didn't immediately comply. He was family. Family didn't generally present their cards when visiting. But Graves didn't give over.

Perhaps old Graves is beginning to lose hold of his faculties.

Reed pulled his card case from his jacket pocket and took one out. He handed it to the butler, unsure what to expect. The butler dipped his head and disappeared up the stairs.

Poor man must be feeling off today. He left me waiting here as though I were a presumptuous mushroom rather than a member of the family.

The grandfather clock near the door loudly counted off the seconds as Reed stood in solitary silence. Even if Lucy had left already, Reed's parents-in-law should have welcomed him in with none of the formality generally required of a caller.

Lucy's mother appeared at the top of the stairs. "Mr. Stanthorpe. What a pleasure to see you again."

She didn't come toward the entry way, but stood looking down on him, her bearing regal and unfailingly polite. And she'd called him "Mr. Stanthorpe," a formality they'd done away with not long after he'd married her daughter.

"Mother Harrison," he greeted, trying to clamp down his growing confusion. "I had hoped to speak with Lucy. I understood she was here."

She gave him a patient smile. "Now, now, Mr. Stanthorpe. Our at-home day is Friday. Today, as you must know, is Thursday."

What the deuce did their at-home hours have to do with the matter? He'd come for his wife. He wasn't some hapless suitor or socially inept neighbor.

"Do come by tomorrow during our at-home," Mrs. Harrison said. She gave him a quick smile and turned about, walking away with no further explanation.

What the blazes was that about? A few of his cronies had spoken of their mothers-in-law in terms one generally reserved for rabid and difficult dogs, but Reed had never seen Mother Harrison act the part of a dragon. She'd always been kind and affectionate toward him.

"Psst."

Reed glanced about but couldn't identify the source.

"Psssst." The sound was louder, more urgent than before. "Reed, my boy. Up here."

He followed the voice and spotted his father-in-law on the first floor-landing above. Mr. Harrison waved him up.

"Quickly, son, before the ladies spot you."

Reed heard in Mr. Harrison's voice the promise of an explanation and didn't hesitate. He took the stairs two at a time then followed Mr. Harrison down the corridor. He'd never before thought of his father-in-law as spry, but the gentleman was making short work of their journey.

Mr. Harrison pulled open the door to his book room, a room Reed had been in more than once. "Inside. I don't think they've seen you."

Why was not being seen so important when Reed had come specifically to see someone? He stepped into the book room and found it wasn't empty. His brothers-in-law, both of them, sat near the fireplace, watching his entrance.

"Robert," he said. "Charles."

"Good afternoon, you twit," Charles greeted him with a smile. He was married to Lucy's older sister and was the closer of the two gentleman to Reed's age.

Mr. Harrison had taken his place in a leather armchair near his sons-in-law. All three watched Reed with looks of almost comical concern.

"What is this?" Reed asked. "A council of war?"

"We are staging a daring rescue." Mr. Harrison's tone was utterly serious, though his eyes twinkled with a bit of mischievousness.

"And whom are you rescuing?" Though he asked the question, he suspected he knew the answer.

"Have a seat, son." Mr. Harrison motioned to the empty spot on the sofa. "We are here to save you from yourself."

Reed looked at them each in turn. "Save me from myself?"

"Apparently, brother," Charles said, "you told your wife

that husbands aren't required to squire their wives around, and that attending social functions is a distasteful chore."

"But it *is* a distasteful chore."

"Oh, we all know that," Robert, Lucy's brother, replied. "But we have the sense to not say as much to our wives."

"I—" Reed had a sudden realization. "How do the three of you know about that conversation?"

"Lucy arrived this morning with a bee in her bonnet," Mr. Harrison said. "She and her mother closed themselves up in the sitting room for a full hour. Then the flood of Harrison ladies began."

Robert took up the tale. "Mother sent notes to Clarissa and Amelia, insisting they were needed 'immediately' to sort out a problem of 'unparalleled urgency.' Your fateful error was revealed, and here we all are."

"So Lucy *was* here." He hadn't managed a straight answer from Mrs. Harrison.

"*Is* here, my friend." Charles looked ready to burst out laughing. "Lucy *is* here."

"Perfect." Reed stood up. "Nice to see you all again."

"Sit, you muttonhead." Charles went so far as to roll his eyes. "You are in far too deep to get out that easily."

He slowly lowered into his seat. "I think you had better tell me the whole story."

"First," Charles said, "you never tell your wife that time spent with her is a 'chore.' She'll think that means you don't care for her company."

"But that's not what I said."

"It doesn't matter what you say," Charles insisted. "All that matters is what she hears, and the two are often very different from each other."

"Furthermore," Mr. Harrison said. "There is nothing a husband is permitted to believe he is no longer required to do once he is married. Though the list of things we'd *prefer* not to do is long and detailed, we keep that list to ourselves."

"Are you trying to say that I'm in trouble with Lucy?"

"You have moved far beyond *trouble*," Charles said.

All three men were clearly laughing at him. Either Lucy wasn't as upset with him as they were letting on, or they were enjoying the thought of his apparent impending doom. "And I am in my wife's black books because I told her that gentlemen don't actually enjoy balls?"

"Yes," Mr. Harrison said. "And that spending time with her was unpleasant."

"I never said that."

"Again," Charles jumped in. "What you *said* is of little importance."

Mr. Harrison continued with his explanation. "Lucy told her sympathetic female relations that you haven't attended any balls with her since arriving in London. You have refused to attend any number of Society functions—most of them, in fact."

Reed leaned back, eyeing them each in turn. He could feel something like a smirk tug at his mouth. "So you are all envious, that's what this is. You have been forced to attend those things and can't believe I managed to get out of the obligation."

"Envious?" Robert actually chuckled. "Our wives aren't in the sitting room conspiring against *us*, Reed. I think you are the one who ought to be jealous."

"Conspiring against me?"

Mr. Harrison's grin only grew. "The ladies of this family mean to teach you a lesson, son. And if I know them as well as I think I do, they will succeed."

"What is it to be, then?" Reed asked. "Am I to be stretched on the rack or locked up in the dungeon?"

"Worse even than either." Mr. Harrison's eyes danced with amusement. "You are to be forced to court your own wife."

"Oh, good heavens," Reed muttered, beginning to understand what his father-in-law was hinting at.

"You are to be subjected to at-homes and requesting

permission to dance at balls and visits to the family box at the opera. And I have been instructed to make it difficult for you." Mr. Harrison's look of empathy clearly indicated he would do nothing of the sort. "Never tell your wife that you're not required to court her unless you are fully prepared to do so."

Reed shook his head in disbelief. "Where in the world did this come from? Lucy didn't seem upset last night."

Charles and Robert exchanged knowing looks. Reed eyed them both. Charles took pity on him and explained.

"Considering the number of social functions we have not seen you at this Season, I am certain Lucy has been stewing over this for some time. She might not have seemed upset last night, but I can guarantee she was."

Robert nodded. "And since all of our wives have, at one time or another, been upset with us over our disinterest in squiring them about, Lucy has found an entire house full of sympathizers."

"I will have to go through with this, then?" Reed slumped lower in his seat. This Season was supposed to have been simple and easy.

"*Yes.*" Mr. Harrison pulled the single syllable out long. Spoken in that way, his yes sounded far more like "in a manner of speaking."

Reed's companions looked at him pointedly, their expressions growing instantly conspiratorially.

He leaned forward. "What do you have in mind?"

Four

Lucy sat in her parents' drawing room, chatting amicably with many visitors, as she had the previous two Seasons. And, as she had the year before, she found herself watching the door, hoping each new arrival was her Reed. A flutter of anticipation seized her with the very first visitor and only grew as time passed.

I have missed this.

Though last Season, not knowing if he would visit or dance with her, or invite her to ride out with him had been a source of worry, every time he had come by or had spoken to her or sent her flowers, she'd known with absolute certainty that he cared about her. She'd known he thought her worth the effort. *That* was what she'd missed—the little things that said he valued her.

Their at-home hours were nearly gone. Lucy caught her mother's eye, silently asking the question on her mind. *Where is Reed?*

Mother's eyes softened, and she gave a quick nod of reassurance. She had insisted, along with Lucy's sister and sister-in-law, that Reed would most certainly come call on her. Husbands grew lonely for their wives, they said. Having not seen her in a day and a half, Reed would realize how much he enjoyed her company and would do whatever he must to see her.

That was the crux of their plan, at least. Reed took her for granted. Requiring him to make even a minimal effort would show him how fortunate he was to have her as his wife. Perhaps he would decide that dancing with her and accompanying her to Society functions were not such chores after all.

Only a moment more passed, and there he stood. Reed greeted Mother first, as was proper, she being the hostess of this at-home. He smiled and nodded at the others in the room, a quick and unexceptional means of acknowledging everyone without taking time to do so individually.

Which will mean more time for the two of us to converse.

Reed took the empty chair nearest her. She kept her eyes trained on him, her smile feeling more natural by the moment. He was here. He had come.

His eyes met hers. She held her breath, excitedly anticipating the twinkle of mischief she'd so often seen there. But his gaze was little more than polite.

"Good afternoon, Mrs. Stanthorpe," he said, his voice low enough to not be overheard by those conversing with her mother and sister. "Fine weather we are having."

Mrs. Stanthorpe? They had on occasion resorted to formal address with each other when in public, especially amongst the older set, who were quite particular about that. But it was decidedly odd for him to not call her by her Christian name in her own parents' house, when they were the only two taking part in the conversation.

And had his first words to her after more than a day apart truly been a comment on the weather?

"Yes," she managed to reply. "It has been very dry."

Reed wore the same smile as when he'd first stepped inside. There was nothing particularly personal in it. "I understand the Hombolts' ball is this evening."

Now they were getting somewhere. "It is indeed." She didn't entirely manage to keep the eagerness from her voice. "Are you planning to attend?"

He shrugged a bit as he reached for a cucumber sandwich. "It will, no doubt, be a terrible crush. Any gentleman with a modicum of sense will stay home."

"Oh." What could she say beyond that? He didn't mean to attend. Perhaps he thought she wasn't attending. That would certainly explain it. "I am quite looking forward to the Hombolts' ball."

He made a vague sound of acknowledgement. "This cucumber sandwich is excellent." Reed turned his attention to Mother. "An exceptional sandwich, Mrs. Harrison."

"Why, thank you." Mother's eyes darted to Lucy, a look of triumph in her eyes. Did she honestly think Reed's compliment of her tea offerings was a sign of success?

"Well, ladies." Reed stood and took in the room with a quick sweep of his gaze. "It has been a pleasure visiting with you all."

And with that, he left. Two days apart, and Reed visited with her only for two minutes and spoke only of the weather and cucumber sandwiches. What an utter disappointment.

She rose from her chair. "If you will excuse me, Mother," she said quickly, and left the drawing room with as much dignity as she could summon.

The moment she reached the corridor, she took up a brisk pace, rushing up the stairs to her bedchamber. She hurried to her window, drew back the curtains, and looked down at the street below. Reed walked from the house at a leisurely pace, swinging his walking stick as though he hadn't a care in the world.

She pressed her open hand to the glass, watching him

leave her behind without a single backward glance. "Haven't you missed me at all?" she whispered.

<hr />

"I am not convinced this is a wise course of action." Reed resisted his brother-in-law's efforts to nudge him into the Hombolts' ballroom.

"Nonsense," Robert insisted. "Everything is working perfectly."

Perfectly? If everything was so perfect, why was he keeping company with his brother-in-law instead of his wife? Reed considered that a significant step in the wrong direction.

"Stick with the plan, Reed," Robert said. "You'll not only settle your current contretemps, but you'll save yourself a great deal of misery down the road." Robert gave him a significant look. "You're a married man now. If you don't put your foot down, you'll soon become extremely well-acquainted with misery."

"That is a fine thing to say about your own sister."

"You are the one who married her and turned her into a *wife*. She was a fine, sensible sort of lady before that." Robert gave him one final nudge, forcing him into the ballroom. "Time to face down the dragon."

Reed straightened the cuffs of his jacket. "First she's a wife, and now she's a dragon. How much worse can this get?"

"Your mother-in-law is approaching," Robert answered.

"So quite a bit worse." He shot Robert a grin.

Robert laughed as they walked around the edge of the ballroom. "Mother isn't so terrible as some."

True. He was exceptionally fond of Lucy's family, even if its ladies were currently making life difficult for him.

"Mrs. Harrison," he said. "It is indeed a pleasure to see you again."

She smiled. "I know the look of a suitor when I see one. I daresay you've come to ask permission to dance with our Lucy."

Robert pierced him with a significant look. Reed gave a subtle nod. He knew his part. "I am promised already for the next several dances," he said. "But should I have a dance free before I quit the ball, I will be certain to seek your daughter out."

Mrs. Harrison's eyes pulled wide with shock. Reed offered a very appropriate bow and took leave of his mother-in-law. He glanced back only briefly. Robert, who still stood by his mother, gave him a firm nod of approval. Their plan was moving along nicely.

Why, then, do I feel so utterly dissatisfied?

He saw her in the next moment—his Lucy. She stood amongst a group of her friends, chatting away. Even from a distance, he could see the sparkle in her eyes. The first time he ever saw Lucy was at a ball, like this one. She'd been standing, as now. At first he'd taken only a passing notice of her. But then she'd smiled, and Reed hadn't been able to look away.

He hadn't managed to summon the courage to pay her court until the start of the next Season. Fortunately, he'd not turned coward then. He'd asked her to dance, and she'd agreed. At the end of that Season, he'd asked her to marry him, and she'd agreed.

What went wrong? Why has this *Season been so miserably disastrous?*

She hadn't been satisfied with his company any longer. Every evening, it was the same complaint—she didn't want to be at home with him. She wished to be out with Society and her friends.

Mr. Harrison appeared at his side unannounced,

"You're not turning lily-livered on us, are you?"

"Not lily-livered. I only—" His eyes returned to Lucy. "I was only wishing things were different between Lucy and me."

"They will be, my boy." Mr. Harrison slapped a firm hand on his shoulder. "Your marriage'll be happy and loving again, just as soon as you've ignored your wife properly."

"I am beginning to suspect, Mr. Harrison, that your entire family is a bit touched in the upper works."

"Nothing mad about it, Reed. It's a fine plan."

He was attending a ball, something he generally did his utmost to avoid, and his wife, whom he'd not really seen in two days, was there. This "fine" plan required him to not dance with her—indeed, to not even talk to her. That seemed a little daft.

But he had only been married a few months. His father-in-law and brothers-in-law had more than forty-five years of marriage experience between them. They understood the issues better than he did. And if their plan worked, and he and Lucy could have the happy and contented stay in Town he'd anticipated, the entire ordeal would be worth it.

That was what he told himself as he tore his gaze from Lucy and walked away.

Five

Lucy's patience was nearly spent. She had sat through four nights of Society functions waiting for Reed to rush to her side and declare he couldn't bear to be away from her another moment. She had even seen him at most of the gatherings, but he never said so much as a word to her. He smiled and made friendly conversation with any number of people then left without ever noticing her.

She stepped into her parents' sitting room, where her mother and sister-in-law, Amelia, bent over their needlework, discussing someone's choice of gown the evening before.

"This is not working," Lucy declared with all the authority a youngest child could manage.

"Nonsense, dear," Mother said. "Our embroidery is coming along nicely."

"Not the embroidery." Surely her family had noticed her dilemma. "This plan we've concocted to remind Reed how lonely and miserable he was as a bachelor so he'll come running back to me and declare he'll never neglect me again. *That* is not working."

Mother looked at her over her needlepoint. "Why in heaven's name do you think that?"

Lucy looked from one of them to the other. Surely they weren't so blind as to have not noticed the lack of results their scheme had produced.

"Reed is living as a bachelor and couldn't be more pleased about it," she explained. "I have never seen him look happier at a ball or musicale as I have this past few nights. He pokes his head in, chats amicably with a few people here and there then gladly leaves with his cronies, no doubt to spend the night at their club. He's gleeful."

Mother and Amelia exchanged knowing looks.

"Clarissa said Lucy's determination was flagging," Amelia told Mother.

As Clarissa was not currently present, Lucy could only assume her "determination" had been a previous topic of discussion among them.

"This is not a question of determination," Lucy insisted. "I miss my husband. I miss seeing him each day and talking to him. That isn't a bad thing. I love him enough to have married him, after all. Wishing he were with me is to be expected."

"Of course it is," Mother said, but she didn't sound as if she actually agreed.

"He may not like to attend balls and soirees and such, or perhaps he doesn't like attending them with me—he has, after all, made more appearances at social events these past few days than in the weeks prior—but I would rather have his company quietly at home or doing something he enjoys than to not have it at all."

Amelia gave her a commiserating look. "And are you prepared to make that sacrifice every day for the rest of your life? You would be telling him that his preferences are the only consideration in your marriage."

"But by staying away, aren't I insisting that my preferences are the ones that must be bowed to?"

"Come sit, dear." Mother patted the space beside her on the sofa.

Lucy sat beside her, feeling more confused and frustrated and tired than she had in some time. Nothing about this Season had gone as planned. She longed for Reed's company. She missed the little gestures of kindness she received from him—his arm when she walked, the way he adjusted her wrap when they were out, their shared excitement over antiquities and ices. She missed his smile and his laughter.

Mother set aside her embroidery. "Reed has been in consultation with your father, Robert, and Charles." She made that fact sound like a terribly ominous thing. "They realize we mean to teach Reed a lesson in valuing his wife, and they mean to teach us a lesson in return."

"What lesson is that?" The only thing the past week had taught Lucy was that being a wallflower as a debutante is being a wallflower as a married lady. The former was disheartening, while the latter was simply heartbreaking.

Amelia, sitting in a chair facing them on the sofa, leaned forward. "The gentlemen mean to show us that we are the ones who cannot live without *them*, that we are more miserable in their absence than they are in ours. They are determined to prove that we will give over first and go running back to them, begging for their company. To make us admit that we miss them when they are gone."

Mother nodded her agreement with Amelia's explanation.

"But I don't know that I can live without him," Lucy said. "What is so wrong with telling him so?"

"And deal a blow to ladies everywhere?" Amelia scoffed. "No, dearest sister-in-law. Your victory in this battle will give hope to your fellow wives. You will be a revered warrior."

"'A revered warrior'? How utterly ridiculous. I only wanted Reed to take me to balls and such. When did this turn into a war?"

Mother waved off the question. "When? Adam and Eve, darling."

Lucy felt unaccountably exhausted. "How much longer do I have to keep 'teaching Reed a lesson'? This has been a long week for me. I don't get to go home to my husband as you do. I am alone every night and every morning and most of the day. I haven't danced at any balls, nor have I had the man I love to whisper with at the theatre. Your endurance may be endless with those things buoying you up. But mine is quickly running out."

"Do not fret," Mother said, retaking her embroidery. "The tide will turn tonight. We have it all in hand. You'll see."

***

That night, Lucy watched her mother and sisters assume their positions at the ball and couldn't help thinking that the undertaking rather resembled the positioning of troops on a battlefield.

Reed had arrived, flanked by the Harrison men. As they had during the past few evenings, the gentlemen quite obviously headed in the opposite direction of Lucy. But the Harrison ladies had anticipated the maneuver. Mother was waiting for them. They were too far distant for Lucy to overhear their conversation, but she could easily guess at it.

Mother offered a greeting, doing a poor job of pretending to be surprised at having bumped into Reed. He made some kind of polite reply, all the while glancing at his companions for some indication as to what he might do to counter the ladies' strategic victory. Before anyone could speak to the contrary, Mother had her arm threaded through Reed's and was leading him rather forcibly in Lucy's direction.

How utterly humiliating. All I wanted was for him to accompany me to Society functions, but here I am now watching him be bullied into even talking to me.

Reed reached her side a moment later. He wore the same vaguely polite expression he had at Mother's at-home a week earlier. "Mrs. Stanthorpe." The same emotionless greeting as before.

Oh, Mother. This had better be worth the heartache. "Mr. Stanthorpe," she replied, as her female relations had advised her to.

"As luck would have it," Mother said, "Our Lucy has this next set free. How fortuitous."

Reed hesitated for just a moment. Would he truly turn down such a pointed request? "I—"

Father interrupted whatever Reed was about to say. "Oh, dear, ladies. I do believe Mr. Stanthorpe told me he didn't mean to dance tonight."

Lucy kept her gaze on her husband. "Is that true?"

"I . . ." His eyes darted to Father then to Robert and Charles gathered nearby. "I am not particularly in the mood for dancing, and it would be unfair in the extreme for a person to be forced to do something he did not care to do." Something about the declaration felt practiced.

Reed has been in consultation with your Father and brothers. This, then, was what Mother meant. They were combatants. Indeed, Amelia and Robert seemed almost gleeful at the prospect of debating the topic.

"By that logic," Amelia said, "a lady who does not care to be left at home evening after evening shouldn't be forced to remain there by a husband who refuses to take her out."

Robert answered his wife's argument point by point. "Requiring a gentleman to undertake something he finds truly distasteful is hardly comparable to a lady spending a quiet evening at home."

"Distasteful?" Amelia clearly objected to the word. "If you found squiring me about all these years so torturous, why did you even bother?"

"I didn't have a choice," Robert answered. "I was never given the opportunity to stand up for myself and for husbands everywhere. But Reed here does. And I, for one, applaud him."

Lucy looked to her mother. Was this truly the great victory she'd promised? This was "having it all in hand"?

Mother didn't seem swayed in the least. "If Mr. Stanthorpe does not mean to dance, surely he would have no objection to taking a turn about the room. You would have been doing precisely that as it was."

As far as logic went, that was rather water-tight. Reed made a nod and small bow of acknowledgement. Lucy stood and took the arm he offered. They stepped away from her family, looking for all the world as though they were taking an unexceptional turn about the room. Inside, however, Lucy was a tangled mess of emotions.

She had missed him, missed him to the point of misery. But he didn't seem to have suffered at all in her absence. She didn't want to spend the remainder of her Season without him, but neither did she wish to dig up this old argument every summer, having to beg and plead for every outing. She didn't want them to bicker in public the way Amelia and Robert were, or secretly conspiring against each other the way her parents were.

She held more tightly to Reed's arm, grateful for his presence even in her uncertainty. He set his hand on top of hers. That light touch took her back a year to their courtship when that was all they were permitted. Her heart pounded at the feel of his hand on hers. Lucy settled herself into that fleeting connection, finding a wonderfully welcome helping of peace by having him at her side again.

He broke the silence between them. "We are having very fine—"

"Don't you dare speak of the weather, Reed Andrew Stanthorpe."

He abruptly stopped. His eyes pulled wide and his mouth hung the tiniest bit open. She didn't apologize for her vehemence, didn't take back her words. An entire week they'd been apart, not seeing each other, not speaking. She would not endure a stilted and insincere conversation on topics neither of them cared the least about.

He seemed to fumble about for the right thing to say. "Weather is a commonplace topic between two people."

She pulled her arm free, shaking her head in frustration. "We've not seen each other in a full week, yet you have nothing to say to me beyond 'commonplace topics between two people'?"

"Lucy—"

"Either you are wounding me on purpose, or you really are utterly indifferent to me." The thought brought a fresh threat of tears. "I had thought you were as miserable as I was, that you missed me as much as I missed you. But Mother was right. You didn't. Not at all."

"Lu—"

She couldn't bear more empty words. Not caring that she was likely making something of a scene, Lucy hurried away toward the doors. The Barringtons lived but a few doors from Lucy's parents' home, and therefore, she could return there without waiting for the carriage to be summoned. The Barringtons' butler insisted on sending a footman to accompany her. Lucy didn't object, but neither did she wait.

The footman caught up to her a moment later. He accompanied her in appropriate silence, leaving her thoughts ample opportunity to turn and twist about. Her parents' butler opened the door to let her in and sent the Barringtons' footman off. Lucy was grateful the butler didn't inquire after her early return. She had no desire to explain.

She rushed up the stairs and to her bedchamber. Tears flowed by the time she dropped, exhausted, onto her bed.

Their plan had seemed so ingenious at first: some time away would show Reed how much he really enjoyed their time together. He would appreciate her company enough to be willing to take her to all the Society events she'd longed to attend. Though she knew she would miss him, she'd thought he would come to his senses quickly, that they wouldn't be apart for long.

And he doesn't even care. He hasn't missed me at all.

By the time Reed reached the front of the Barringtons' home, Lucy was gone. He stood looking out into the dark night, worry tying his insides into knots. How had things come to this?

"The scales have tipped decidedly in our favor." Mr. Harrison slapped a companionable hand on Reed's shoulder. "We'll have the ladies agreeing to let us stay at home every night of the week soon enough."

Robert and Charles had come as well, both looking pleased as could be.

"Another evening or two, and we can declare this a decisive victory for the gentlemen," Robert declared.

"No." Reed snapped out the word.

"What do you mean, 'no'?" Robert smiled, even laughingly elbowing Charles. They all thought this a great joke.

"I mean there will be no more evenings like this. No

more." Reed stepped back into the entryway. "My hat and outercoat," he instructed the butler. "And send for my carriage."

A moment later, the items were in his possession and he was waiting in the vestibule for his equipage.

His in-laws closed in on him. "You are quitting the field?" Robert asked in a tone of surprise. "But we are winning."

Reed eyed them each in turn. "Gentlemen, this has gone too far. I saw tears in my wife's eyes tonight, and that is something I will never abide. Not ever. This ends now."

They looked at him as though he had lost his mind. "If you give in now, Lucy will be leading you about by the nose the rest of your life."

"So be it."

His carriage pulled up, and Reed was grateful for the escape. He preferred staying on friendly terms with his wife's family, but if they continued insisting he treat her with less kindness than she deserved, he would be hard pressed not to call each and every one of them out.

He'd gone along with the plan because he hadn't expected it to wound Lucy the way it obviously had. They'd convinced him she was playing along, that it was a friendly bit of rivalry between them. A bit of lark was all. In the process, he had hurt his wife, his darling, wonderful Lucy.

To his surprise, Mr. Harrison climbed in the carriage with him.

"If you mean to try to change my mind—"

But Mr. Harrison held up a hand. "Actually, I mean to admit to you that you're right. We took this game too far."

"That seems a very abrupt change of position." Reed wasn't generally a suspicious person, but he'd seen an underhandedness in his in-laws over the past week, albeit it a good-humored underhandedness, and it made him wary.

"Robert, Charles, and I were thoroughly enjoying this little rivalry with the ladies. And I know from speaking of it with my wife that she, Amelia, and Clarissa have been amused as well."

"Forgive me if I haven't found it overly amusing."

Mr. Harrison acknowledged Reed's position with a quick nod. "I am not at all happy with how things have turned out myself. We didn't mean to hurt Lucy's feelings."

"I need to apologize to her," Reed said.

"Oh, son, you must do far more than that."

The declaration was not a promising one. "Did you have something particular in mind, because I am currently at a loss."

Mr. Harrison's expression turned ponderous. "I might. I just might."

Seven

Lucy's tears dried by morning, though she kept to her room all the next day. She didn't want to hear any more of her family's schemes nor see the glint of triumph that would, no doubt, be in her father's eyes. The gentlemen had scored a decisive victory, with Lucy's broken heart being the spoils.

Over the past months, when something worried or upset her, she'd turned to Reed, and he'd listened as she talked it through. That always made her feel better. But he wasn't here, and he'd made it quite clear over the past week that he didn't really care to be.

She could go to their house not many streets away, ask if she could come home, and they could forget the rivalry they'd been entangled in the past few days. But there would always be the knowledge in the back of her mind that he hadn't asked her back and didn't really want her there.

When the dinner bell sounded, Lucy instructed her abigail to have her meal brought up on a tray. She simply wanted to be left alone. But the minutes stretched out, and her food didn't arrive. After nearly thirty minutes had past, Lucy began to suspect something had gone wrong.

She opened her bedchamber door a crack and peeked out. The corridor was empty. The family would be at their meal already. She tiptoed down the stairs, not wishing to draw attention to herself. They would want to talk, but she had no desire to. The corridor where the dining room stood was silent.

Now that is *odd*. She glanced around, trying to sort it out. It was the dinner hour, and her family was not one to miss a meal. She was nearly certain that Robert and Amelia, and Charles and Clarissa intended to take dinner with them that night. With six people sitting down to a meal, there ought to have been quite a bit of chatter.

Perhaps they had decided to eat elsewhere. The staff always seemed to know more about the comings and goings of the family than anyone. She stepped into the dining room, intending to tug the bell pull, but the sound of voices down the corridor stopped her.

She listened. Definitely voices. Lucy moved toward the sound. *The drawing room?* Why were they gathered in the drawing room? She pulled the door open a bit and looked inside. Seven pairs of eyes darted toward her. Then the room seemed to spring into action.

"Oh, no you will not, you lying blackguard!" Father declared in ringing tones, pointing an accusatory finger at Reed, of all people.

Lucy opened the door more fully.

"I will not be deterred, old man," Reed replied, in stilted and overly dramatic tones. "Resign yourself."

Mother pressed the back of her hand to her forehead and dropped against the sofa. "Whatever shall we do?"

Amelia and Clarissa rushed to Mother's side, waving

smelling salts and patting her hands as if consoling her.

Robert rose and stood next to Father. Though his expression was serious, Lucy knew the look of laughter hovering in the back of her brother's eyes. "You will not get away with this dastardly plan, Mr. Stanthorpe."

"Oh, but I will," Reed said. "You will not keep us apart a moment longer. If I must move mountains or cross oceans, I will. For true love always wins in the end!" He spun about, facing Lucy. "Never fear, my lady, I have come to rescue you from this vile place of imprisonment."

"What in heaven's name—"

Reed stepped up to her and wrapped his arm around her waist. He looked back over her family, assembled in an obviously preplanned pose. "Do not attempt to follow us," Reed warned. "For I will allow nothing to come between me and my true love again."

"Reed, what is going on?" Lucy asked.

He looked down at her, and her heart nearly stopped at the intensity of his gaze. "Our long nightmare is over, love. I've come to take you away from this place."

"Have you really?" The words emerged as little more than a whisper.

"I have, indeed, and should have long ago." To her family he said, "Au revoir!" then swept her from the room and down the corridor.

A footman waited at the front door, clearly anticipating their departure. He held the door, and they stepped out. Reed's carriage sat in readiness, the driver already perched atop. They were quickly settled inside—Lucy on the forward-facing bench and Reed on the rear-facing—and the carriage lurched forward.

Her mind was in a whirlwind. What had just happened? Reed came for her, that much was certain. Though why he had remained a mystery. She would not allow herself to believe he had missed her and longed for her, when so much silence had stretched between them.

And, yet, he *was* here.

"Lucy?" His voice was a bit uncertain. "I need to say something, and I hope you won't take it the wrong way."

She braced herself. Heaven only knew what he meant to tell her.

"I have always liked your family; you know that. But darling, they aren't very bright."

"What do you mean?"

Reed moved and sat directly beside her, taking her hands in his and looking into her face. The streetlamps they passed illuminated his expression enough for her to see the earnestness there. "I realize you first came to your parents' home because I was being an utter featherhead and you needed someone to listen to you. By the time I realized where you were, your mother and sisters had already convinced you that this miscommunication we were having was worthy of a drawn-out battle."

That was true enough.

"Upon arriving, your male relations pulled me aside and convinced me of the same thing. Though I would have far preferred to simply bring you home and talk it through, I bowed to their years of matrimonial experience, thinking it gave them insight. But, Lucy, darling, they are idiots, the lot of them."

She actually laughed out loud. She knew Reed really did like her family, but considering the turmoil of the past week, she had to agree with his assessment of their mental faculties.

He brushed his fingers along her cheek. "We should never have listened to them, my love. And I am sorry their schemes hurt you and sorrier still that I had any part of it."

"We were both rather blinded by them," Lucy said. "We ought to have simply told them all how bacon-brained they were being and fixed the problem ourselves."

"Indeed." He cupped her face gently in his hands and placed a tender kiss to her forehead. "And now that I have rescued you from the dungeon of despair they were keeping you in—"

She smiled at the theatrical tone he had adopted once more.

"I think we had best set our minds to resolving the difficulty that caused all of this trouble."

Lucy leaned into his embrace, resting her head on his shoulder and her hand against his chest. "I know you don't care for Society functions," she said. "And I don't want to force you to endure them all the time."

His arms held her ever tighter. "And I know how much you do enjoy them, and I don't want you to miss them all."

"Perhaps . . ." She pressed a kiss to his cheek. "We could pick a few events each week I would particularly like to attend, and on the other nights, we could stay home."

Reed kissed her temple. "I believe that is an excellent solution."

Lucy shifted enough to more fully face him, brushing her fingers along his jaw. "And if there is ever anything you desperately wish to avoid attending, you tell me, and we'll stay home."

His hand slipped behind her neck, his fingers weaving into her hair. "And if there is anything you desperately wish to attend, you tell me, and we will make certain we are there."

"And"—she feathered a kiss on his lips—"we will never"—another light kiss—"ever"—and another—"listen to my family again."

"Agreed."

Reed pulled her firmly into his arms and kissed her thoroughly. The heartache and loneliness of the past week simply melted away. He did love her. He always had. If not for the poor advice and insistence of meddlesome relations, they might have resolved this difficulty very easily.

But, she told herself as he continued kissing her and

holding her, that without the argument, they'd not be enjoying a reconciliation.

The carriage came to a stop in front of their house. Reed pulled away, letting down the window.

"Circle the block a few more times, man," he called out to the driver. "And drive slowly."

He put up the window once more and drew the curtains. She felt his arms slip around her and his warmth settle over her once more.

"Now, my dearest Lucy, where were we?"

ABOUT SARAH M. EDEN

Sarah M. Eden is the author of multiple historical romances, including the two-time Whitney Award Winner *Longing for Home* and Whitney Award finalists *Seeking Persephone* and *Courting Miss Lancaster*. Combining her obsession with history and affinity for tender love stories, Sarah loves crafting witty characters and heartfelt romances. She has twice served as the Master of Ceremonies for the LDStorymakers Writers Conference and acted as the Writer in Residence at the Northwest Writers Retreat. Sarah is represented by Pam van Hylckama Vlieg at D4EO Literary Agency.

Visit Sarah online:
Twitter: @SarahMEden
Facebook: Author Sarah M. Eden
Website: SarahMEden.com

MORE TIMELESS ROMANCE ANTHOLOGIES

For the latest updates on our anthologies, visit our blog:
TimelessRomanceAnthologies.blogspot.com

www.ingramcontent.com/pod-product-compliance
Lightning Source LLC
LaVergne TN
LVHW021758060526
838201LV00058B/3143